Prince and the Throne

Book Two

Brien Feathers

Copyright © 2024 by Brien Feathers

All rights reserved.

No portion of this book may be reproduced in any form without written permission from the publisher or author, except as permitted by U.S. copyright law.

Any references to historical events, real people, or real places are used fictitiously. Other names, characters, places and events are products of the author's imagination, and any resemblances to actual events or places or persons, living or dead, is entirely coincidental.

Without in any way limiting the author's exclusive rights under copyright, any use of this publication to "train" generative artificial intelligence (AI) technologies to generate text is expressly prohibited.

Cover designed by JV ARTS.

Contents

Content Advisory — 1
1. Friends and Lovers — 3
2. Rosewater and Sunshine — 17
3. A Misunderstanding — 27
4. Tales in the Den — 35
5. Book of Darkness — 47
6. Teo's Crown — 57
7. Duel of Honor — 73
8. Wolf of the Red Den — 81
9. The Stone House of Cuckoo — 87
10. Save Me — 97
11. God — 105
12. Lover's Heart — 119

13.	Charlatans and Buffoons	129
14.	Sunshine	143
15.	It Belongs to You	157
16.	Illuminate	167
17.	House of Silver	179
18.	Something Nice	189
19.	An Old Fool	199
20.	Break You	209
21.	Hello, Soful	219
22.	Ridiculous	231
23.	Games We Play	241
24.	Father	253
25.	Define Gone	261
26.	I Told You So	271
27.	The Plan	283
28.	Slowly, Terribly, Poorly	291
29.	Good, Bad, Terrible	301
	Tsar and the Throne	317
	Author Newsletter	319
	Also by Brien Feathers	321

Content Advisory

This book contains strong language, graphic violence, and intimate situations.
Reader discretion is advised.

One

Friends and Lovers

The weather turned wretched with icy sleet, and the wind howled like a pack of wolves. The scenery outside was completely white and the carriage rocked, the doors rattling with the strength of the gale. Sofia had been leaning against the window, trying to make out where they were, as though she'd know, when her door swung open and a sentinel with a black cloak came in.

Crouched, he shed his frozen cloak before plopping down on the powder blue velvet seat across from her. He shook his white curls, releasing the ice and snow, though his hair was white with or without the winter's kiss, and lit the silver pipe he brandished from his pouch while muttering, "I hope you don't mind, Lady Sofia."

A hundred sentinels were traveling with the prince to Sarostia, and though she didn't know most of them, she knew Ignat. His wavy hair and arched brows were so blond they appeared white, and Ignat was one of the few favored by his captain. He darkened his eyelids with black mineral powder, jarring against his pale complexion. The black was now smeared and looked as though Igant had rubbed soot on his face.

"How are you doing on this fine day, my lady?" He smiled, and whatever he was smoking smelled sweet with a tang of spice.

"Aleksei sent you?" Sofia yet again found herself asking about Aleksei rather than speaking to him.

"Why, my lady? I'm an excellent company if you'd give me the chance."

"Where are we going?" she asked when she felt the carriage turn.

"We're turning into an inn, my lady." He tapped his pipe on the side of the door. "The light is falling, and we can't travel through the night in this weather."

"Is your captain outside?" Sofia asked. "He shouldn't be. His bones are mending, and he's injured still."

"It's not my call, Lady Sofia." Ignat shrugged. "But he's with the Chartorisky. If your concern is truly for his wellbeing, take comfort that he's not outside."

He was mouthy like this and gave Sofia cause not to like him. They'd been on the road for nearly three weeks, and she'd spoken with Aleksei less than a handful of times. He was more often in the Chartorisky carriage than not, and he wasn't there to see Daniil. They'd quarreled, Zoya and Sofia, for all the sentinels to see and hear and Aleksei hadn't taken Sofia's side.

When she would bring it up to Aleksei, he'd say, *'She's a friend,'* and look confused as to why Sofia was displeased but he wasn't dense. He just didn't want her anymore was Sofia's guess, and to be fair, he'd already said as much before they even left Krakova.

Sofia knew Aleksei had been *with* the queen when she brutalized him so badly it took a hundred and seventy nails and splints and two months of Baltar's care to put him back together, and she wanted to give him the time and the space to heal without suffocating him. She'd understand if that was all, but that wasn't all because he was *always* with Zoya.

"You look sad, my lady. Anything I can do to help?"

Sofia turned from the blizzard outside and looked at Ignat who wasn't Aleksei. "No," she said.

"If you're upset with the captain, it might be helpful to tell him why."

"He knows." Sofia sighed because her heart ached. "How far to Sarostia?"

"We're riding through the province of Sarostia." The many gold tassels dangling from the cabin roof swayed, and Ignat reached up and held one as though it was a flower. "But we should reach the Red Den tomorrow if the weather lets up."

"The duke's wife is Chartorisky?" Sofia asked.

"Duchess Elena is from the House of Chartorisky," he said.

"They are all beautiful, aren't they? The Chartorisky women?"

"Their men, too," Ignat said. "And so are you, my lady. I find everyone is beautiful in their own way, like the crystal flakes of snow."

"You thought Queen Kseniya was beautiful?" she asked.

"In her own way, she was," he said. "But she did many hideous things." He puffed his cheeks and cocked his head, studying her. "My captain, he's not good with women."

"Oh, I don't believe that."

"It's the truth, as witnessed by how he's made you sad. I've never made a lover sad, but I've also never loved. The heart complicates things, the poets say, but perhaps they have it the other way around. Maybe love makes us stupid, leaving us unable to solve the simplest of affairs."

"He doesn't love me," Sofia said out loud, the harrowing truth slowly dawning like the sun on a cold grey morning.

"I don't know. I can't see into another man's soul," Ignat said. "But it's possible he doesn't know what that is. We don't end up as Imperial Sentinels, as killers and harlots, because we were abundant in love."

"How did you end up here?" Sofia asked.

"I'm my father's gift to the queen. I should be flattered, I suppose."

"Who's your father?"

"Lord Fedya Pulyazin. My mother was a servant, so I don't count."

"That's a big name," Sofia remarked.

"Sure is." He smiled.

"Can you perform water alchemy?" she asked.

"A little." His eyes were grey but not dull, as they were full of lively mischief. "Every boy tries to impress his father, I suppose... Though you might find me abrasive, I like you, Lady Sofia. So, here's my unsolicited advice. The Chartorisky are an alley of the Shields. Lady Zoya and the captain have known each other since they were children. She's familiar, she's safe, and the captain doesn't offend her when he's short with her or when he refuses her. You're none of those things, my lady, and I don't mean that in a bad way."

Sofia watched the silver pipe twirl in his fingers, waited, then asked, "And where's the advice?"

"That was it," he said. "Information framed in a useful way *is* advice."

"I see." She saw nothing and sank into her seat feeling like the weather, whiny and cold.

Ignat remained with her till they were pulling into an inn and stepped out then. It had been less than an hour, but the day had fallen breathtakingly quick, and it was nearly dark.

Taking her book and satchel, Sofia exited the coach and saw the inn was two floors and large by the number of windows alight. It had a watchtower, she supposed, because a single light flickered high up like a torch held by a giant, but what they watched in this weather, she didn't know. Probably nothing but darkness and the slush of the last rain of fall turning into the first snow of winter, visible only in the lanternlight. All else was blindness.

Sofia didn't know where Aleksei was and went ahead into the inn alone. A servant greeted her and took her cloak. The hall was large with multiple fireplaces, and she saw sentinels and assumed Aleksei had sent them ahead to vacate the place and inspect it for assassins and what not. They'd been sitting and eating but all rose when Niko entered.

"It's nice," he said, handing his cloak to Eugene who'd come in with him, and taking off his gloves. The prince went to warm his hands by the fireplace without telling the curtsied servants and bowed sentinels they could rise. They remained frozen in place till Niko turned around and said, "Oh, please continue. Don't mind me."

The entourage poured in after the prince, and the kitchen did their best to rush out the food. Niko took a table by the fireplace and the Chartorisky siblings joined him. Zoya laughed often and touched Niko a lot, and Eugene eyed the girl each time she did it.

So close to the den, it was clearly a Shield inn, and the red banners hanging from the walls, the dark wooden furniture, and the bare brownstone floors made the hall dim despite the candles lit on every table, the light from the fireplaces, and the oil lanterns.

The dining hall fell short of accommodating the full numbers in the prince's entourage, and soldiers sat on the floor, but Sofia's table remained empty. She'd been reading by the fireplace and drinking wine after a dinner of roasted goose and potatoes when someone came and stood by her. A sentinel, she knew. Not Aleksei, she also knew before looking up from her book.

"Do you mind if I sit with you, Lady Sofia?" He was pretty with curly brown hair and brown eyes, perfect everything including his skin. "I'm Dominik, my lady."

They hadn't spoken before, but Sofia knew who he was. "Where's your captain, Dominik?"

"Outside," was all he said.

"Doing what?"

"Forgive me, my lady, but the captain is not in the habit of reporting to me."

Sofia returned to her book, but seeing as there was nowhere else to sit, she said, "You can take the chairs if you want."

He took that as he could sit at her table but she didn't want to be rude and said nothing. He said her name after a while, but she pretended not to hear him because the hall was loud with all the chatter.

"Sofia." He leaned in, his hand on her knee.

She lifted her gaze from her book and found him smiling. He retrieved his hand because she'd frowned. He studied her for a moment, his brown eyes keen. Then he laughed. "You didn't request my company, did you?"

"No."

"Misunderstanding, forgive me, my lady."

"Who told you I wanted to see you?" she asked as he got up.

"Can't say, my lady."

After he left, Sofia narrowed her eyes at Zoya a few tables over, and the blonde girl laughed. The Chartorisky girl was playing, as she seemed to do often, but it said much that Aleksei's men didn't know she was supposed to be his. She'd lost the appetite to be in the company of others and asked the servant to show her to her room.

After taking a long, hot bath in the tub, Sofia sat on the large bed in her nightgown and brushed her hair. Though the weather outside sounded terrible still, it was warm inside with logs crackling in the slow fire.

"Do you need anything else, my lady?" one of the servants asked after they drained the bathwater and cleaned up after Sofia. The place was well serviced.

"Yes, can you go tell one of the sentinels Lady Sofia is asking for Captain Aleksei?"

"Yes, my lady."

"That will be all. Thank you."

The women left. The room had two beds, a larger one for the lord and a narrow one against the wall for the valet. There was a wooden trunk between the beds, which Sofia inspected hoping to find something someone left behind, but it was empty. She took a candle and passed the time by looking at the books on the small shelf. No codex, but she found a Shield soldier's handbook—not Imperial Sentinels—and looked through it.

Containing the mundane affairs of a soldier's life, including how to care for horseshoes when traveling through rocky terrain, they'd gone through the trouble of producing such things and distributing them to inns.

Next, she went through Shield military law and found a surprising amount of liberty, including the right to challenge the commandership of a superior officer for those whose birthright allowed it. For the common soldier though, every punishment was death. Desertion, death. Mishandling of equipment, death. Theft, death. Cowardice, of course death.

She put the book away when her door opened. Aleksei had knocked, a far cry from when he broke into Papa's house, twice, to be with her.

"Did you ask for me?" He left the door open but took off his exoskeleton and shook his hand, making Sofia wonder how cold it must be to wear so much metal in winter.

"Did you eat anything?" she asked.

"Yeah," he lied.

"Out in the blizzard?" she asked.

"What do you want?"

She wanted him to eat something but that would mean he'd leave the room, so she said, "I want you to sleep." At this rate, she was turning into the mother he never had. She wished for them to find their way back, for him to return to her, for her not to have him in reins like this, but if she let the lead go, he'd wander off further and further away from her till she lost sight of him, and he'd never come back.

"I'm fine," he said.

"Please."

He sighed as though she was burdening him but closed the door, hung his cloak, wiped his boots before crossing the room, and sat down on the valet's bed. He sat for a while, staring, then went to the washing table.

"How far is Sarostia?" Sofia asked. She hadn't forgotten Ignat had already answered her but wanted to make conversation with Aleksei and couldn't think of anything else.

"We're in Sarostia," he said, wiping his face. "But we should be at the Red Den tomorrow if the weather allows."

"That's the duke's fortress?"

"It's a Shield fortress the duke oversees. It's right at the border of Elfur. I believe you can stand on the wall and see it."

"Did Niko ever tell you how he killed the queen?" Sofia asked.

"No, and please don't say such things in the den."

"Of course not, Aleksei. I'm not stupid."

"Didn't say you were."

Sofia let it drop. The last thing she needed was a quarrel with him over semantics. "A sentinel approached me." She withheld the name because she didn't want him in trouble, should there even be one, but she *had* to know if he even cared. "He asked if I wanted company."

"Did you?" he asked.

Sofia got up and marched to the washing table. "Aleksei."

He looked up from cleaning his nails with a bristle, and she slapped him across the face. She hadn't held back either and his cheek turned red with her handprint. Her palm and even the tips of her fingers stung.

He stood there for a while, looking down, then tossed the bristle and turned for the door. Sofia ran around him and blocked the door as he grabbed his cloak from the hook on the wall.

"I'm sorry," she said. "But you shouldn't speak to me that way."

"Hit me more if that makes you feel better." He waited. "All right, then, goodnight, Lady Sofia."

For all the saints... She dropped her hand from the door handle and moved out of his way.

The door closed behind him. This was done. She felt it. She knew it, but she couldn't believe it. She blamed the archmage for erasing her from Aleksei's memory because their relationship couldn't and didn't recover from it. Aleksei may claim the love remained but he treated her like a stranger, and to him, she was.

For a long time she stood by the door, then put on her boots, draped her cloak over her nightgown, and stepped out into the corridor. She took the stairs down, passed through the dining hall now nearly empty, and walked out of the inn.

Branches had bent with the weight of the snowy slush and the shrubbery along the bank lay on the ground as though the weight of the world sat upon their backs. The river flowed loudly, and it wasn't too cold as the dawn broke grey and silver, promising more moody weather but calm for the time being.

Sofia sat with her back to a birch tree, her father on her mind. Not Papa, but her father whose face she'd forgotten. Moriz of Dohnan, he'd been an Elfurian *graf*, count—she remembered that. The invisible stranger, not so invisible then, kept her company. The shadow sat beside her, the snow under him undisturbed. The archmage had called him a darkling, but she was yet to learn what that was.

"Why did you kill my uncle?" she asked.

"Yelizaveta gave us his name."

"I'm not her. She was my mother." Even phantoms confused Sofia with Lady Yelizaveta, another testament to how little she mattered. Her mother had been loved. The archmage loved her. Papa loved her. Count Moriz of Dohnan loved her... It was unfortunate she'd died bringing Sofia into this world, and a pity none of the love had been inherited by her.

"We love you."

"You don't exist."

But he did though. The archmage and the synod were still very much dead.

Dogs barked, probably from the inn as the royal entourage had none, horses nickered, and sentinel voices echoed as they had been throughout the night. Two hounds ran by her, one turned and wagged its tail but the other found her cloak by the river, and excitedly barked—they were both good boys.

The one who'd found her came to receive his pats from her, while the other barked and barked, sniffing her cloak. It was still somewhat dark, the sight just returning to the world, as Charger blew past Sofia, and the captain of the sentinels jumped off his horse by the river, grabbing the cloak from the hound. They'd been calling her name and looking for her all night, but she was having a moment, throwing a tantrum as though she was five years old and had run away from home.

She could have called Aleksei but just watched him instead. He was showing her he still cared and that she'd frightened him. His mind was so frenzied he didn't see her less than twenty yards away. Was it wrong that it pleased her?

"Give us the boy's name. He doesn't love you."

The dog didn't sense him, but Sofia turned and frowned. "Don't ask me such a thing again. Matter of fact, be gone."

Without another word, the shadow vanished in the silver light.

The water was deeper than it appeared and Aleksei struggled with the current for a while, falling and losing his cloak, before it occurred to Sofia that Niko had nearly drowned when he was a child and that she was frightening Aleksei more than she meant to, making him relive a nightmare.

"Aleksei!" she called.

He didn't hear her over the current. She got up and approached the bank, and stood there calling, the dog at her feet barking, till he saw her, and marched out of the river, drenched, and grabbed her by the throat, screaming, "What is wrong with you? What is wrong with you!"

They stepped backward together, and he shoved her and slammed her against a tree, the hand with the exoskeleton around her throat. "What is wrong with you!" The scarlet eyes were bright but the expression dark. The alchemy on the vambraces glowed as though he meant to kill her.

"What is wrong with you!" He shook her by the throat till he realized what he was doing and dropped his hand, breathing, "Fuck."

Aleksei shivered. Not from the weather but from distress. He sat in the tub for a while, his head on his knees, then got up and got dressed. The room had one small window by the beds, the light through it pale, and the candles were still lit. Sofia sat on the bed and watched Aleksei as he mumbled to himself, tossing this and that, looking for something. She'd given his uniform to the servant to be cleaned and dried, and he was in cotton trousers, strapping his vambrace to his naked arm as he didn't have a shirt on, but he let that drop to the floor and came to her.

He bent and kissed her, desperate.

"Aleksei," she whispered as he continued down her neck. "Aleksei, stop."

Anxious and his breathing strained, he knelt in front of her and pushed up her skirt. Sofia put her hand under his chin and lifted his face to her, her other hand holding the back of his head.

"Aleksei, get up."

He'd cried and his eyes were wide. "Is this not what you want? What do you want?"

She wanted what they had once, love. But it was gone now, wasn't it? Sofia would always love him, this was true, but Aleksei's love had been so innocent because it had started when he was a boy, before the world hurt him so much that he no longer knew what it was. That, they couldn't replace. So this was done. By being here, unfairly asking him for what he couldn't give, she was just hurting him more.

"I'm sorry I frightened you." She dropped her hands from his face, but he was still knelt in front of her and they looked at each other. "That was unfair and I won't do it again. Let's try and be friends at least." It hurt her to say it. "We'll meet the duke and I'll be an ally, but afterward, I think it's best I go to Lev."

Silent a while, he nodded. "Thank you." He rose.

"Mmm." Sofia's throat clamped, and the tears she held back drowned her words. She took a pillow and a dry wool cloak, went to the valet's bed, and laid down turning her back to the room.

"Did you not want the larger bed?" Aleksei asked, but she pretended to be asleep and didn't answer. She was crying and didn't want him to know.

Two

Rosewater and Sunshine

The Red Den was the size of a mountain. Its high walls wrapped around the hill like a titan snake, around and around for miles. It had appeared daunting from afar, but the monstrous size made Sofia feel like a fleck of dust or a grain of sand, as the prince's entourage waited an unpolite amount of time for the draw bridge to be lowered over the gap in the earth deep enough to be black in the afternoon sun of a clear day, and perhaps even reach the necromancy hell.

The fortress housed *tens* of thousands was Sofia's guess, when the bridge was finally lowered for the prince and the royal carriage, and she looked out the window at the ivory walls touching the blue skies.

The ascent to the main castle took a long time and felt as though they were voluntarily riding into the mouth of a beast. The battlements were lined with soldiers, and Sofia closed her curtains when she'd seen enough of them. Now she also understood why the throne was bankrupt, for the stomach of this serpent must be a bottomless pit for silver, copper, and grain.

As alarming as it should have been, unable to shake off the melancholy Sofia could hardly be bothered. The world seemed so heavy just then, and feeling as though slogging through water she was dying a bit at a time. Her chest was tight and her physical heart hurt. She'd been looking down and staring at the codex, reading the same line over and over and not comprehending it, when her door opened and Aleksei came in.

He took a seat across from her, propped his restless leg's ankle over his knee, and sat vibrating both. "It's a lot larger than I thought. If this turns shit, I might not be able to get us out of here."

"Mmm." Her mind blinked blankly before coherent thoughts trickled in painfully slow.

"Are you all right?" Concern knotted his brows.

"Ah, yes." She sat up. "Um... yeah." She couldn't remember what he said. "It's large, the den."

"Look, Sofia, there's no need for you to be here. I'll have Ignat take you to Usolya." He nodded to himself and reached for the door. Then his face dropped. "I'm so sorry." He didn't know what to do and looked afraid because she'd cried. She couldn't help it. "I'm sorry," he mumbled. "I'm so sorry."

He didn't mean to hurt her but kept doing it, and she didn't want to burden him but now he was apologizing, begging, holding her hand when he should be minding the den and the duke. This wasn't working.

"It will look strange if I turn around at the gate," she managed to say after calming down. "I'll go in and greet the duke and stay for the customary pleasantries, but I'd like to leave tomorrow. If Niko wanted to send a letter to my brother, would you make sure it's drafted by then?" She dabbed her eyes with her handkerchief and sniveled.

"Yeah," he said initially, but deflated completely. "I... I keep making you sad, and that's not my intention. Will you please tell me what you want? I thought you wanted intimacy, but you turned me down. I don't understand what you want. *Please* just tell me."

"Is that what you want? To be with me?" she asked.

"I'm going to say the wrong thing." That was answer enough.

"Never you mind," she said. "Worry about..." Twirling her finger she gestured 'around'. "I'll speak with you later. I suppose I'll be expected to stay for dinner."

After Aleksei stepped out Sofia shook her head, trying to see if that would wring out the sadness—it did not. So she tried to stuff it full of current concerns to distract herself and failed at that too. It was hard to care about Niko's throne when the thought of dying at the den sounded like a relief.

It took nearly an hour of climb before they reached the castle, and the sun had passed its peak and begun its westward arc by the time the prince and the highest esteemed members of his entourage, which included the Chartorisky and Sofia, found themselves in the duke's courtyard.

The garden was meager with some shrubbery which had died in the recent blizzard, and there was a hole at the center of the attempt at greenery where a fountain used to be, but the keep, the towers, the wall, all the stone structures were tremendous. The den was bigger than Raven and Sofia had never seen such a large castle.

The Shield red banner hung behind the duke who was dressed in all black. The darksteel gear he wore glinted. His long thick hair and the beard touching his breastplate were salt and pepper, but the grey strands of age didn't soften his stern red eyes. The years had made Papa kind, but this man had gone the opposite way.

He had men standing to either side of him, and from the expensive gear, Sofia assumed they were generals or captains—highborns. The red tint in their eyes was a dead giveaway even if their darksteel hadn't been embellished with gold enough to be a fortune. They stood on the tall granite steps and did not come down to welcome the prince.

The duchess, the blonde Chartorisky, fluttered down the stairs. She greeted her own, Zoya and Daniil with an embrace, and curtsied to the prince, a passing cold smile as sharp as a knife's edge.

The courtyard was surrounded by armored soldiers, purposefully, Sofia thought. Their uniform was different than that of a sentinel, and they wore red tunics and leather armor over black trousers and boots. Their weapons were plain steel and they carried no alchemy.

Three lords and a lady stood below the granite steps, and the woman with them was puzzling. Darksteel gear on her, including exoskeletons on both hands, she wore trousers as though she meant to go riding, hardly appropriate attire for greeting the prince. A soldier, Sofia would have placed her, had she not been standing next to lords. A woman soldier wasn't heard of in the Guard ranks, but Sofia had heard Queen Kseniya had been a warrior when she was younger... So, perhaps they had female soldiers at Shield.

The woman confused Aleksei as well, walking up to him and giving her hand as a lady would, but when he bent to kiss her hand, she yanked him forward and laughed because she'd thrown him off balance.

"I'm Oleksandra, but just call me Sandra." She patted Aleksei on the back. "Welcome to the den, cousin." She bowed to Niko as a lord would. "Your Highness."

Then she turned her back on the prince and strutted back to her group, the three lords and the young lady all laughing now. Oh, this was trouble, Sofia realized at once, because they were Rodion's children. The duke had three sons all bigger and older than Aleksei, and even one of his daughters was larger than the captain of the sentinels. The younger one, well she was Zoya in another form—a brat—and without the subtlety of the Chartorisky to soften her crooked sneer, she looked like a rat.

The duchess completely ignored Sofia. Pity, because then she would have remarked on the sorry state of her garden.

Then came the false pleasantries of everyone greeting each other, and Sofia was announced as Lady Sofia of White Guard. All eyes turned to her, but she would take the time and decide how she would proceed. The throne of Fedosia was a weight on Aleksei's back, the fate of tens of thousands as they were at war, but Niko wouldn't carry his share. He walked around waving, and saying, "Hello."

Sofia was a Guard and not just some woman accompanying Aleksei. Rejected by her lover, she'd been crying earlier but they didn't know that. She had to gather her scattered self because she was representing her house as well.

She greeted the men as though they were courtiers, and held out her hand to whom she thought was the oldest son of the duke.

"My lady." The lord kissed her gloved hand.

To the others, she gave a passing, "Hello, and how are you?"

She climbed the stairs and curtsied only to the duke, "Your Grace."

Turning her back on everyone in the courtyard, she carried herself into the keep leisurely. Any other day she might have been terrified, but at the moment she couldn't give a damn. She was carrying her brother's name and would take care not to drop it, but the hell with the duke. Had Aleksei turned on a copper coin like this on his own, she'd say the hell with him too, but he hadn't. He'd loved her with all he had, and she couldn't get out of her mind how terrified he had been that morning in the narthex of the Church of Murmia.

'What am I to do without you?' had been the last thing he said before the archmage called him a whore and threw him out.

Oh, how she hated that old man even beyond death. On second thought, she wasn't sorry at all she killed him… probably.

Inside the castle everything was large, the tables, chandeliers... and the arched doorways were so tall Sofia had to wonder if the den had been designed for giants. Intricate woodwork on the high ceiling and the overlay of the beams gave the den the aura of a church, but in the Shield fashion, they had a lot of red, including crimson wool carpets and heavy curtains.

In her quarters the walls were saffron, pleasant though the paint was old. The well worn carpet warmed the floor and the windows were arched and slender. Sofia complained about a headache and was told it was the high altitude, though she suspected the copious amount of wine she'd guzzled to mend her broken heart had something to do with it.

She'd been hiding in her room, sitting on a satin settee with her eyes closed, when the steward came in to ask if she'd be joining the duke for dinner and dance. She had to attend, she supposed, and informed the thin man she would indeed be coming down for 'dinner and festivity' whilst wondering where she would find the energy for such a thing.

A knock came on her door, and she yelled, "I'm indecent!"

"I'll wait." It was Aleksei.

She had to take a moment to decide if she wanted to see him, but in the end, as sad as it was, he was her darling. "Come on in."

Aleksei entered and closed the door. "They told me you weren't feeling well."

"I'm all right. I just didn't want the maids in the room and told them I had a headache... What should I wear for the dinner?" She looked at the wooden trunk which she hadn't taken the dresses out of. No point since she was leaving tomorrow.

"Whatever you wish," he said.

"Can I be naked, then?"

He frowned. Perhaps he'd forgotten his sense of humor too. Since she would be attending a grand total of one event, Sofia thought to go straight for her ivory dress embroidered with gold threads and asked for Aleksei's help since he was there anyway.

He took out the dress she'd asked for, stretched out the fabric on the bed, and proceeded to release the travel wrinkles with an alchemy iron, as she watched with some fascination.

"What do you iron?" she asked because he'd had that on him. Apparently, one of the settings of his darksteel was an iron.

"My cloak, trousers, and shirt," he said.

"No wonder you look so sharp." She couldn't help but smile. "Oh, I should probably brew a few portions of tonic for you before tomorrow." She thought to get up but she was truly tired from traveling in coach for three weeks and running around in the forest instead of sleeping the only night she'd had a bed since they left Krakova. Now, she'd be on the road even longer. "How far is Seniya?"

Aleksei thought, lifting the iron so as not to burn her dress, then said, "Nearly eight hundred miles. You were far closer to it in Krakova. From the capital, it's only two hundred miles through flat terrain."

"Eight hundred miles?" The thought exhausted Sofia. "Is it closer if I just ride to Usolya rather than go to Seniya?"

"That's over four thousand miles," he said. "You have to take the train. There is no other way in the winter."

Disheartened at the whole thing, Sofia dropped her gaze to her lap and twirled the loose thread she pulled from her dress.

"All done," she heard him. "Rosewater and sunshine," he mumbled.

She stole a look and saw him sniffing the bodice of her dress. "What does sunshine smell like?" she asked.

"Outside," he said. "When you dry clothes on the line out in the sun, it smells like this, like clean…" He flicked his gaze, saw her watching him, blushed, and set her dress down. "It's ready." He gestured.

"Thank you. Do you know what you smell like?" she asked.

"Is it bad?" He pressed his sleeve to his face, wrinkling his nose.

"No," she whispered, watching the evening light, gold and warm, trace the curves and the angles, the sharps and the softs of his face, neck, collarbone… "You smell of leather and steel, clean attire too, and earth."

"Dirt?" he asked.

"Dirt is only but a part of earth," she said. "Aleksei, may I ask you for a favor?"

"Anything, my lady."

"I hear there will be a dance tonight. I don't want you to dance with Zoya." There she'd said it and now she puffed her cheeks.

"I wasn't going to," he said. "I can't dance."

"It doesn't matter. She's going to ask you, and I want you to decline. You can do whatever you wish after I leave, but tonight, I want you to stay by my side. Is that all right?"

"Of course," he said. "Are…" He hesitated, scratching his head. "Are you… jealous of Zoya?"

"I'm jealous of anyone who has your attention." She was petty, but so what.

"She doesn't, but all right."

"Good."

"I'm going to go check on Niko." He turned for the door. "I'll see you tonight. I've posted sentinels at your door. If you need anything, please let them know."

"Sure."

He left and instead of getting up to get ready, she closed her eyes thinking it'd be for a moment, but she'd fallen asleep and dreamt of home, Elfur, of a castle and the frozen lake beyond it. She was running after her father, she thought, but he turned, and it was Grigori. She ran away from him, then it was dark and she heard voices.

"Give me a name to feed the darkness, give us his *name. Give me life, Yeliza, so we can be together."*

Three

A Misunderstanding

The stone walls, the narrow slit of windows, the domed ceiling, the great hall, and much of the den reminded Sofia of a church, and the dining hall was no different. It would be a nave had there been an altar and saints instead of a long table and chairs. It felt sacrilegious to be eating meat in the hall of prayers and Sofia kept herself to fruits. The duke served a whole boar, and the nearly alive creature perched at the center of the table.

The chewing sound was revolting because there was no music. They hadn't waited for the prince and just ate as Sofia sat alone. Aleksei hadn't come, either.

The Chartorisky siblings sat on the duchess' side of the table and across from Sofia who was on the duke's side. Down the table were the duke's five children along with Shield commanders and their wives whose faces were obstructed by the boar.

"So, Lady Guard, what is your business with my nephew?" The duke stroked his beard. He had a thick gold ring with a ruby setting on his thumb and held a gold cup in his other hand. He slurped wine loudly, wiping his mouth with his hand, and talked while he chewed.

"His Highness, you mean?" Sofia dabbed her lips with the napkin, realized it didn't smell clean, folded it, and set it on the table. "I'm here to negotiate the terms of peace on behalf of my brother."

"Isn't your father a necromancer, not Pyotr Guard?" Oleksandra, the lady who wore a stableboy's attire to her father's table, pointed her fork at Sofia.

"It's true," Zoya butted in. "Her father was an Elfurian necromancer, and the archmage burned him at the stake."

"Family drama, am I right?" Oleksandra wore darksteel gear to dinner, and the cup she held was gold like the duke's. The whole family drank from gold cups. It was a mark of paranoia because gold changed color with the touch of poison. The duke thought someone might poison him in his own house.

"Every great family has drama," Sofia said.

"Some more public than others," Zoya remarked.

The duke's three sons, Dragan, Fedir, and Vukhir sat in a row like three carrion crows, from oldest to youngest. Dragan, the oldest, was a large man with a fur lined collar but he wasn't unpleasant to look at. The other two were different. The middle son Fedir wasn't much different than the boar on the table with pudgy short fingers with dirt under the nails, and long sharp teeth like tusks. He ate the raw part of the creature, and his mouth was red with blood when he chuckled at something one of the commanders said. It was too far and too quiet for Sofia to have caught it.

The younger two, Vukhir and Teo, both resembled rodents. Showing astonishing disrespect, Teo the brat girl wore a coronet to the table when they were expecting the prince, and Vukhir kept shoving things into his mouth while it was still full, further reminding Sofia of a marmot.

Zoya was whispering in her aunt's ear, both women giggling, and Daniil and Dragan speaking in hushed voices wearing serious faces, when the door flung open with a loud slam against the stone walls, echoing through the hall.

"Why isn't my brother allowed to come to dinner?" Niko's voice rang, and all Sofia heard was 'brother' and flinched inside. Correcting him now would only draw attention to it, though, and she rose in a hurry, trying to curtsy.

"His Highness Prince Nikolas!" The steward ran in to announce, out of breath at probably having chased after Niko.

Niko stood by the door, fuming, and Eugene lurked behind him in the hall. The sentinel had his full gear on and kept his hand on his hilt. He typically carried his darksteel as a blunt rod, but in the den, he'd shaped it into a proper sword.

No one had gotten up except for Sofia who managed a curtsy, and the duke asked, as he slurped loudly, "What are you going on about, boy?"

"Not a boy, I'm your prince, and I demand to know why Aleksei wasn't invited to dinner?"

"He's a sentinel, Prince," the duke said. "Common soldiers don't eat at the lord's table."

"He's not common. Burkhard outranked you, Rodion." Niko didn't acknowledge Sofia, so she didn't rise, and kept her head bowed. "Also, you refused to feed my sentinels? Why?"

"Since your mother was so keen on feeding the Pulyazin rather than her own, we don't have the grains to spare, Prince, not with the winter coming," the duke said.

"Mother sent you plenty. Maybe he ate it all. Look at him!" Without looking, Sofia knew Niko was pointing at Fedir. "I want food for my sentinels or I'm leaving!"

"Go where, boy?" the duke asked. "Back to the capital you're most definitely going to lose without my men? I hear Lev Guard gathers his allies and he's coming for your head, not mine. So, sit, eat, and don't disrespect my family."

That was it. Sofia's legs hurt anyway. She rose and stood by Niko. "Well, with my coming here, I hoped to assess if the duke was a suitable guardian for the young prince. But since he appears to be in dire straits, unable even to feed his own men, I hereby nominate Lev of Guard for tsar regent and the guardian of the prince till he is of age.

"That will end the conflict, Your Highness. All you need is to assemble the *Boyar Duma* once you're in the capital," she said.

"You have no right." The duke glowered at Sofia, taking her into his crosshairs.

"Your Highness, who is your father?" Sofia asked.

"Saint Neva of White Guard," Niko said.

"Of White Guard," Sofia repeated. "It appears we have every right, Duke Rodion."

"That's not true. She has no authority," Zoya said. "I thought you fought with Aleksei and were leaving?"

She had long ears. Sofia wondered if Aleksei had told her that, but she wouldn't fight with Zoya over a man when they were discussing the Guards claiming the throne.

"I didn't say she fought with Aleksei. I just said she was leaving, and Aleksei was upset." Niko stumped his boot on the stone floor. "You're stupid, Zoya! You said it'd be funny to send Dominik to Sofia, but it wasn't, and Aleksei got mad at me. I thought you were a proper lady, but I found out you entertained many men including Lev Guard. You call him a dick licker, yet you kissed him on the mouth, anyway! This wedding is off. I don't like you and I'm not marrying you."

Niko turned and grabbed Sofia's arm. "Get your things. We're leaving. They're stupid and this place is terrible." Then he yelled at Rodion, "I don't need your help. Lev is dead anyway. But I won't be sending you any more grain! Or steel! Or money!" The prince turned on his heels and strode out dragging Sofia behind, whilst shouting, "And she's wearing a coronet! Off with her head!"

"What the fuck?" Aleksei mouthed to Sofia as she came out into the courtyard with two servants from the duke's household carrying her things.

Niko was behind Aleksei, stubbornly demanding to leave already while Eugene stuffed his things into the royal carriage. The sentinels were all outside, some mounted already, and the prince's carriage was hitched to six black horses.

"My lady." Ignat the white haired sentinel bowed and took Sofia's trunks from the servants. Her coach was ready as well, two white horses pawing restlessly.

"I don't know. I'm sorry." Sofia stood with Aleksei and whispered in the courtyard filled with lanterns, neighing horses, jingling tacks, and sentinels relaying orders.

Their mounts were tired. They had no provisions for the three week trip back to Krakova because they'd relied on resupplying at the den, they'd lost the Chartorisky as an ally, and come spring, Lev would arrive not to pat Niko's head but to take it. He was upset about Papa's death, Sofia imagined, the way he'd beheaded the envoy and sent his head in a box with flowers.

"Brother, let's leave! They are insolent!" Niko shouted all over the courtyard.

"This is a shit show," Aleksei breathed. "Fuck."

"Should we wait for the Chartorisky, Captain?" Dominik asked.

"No!" Niko yelled. "She's stupid. I'm not marrying her."

"Simmer down, Niko," Aleksei said, but guided Sofia to her coach anyway. He barked at someone to check the wheels on the royal carriage, claiming it looked lopsided, but he was stalling.

He climbed into the coach with Sofia and once he closed the door, he let out a long line of colorful curses, then buried his face in his hands. Seven years older than Niko, he was only twenty-two and at his wit's end. "What am I to do?"

"We have to leave," she whispered. "The prince said he would, so we must."

"What happened with Zoya?"

"Someone told Niko she'd been with Lev... Is it true?"

"Why does that matter?" he asked.

"It matters to Niko," she said. "Come on, Aleksei. We'll figure out the rest later, but we have to move now."

"Yeah, yeah..." Aleksei tutted. As he reached for the door, it opened from the outside, revealing Lord Dragan, the duke's oldest son.

"The prince will not hear me, but may I have a word, cousin?" Dragan asked, after acknowledging Sofia with a courteous nod.

"Speak." Aleksei leaned back in his seat, casually spinning a dagger in his right hand.

"I believe we got off on the wrong foot. There is no need to leave in the middle of the night, cousin. We are family, and our support is with the crown prince. Please come inside so we may talk this over tomorrow while laughing about tonight."

"I'm laughing already," said Aleksei. "What say your father?"

"My father sends me, cousin."

"Then perhaps he should be the one to say it," Aleksei said, his scarlet gaze cold and arrogant as he glanced at Dragan standing outside.

"Come on, Aleksei, be reasonable." Dragan cocked his head. "Father is now head of the house. He's not coming out to apologize to a child even if the child is a prince."

"I suppose we're leaving, then," was Aleksei's answer. He reached over to pull the door, but Dragan held it.

"You should know there *will* be war should Lev of Guard come anywhere *near* the throne," Dragan said.

Aleksei flicked a look at Sofia, and she was glad the lack of light in the cabin concealed her burning face. Though she meant to help, she certainly had overreached.

"Good," said Aleksei. "Then Elfur can come pouring through the Narrow while we have a pissing contest in Krakova."

"You presume you can go to Krakova." Though the smile remained, the lord didn't look too warm just then.

"That sounded like a threat, cousin." Had there been any self-doubt in Aleksei, it blinked out in a beat, as he shoved Dragan back, surprising the lord with his strength, and stepped out. "Are you threatening the prince?"

"Aleksei." Sofia rushed out after them to put herself between the captain whose alchemy glowed on his darksteel vambraces and the lord who wasn't used to dealing with sentinels and was surprised at how quickly that escalated. She held Aleksei's sword hand, though if he wanted to, he could easily shake off her grip. "Lord Dragan misspoke, I'm sure. Right?" She turned to the lord, all but begging.

Dragan's eyes checked the battlement where his men were, then scanned the courtyard now glowing with alchemy as numerous as the lanterns. Dominik was right behind him, his fingers tapping the hilt of his sword.

Ignat's attention was on the ramparts, walkways, and rooftops where shadows flickered as soldiers lined up with their crossbows. "Captain?"

"Put out the light," Aleksei said.

The lanterns blinked out at once as though someone had blown the candles, and Sofia saw the confusion on Dragan's face, perhaps realizing for the first time that a hundred sentinels might be more trouble than he bargained for—he lost track of them in a beat. Ignat who'd been right by them had vanished, Dominik too, and the royal carriage was open but empty inside. The courtyard fell silent and dark at once.

"Lord Dragan misspoke, I'm sure, right?" Sofia repeated, and this time the lord slowly nodded.

"Misunderstanding, cousin," he muttered. "Let me go speak with my father."

Four
Tales in the Den

Shield commanders held more power than Sofia would have imagined. One man in particular, Volg, had much to say about family, honor, and the greatness of the Red Shield, and acted as a mediator between the prince and the duke. The man looked like a grey wolf and the wide grin with pearly rows of perfect teeth didn't change that. She could sense the hidden fangs.

The night had spiraled out of control after Aleksei took Dragan hostage to cross the draw bridge, and the sides negotiated while standing over a bottomless pit.

Draped in Eugene's hooded cloak, Niko stood indistinguishable from his sentinels and smirked the whole night, finding the affair amusing. The boy was learning to play with power. But Sofia didn't see the humor in Aleksei having to bet with real lives including his own to save face, to not give too much ground to the duke though they had nowhere else to go.

Shields lived and died by their own laws, and once the duke guaranteed the safety and the free rein of the prince and his entourage, as witnessed by his commanders and soldiers, the night concluded with them returning to the den. The morning would bring negotiations regarding the throne and the war, but the ill affair which began during dinner had concluded with apologies from the duke's children—for now.

Afterward, Aleksei came into Sofia's room while she was unpacking her dresses and putting them into the wardrobe. Since she'd brought Lev's name into the mess, she had to stay and see through the negotiation.

Aleksei had found a little bowl of food and sat on the stool of the vanity, spooning it.

"How's the prince?" she asked, folding the ruffle of her Guard white dress with a gold sun, the same one Aleksei ironed earlier.

"Niko's Niko," he said. "But Eugene's grating on my nerves." He shook his hand, then grimaced. "Feels off," he muttered under his breath. He'd struck a castleguard in the face, and Sofia had seen he'd hurt his hand. That had been the arm he'd broken in seven places, including three on the hand itself. Also, the shoulder on the same side had been torn.

"You can't get into any scuffles," Sofia said.

"Yeah," was his answer. He set the bowl aside and took off his darksteel gear. "Are you sure you want to stay?"

"No," she said honestly. "But a few days won't matter. I don't want it to look as though the Guard ran off after the altercation." She continued as she arranged her dresses, "You can't give Rodion tsar regent. He'll never give the throne back. Just give assurances that Lev wouldn't be regent, and I'll pretend to be offended, I suppose."

"Why did that come up anyway?" he asked.

"That's something he would seek. You should know that." Sofia was exhausted. She left the dresses for the morning, went to sit on her bed, and kicked off her slippers. Sentinels were posted outside the door, and she didn't worry too much about her throat being slit while she slept. "Claiming the prince sired by the ghost of a Guard isn't consequence free, as it appears."

"I'd hoped the duke would be... family," Aleksei muttered.

"You're guarding the throne of Fedosia. You have no family, unfortunately." Sofia considered getting up to change into her nightgown and found it too much effort. She blew out the candles instead and went to bed. "Goodnight, I'll see you in the morning," she said in the dark.

Silent a while, then he asked, "Is it all right if I stay here?"

"Why?"

"I hear Rodion's sons are betting on who could sleep with you first."

"What?" Sofia sat up.

"There are hundreds of men in this keep alone. I'd like to stay in your room if that's all right. I'll just sit here. I won't bother you."

"You can stay only if you're sleeping," she said. "There's a settee by the fireplace, and if you could stoke the fire, that'd be... good."

"Sure."

As she lay back down and pulled up the cover, she heard him walking about. Then he was by the fire, tending to it. "I'm going to set my *lash* on the floor," he said. "It might look like a snake in the dark, but don't be afraid."

"I know what your *lash* looks like. Goodnight."

"Goodnight."

⁂

"Niko, what's wrong?" Sofia heard Aleksei say. "I can't breathe. Niko, get off me." He sounded asleep.

She opened her eyes, blinking at the dark ceiling.

"I can't breathe," he whispered.

The fire was dying and the room was nearly blind but when Sofia turned, she saw Aleksei's silhouette in the red hue of the ember. At first, she thought he was sitting on the settee, crouched. But that wasn't him. He was sleeping on the settee and something was sitting on him.

"Aleksei!"

Gasping, he sat up, and the thing on him jumped up onto the ceiling and disappeared into the shadow. Sofia screamed and two sentinels burst in, one of them Ruslan and the other a redheaded boy who liked sunflowers, his name escaping her, while she frantically pointed at the ceiling. "Something there! Get him! Get him!"

They brought in more light, searched every inch of the room, didn't find the man, but Shura—that was the redhead, now Sofia remembered his name—tapped on the wall mounted mirror. "This is two way, Captain."

Before Sofia could make horrified noises, Aleksei struck the mirror, breaking the glass. No wonder the fireplace didn't warm the room any, the wall was hollow, Sofia learned as she peered in to inspect for herself, and there was a passageway behind it.

The narrow space was covered in cobwebs, undisturbed for some time, and she didn't think the man had come through there. Besides, now that she'd calmed, she knew what had been on Aleksei—the stranger.

"Ruslan, take her to the prince. She is to stay at his quarters till I return," Aleksei said. "Shura, you're with me."

"Understood," both sentinels replied.

"Aleksei, where are you going?" Sofia asked.

"I'm going to find out where this leads." He stuck his head into the dark space. "Fetch the lantern, Shura."

"No, Aleksei." Sofia found herself grabbing his hand. "Take Niko. I'm sure he's bored, and he can see in the dark far better than you."

"Yeah, I'm not doing that." He turned to Sofia. "Go with Ruslan. I'll be right back."

The prince occupied an entire wing, and his bedchamber had conjoining rooms full of sentinels. The intricate molding and the parquet floor patterned with different colored wood to look like flowers were very reminiscent of the Guard designs, and some gilded fixtures such as candlestands were piled in the corner. The prince was in his nightgown, elaborate black silk, and jumped out of bed excitedly when Sofia came in.

"What happened here?" Sofia looked at the gold things piled in the corner.

"Oh, gold doesn't agree with me," Niko said.

Eugene walked around closing the many doors and leaving only Sofia, the prince, and himself in the chamber, though the sentinels arguing about cards could still be heard from the next room.

"What does that mean?" Sofia asked.

"Blood illness," Niko said. "Are you staying with me?"

"Sure." She patted his head because the child had been smiling and swaying his shoulders.

"Come." He wasn't wearing gloves, and his hand was warm when he led Sofia across the room. He hopped up on his bed and Eugene settled on the narrow valet's bed against the wall. The sentinel was smoking, drinking, and yawning. "Ruslan said there were secret tunnels. Is it true?" Niko asked.

"It appears to be so." Sofia sat down on a red velvet chair bedside, but the prince reached and pulled her to the bed. She could lie down and didn't mind him. So she lay on the large bed horizontally, while the prince sat leaning his back against the headboard.

"I want to see it. I like secret passageways. How exciting," Niko said.

"I told Aleksei to take you but he refused," Sofia said.

"Yeah, Grigori told everyone my blood doesn't clot. I was sick a lot. So Aleksei thinks if I get injured I'll bleed a lot."

"Thinks?" Sofia asked, yawning, catching the thing from Eugene. It was late and she was tired.

"Yeah, yeah. Now I'm looking for a different wife. Do you want to marry me? I like you."

"Um... I'm old enough to be your mother, Prince. It would be better if you pick a bride closer to your age."

"Then she'll be annoying like Zoya."

The bed smelled of years of dust, though Sofia imagined they would have changed the bedclothes for the prince. Perhaps it was just the room. It had been built grandiose but hadn't been cared for since.

"Can you pay the Chartorisky for your brother's horse?" Sofia asked. She didn't like Aleksei owing anything to Zoya. That probably wasn't her business anymore but still...

"What horse?" Niko asked.

"Charger," Sofia said.

"That's Aleksei's horse. He had him before Burkhard died."

"I know. But the queen sold him to an Elfurian baron and Zoya bought it back for him," Sofia said.

"No." Niko folded his arms and frowned. "She owes Aleksei a lot anyway. I'm not giving Zoya anything."

Reminded Zoya had said the Chartorisky owed Aleksei a favor, Sofia asked, "Do you know what he did for them, the Chartorisky?" She was feeling particularly nosy because as soon as Sofia left, Zoya would try to sink her claws into Aleksei.

"Many things!" Niko exclaimed, then looked to Eugene. Sofia could hear the sentinel snoring, so he wasn't going to object. "Daniil was accused of being a spy," he said breathlessly, dropped his arms, then crawled to Sofia and whispered, "Daniil is friends with an Elfurian prince, which is fine because the Chartorisky have a port. But he made a silver model of Raven and sent it to the prince as a gift. You can't do that. You can't send Elfur any maps, information about Fedosia, or you know, the models of our garrisons, fortresses, or Raven. He got in a lot of trouble with both the church and the throne.

"Daniil has no friends, but because Zoya is friends with both Lev and Aleksei, she had Lev take the letter from the church aviary so it didn't get sent to the archmage with the courier pigeons, and Aleksei had to kill the report before it went to the magistrate. I only know because Aleksei asked me to steal a scroll from my mother's things so she didn't find out. *'It's not a big deal, Danny didn't know it's illegal,'* Aleksei said, and I didn't care because it was a tiny Raven inside a jewelry egg, not a real map or anything.

"Then," he breathed scandalously, "he killed his wife's brother."

"Daniil is married?" Sofia gasped.

"No, but he was betrothed to… I forgot his name, some count, but Daniil was betrothed to his daughter. He went to their home to visit, then killed her brother and ran away. It was a whole thing! I know because Eugene knows. That one, Aleksei wasn't so happy about because the brother was little, like twelve or thirteen years old.

"The count was making a huge deal, you know, because his son died, and Zoya tried to have my brother kill him, but Aleksei wouldn't do it. So she hired the city patrol to stab him to death, and that's what happened.

"Then, the whole thing got brought to the sentinels because a count died in Krakova and Zoya begged and begged and begged Aleksei to let it go. The Chartorisky paid a lot of silver to the widowed countess, and in the end, Aleksei didn't pursue the murder because Zoya would have been implicated.

"Anyway, so, I'm not paying for the stupid horse."

"Why did Daniil kill a child?" Sofia was appalled, but also she didn't know how true it was.

"I don't know. He's nearly thirty now and doesn't have a wife. Eugene says it's because he has some type of demon in him."

"Well, most men do," Sofia said.

Then she lay beside Niko, telling the prince the tale of the firebird, a creature so full of magic that even the feather dropped by one contained enough light to illuminate a village, when the prince said, "Lev is a firebird, then. His light is brighter than the archmage's and also he doesn't cast a shadow."

"Lev?" Sofia petted the prince's head. "My brother is just a man. He has a shadow. Everyone does."

"Oh, I meant a different shadow, your reflection on the *dver*. He doesn't have one because he's a source of light. Do you know what shadow alchemy is?"

"Boy," came Eugene's voice. "Stop the chattering and go to sleep. Enough fairy tales for the night."

"He's grumpy," Niko whispered.

"He's right, though. Let's go to sleep," Sofia said.

"All right." Niko bunched up his cover and turned, while Sofia pulled up her wool cloak. "You're not a Guard, though," he whispered, his back to her. "I knew that from the first time I saw you."

"Because I'm not blonde?"

"Because you cast a shadow and Guards don't."

"Boy, be quiet and go to sleep," Eugene grumbled.
"Everyone has a shadow, Niko," Sofia said.
"All right, I believe you. Goodnight."

A hand on her back. Sofia opened her eyes—Aleksei, and it was light outside the windows. Niko was fast asleep beside her. She rolled off the bed without disturbing the prince, slipped on her shoes and followed Aleksei into a conjoining room. The ceiling was blue in that one, like an open sky, and sentinels were asleep sharing the bed and on the floor. Four were awake, playing cards, and rose when Aleksei entered after Sofia and closed the door gently.

"Captain," they murmured and began putting away the cards and coppers splayed on the table.

From the sentinels asleep on the bed, Ignat sat up, squinted with one eye, then got up, yawning and stretching. They were all clothed and had their darksteel gear on.

"Morning, Captain." Ignat went to the washing table, mumbled about the cold water, took the bucket, and stepped out.

The table was cleared, and a sentinel offered Sofia a chair, while another one made tea.

"Thank you," she said, sitting down. She accepted the tea and watched as Aleksei drew on the table with chalk. A map, she saw immediately.

The men slowly got up and gathered around Aleksei, looking at the map.

"There's an undercroft below us," Aleksei said.

"Like a church?" Sofia asked.

"The den used to be a church," Aleksei said. "It was built by the Guards some five centuries ago."

Why didn't she know that? Sofia frowned. She wasn't ignorant of her house history, so this bit must have been neglected, and whenever that happened, it was intentional.

"The tunnels vein out like this," he illustrated on the map, "and run through the entire mountain. The exits appeared sealed off but there isn't a way for me to map it in a single night. So, this is what we're doing," and he began assigning positions for his men to scout. As he talked, he took out a piece of chainmail from his cloak pouch and handed it to Sofia.

Holding the piece of armor in her palm, surprisingly light for metal, she studied it. She didn't know what kind of armor Durnov puppeteers wore, but Shields wore leather armor. Guards wore Apraksin steel cuirass. Skuratov wore full armor but forged of their own iron. The eastern houses, Apraksin, Pulyazin, and Menshikov didn't wear metal armor because it got so cold there that the steel stuck with frost. The two houses whose retainers wore chainmail, Chartorisky and Vietinghoff, were both wealthy and the piece of metal Sofia was holding was incredibly cheap, almost like tin, and the links felt flimsy and not Fedosian made. She didn't imagine the Durnov, the house who could animale steel, would dress like this.

Also, it was perfect. Every single link was exactly the same. It must be machine made, like the printing press, she realized, and said, "It's Elfurian."

"Are you sure?" Aleksei asked. "This metal, the only time I've seen it was from Lev. He shoes his racehorses with it. I thought it might be something Guard, no?"

Ignat had returned and wanted to see the chainmail so Sofia handed it to him, and the sentinels passed it along to each other.

"Makes sense. It's very light," Sofia said. "But I haven't seen it before. Where did you find it?"

"Undercroft," Aleksei said. "It's full of bones."

"Human?" Shura the redhead asked.

"Yes, and not centuries old either," Aleksei said.

"Do you suppose the duke is eating people?" Ignat asked. "Lord Fedir reeks foul."

"Why would Elfurians wear chainmail?" Dominik asked. "They use black powder weapons, I thought. Chainmail won't stop that."

"They might wear different gear at the border," Aleksei said. "To protect them from us, not from each other. That won't stop a darksteel bolt but it might protect from a blade, somewhat."

"What is the old fool doing, then?" Ignat asked. "Why are there dead Eflurians in the undercroft?"

"He's instigating war," Sophia said as it occurred to her. "He's exiled to the border with nothing to do, but if Elfur attacked, that would make him very powerful."

"Assuming he can win…" A sentinel voiced his concern. He'd been cleaning his gear in the corner and shrugged when all eyes turned to him. "We're in no shape for war. The truth is the truth whether it's patriotic or not. The *Boyar Duma* is split. His Highness is very young. Four failed harvests, and if our trade with Elfur stops, Fedosia will starve this winter.

"Correct me if I'm wrong, Captain, but I thought the prince was being betrothed to the Chartorisky because we were going to buy grain with their silver." He sheathed his sword and got up. "But I suppose that's fucked now thanks to old man Eugene."

Sofia had come to see from living at Raven among the sentinels that her impression they were lowborn soldiers had been wrong. Some were of common birth, but many were bastard children of lords, like Ignat, or impoverished highborns like Dominik, and were educated and freely spoken, at least among themselves and with their captain.

"How is the engagement failing Eugene's fault?" Sofia asked.

"He hates the Chartorisky and has the prince's ear," said Ignat. "Without a doubt it was him talking shit about Zoya that changed the prince's mind. He's a liar, a coward, a drunk, and doesn't belong with the imperial sentinels but for through the grace of His Highness."

"He can probably hear you," Sofia whispered.

"I'm sure he can. I bet his ear is pressed to the door," Ignat said. "He knows I loathe him. It's not news."

"That's enough, Ignat," Aleksei said.

A sentinel came in to announce they were being called for breakfast. Aleksei nodded and dismissed him.

"It's probably that oat porridge goo," one said.

"Better than nothing," said another.

"I wouldn't eat stew here, anyway," said Ignat. "The meat on those bones went somewhere."

"Doma." Aleksei gestured Dominik over. "Find me a name. Someone who doesn't like Rodion but has power here in the den."

"Got it," Dominik said.

"Do you want to eat with us?" Aleksei asked Sofia.

"You just don't want me to sit at the duke's table because you heard the young lords fancy me," Sofia teased.

"Better you stay away from them, Lady Sofia. Should they touch you wrong, I *will* kill them." Aleksei wasn't joking. So, Sofia's petty jealousy of Zoya hadn't been unreasonable. At least she hadn't threatened the girl's life.

Five

Book of Darkness

Duke Rodion called a meeting with the prince and his commanders. The negotiation hadn't included Sofia but that was fine, Aleksei was with Niko, and she spent the day in much needed leisure.

Dominik and Ignat followed her a few paces behind, whispering amongst themselves, as she toured the immensity of the den. The hallways were decorated with the portraits and busts of dead Shields, old satin chairs lining the wall as though they had an assembly long ago and forgot to stow the seats afterward. Ignat remarked that perhaps the ghosts of the ancestors haunted the corridors, and that stayed with Sofia because she was still troubled with the stranger's behavior last night.

For as long as she could remember, ever since she was a girl, he'd been an ever present thing, lurking in her mind when no one else was around. The Church of Murmia was the first he'd spoken, and last night was the first he'd affected another—other than the slaughter at the church. She wondered if her acknowledging him, speaking to him, was making him more... real. She shook her head, trying to shake off the unease shadowing her, because it wasn't only the sentinels a few paces behind her.

Ignoring the stranger, she passed through the soldiers' quarters and looked back when Ignat sniggered. The sentinels were laughing about the soldiers training in the courtyard. One of the castleguards was three times the size of a normal man, and Dominik had joked about the length of his sword, which Sofia only later understood had been a reference to the man's privates.

They passed by the Chartorisky siblings in the garden, Daniil using alchemy to fix his aunt's fountain. He nodded greeting her. Zoya sat on the bench braiding her beautiful gold locks—Sofia didn't exist in her world.

By the time Sofia found the Shield gallery of weapons, the stranger had disappeared because she'd forgotten about him, and that was the key, she thought. *She* was calling him.

"That's a lot of fucken steel. How did they use to live in these things?" Ignat bent to read the placard on the watchman's full dark-steel armor on display, red cape and all. "Damn, sixty pounds," he muttered, and stood on tiptoes to open the visor and peer into the armor. Sofia recalled mistaking them, watchmen, for empty armors in the dark corridors of Raven and a shiver passed through her.

After the queen's death, the prince had the rest of the watchmen destroyed. Sofia couldn't say 'killed' because that would imply they had been living. They'd died long ago when they redlined, and it was the cruelty of the queen having them serve her still. They were at peace now, their souls finally free of the red madness.

"Being mad helps, I suppose," Dominik said, referring to the watchmen living in their full steel armor.

"You don't see these often," Sofia remarked about a darksteel poleaxe. She'd seen the castleguards at the den carry them, but theirs had wooden shafts whereas this one was made wholly of darksteel.

"It looks heavier than a donkey," Ignat said, and whistled when he read the placard. "Thirteen pounds. No one carries that much steel."

From Aleksei, and just by being around many sentinels the past few months, Sofia knew the heaviest weapon a sentinel carried was their shield at ten pounds of darksteel, and they only carried it when they were mounted or expecting battle. Otherwise, it was their sword which was three and a half pounds. Shield alchemy was cheap and the gold a typical sentinel carried on their vambraces would last them a lifetime, because there was no cheating in the weight of the darksteel when they shifted between weapons, three and a half pound sword turned into three and a half pound spear, and they were simply performing basic alchemy—which was also why they were so fast.

A Shield crossbow was a self-depleting weapon that fired parts of itself as steel bolts, twelve shots before it spent itself. Very light, the exact weight of the Shield sword, compared to the fifteen pounds of Guard crossbows, and most sentinels carried the extra weight of the bolts as spare steel or just didn't use the crossbow because of the self-depleting nature.

Lost in thought, Sofia had been staring at a fencing sword with an intricate guard when she heard Lev's name and snapped out of the reverie.

Dominik and Ignat were debating Guard alchemy and the cost of it.

"It's three ounces of pure gold," Sofia said because they'd been guessing at the cost of Dragon's Breath.

"Holy shit," Ignat said. "Alchemy of the wealthy, no doubt."

"Well, in Guard alchemy, or spells as we call it, you are creating something out of nothing," said Sofia, "and Dragon's Breath costs three ounces of gold each time it's cast."

"No wonder the archmage had been covered in gold," Dominik said. "He'd go through it in a single day, huh?"

"Not all debt can be settled with gold," Sofia said. "Some light master spells require... sacrifice." The archmage's impotency came to mind but she didn't wish to ridicule the dead.

Nothing came free in alchemy, and speaking to the shadow had dire consequences as it appeared. It was the archmage's death that sent Fedosia on the downward spiral of houses warring, costing thousands of lives, and it was of little consolation to the dead and their families that Sofia hadn't done it intentionally. Lev didn't have a father anymore and it began with her. She'd brought darkness into the church and the debt incurred was being settled with lives. No more, she decided. No matter the situation or the temptation, she'd never be courted by darkness again. She was also afraid of making him stronger because he'd scared her last night.

"Looks like the captain's *lash*." Ignat pointed to a bullwhip. They all knew the serpent like weapon Aleksei's sword turned into was Durnov animation, but no one ever mentioned his mother.

Sofia didn't know if the duchess taught Aleksei puppetry or if he'd learned it on his own to spite his father—it didn't matter. But the weapon was unique to him.

Aleksei had claimed the den was built by the Guards, and Sofia had been noticing the church like architecture of it, but once she saw the library, she didn't doubt Aleksei anymore. Except for some Elfurian manifestos, the entirety of the two-floor library was volumes of light codices.

Most were books she'd seen in the White Palace or at various churches, but a section of mages' writings drew her attention. Scrolls, unbound manuscripts, and centuries old parchments stacked in disarray, they were behind a steel lattice as though they'd been imprisoned, and the 'librarian' didn't know where the keys were.

"It's always been like that," the thin man bent like a question mark said.

Everything smelled of decades of dust and the two sentinels removed the red cloth from the round table and dusted the velvet chairs before settling onto them with a cup of tea. The 'librarian' said nothing as Ignat struck a flint to light his pipe, confirming he wasn't a librarian or a scribe at all. Bring an uncovered flame into a Guard library, you would lose your head for the offense.

The nostalgia hit Sofia like a punch to the gut, and she waited for the moment to pass. Papa, Auntie, the uptight and frigid servants of the Guard household, the knights who'd lost their lives defending the palace, and even the archmage, she missed. They were her family. Only Lev remained as the legacy of once a great house.

Sofia wrested with the guilt because though she still believed the archmage deserved to die, she couldn't deny the chaos his death unleashed. He had been a central figure of Fedosia and his absence had left a power void.

"Are you all right, my lady?" Dominik asked.

"Mmm." Sofia ran her hand along the steel lattice, her fingers turning dirty and grimy from the soot and dust. "Can you open this for me?"

"Of course, my lady." Dominik came and pried apart the netting with his exoskeleton.

"Just take the whole thing off, Doma," Ignat said from his seat. "I don't feel like catching shit from the captain when she cuts her hand on that thing. It's probably rusted too. The state of this place is a disgrace."

Dominik pulled the frame out and left it leaning against the wall. "Anything else, my lady?"

"No, thank you."

Sofia sat on the faded wool carpet and sorted through the documents. A lot of it was written in the language of spells, which she couldn't read, but it was fascinating still to see the signatures of mages, some even sainted and the name familiar, who'd lived centuries ago. Dusty parchments they might be, but she was touching the history of her family.

While she did that, Ruslan came to join them. He was a sentinel of common birth but fit with the other two like the cups of the same tea set. He brought the design plan of the den and they discussed something Aleksei had tasked them with, Sofia gathered, but she was too engrossed in a scroll she found with the seal of Aleksander the Wise. Why didn't she know the Guards built the den? How did they lose it to the Shields, and how could the church abandon such precious documents to be lost to neglect?

"Whose seal is on the plan?" Sofia asked in the passing, having tasked herself with arranging the church scrolls by the date.

"Seventh archmage," said Ruslan. "I don't see a name, my lady."

"We don't refer to an archmage by his given name," Sofia said, and she couldn't stop smiling. "But the seventh archmage was later sainted. I believe you heard of him. Saint Neva of White Guard."

"The prince is in his father's house, then," Dominik remarked.

"Someone tell the duke to take his brats and move out," Ignat said.

"What are you always smoking?" Sofia asked Ignat, returning her attention to the scrolls. "It smells pleasant like herbs and spices."

"Just cloves, my lady," Ignat said.

"Not opium?" Sofia asked.

"Ah, no. The red alchemy is already taxing on the mind. We don't venture into things that make it worse," Ignat answered. "The occasional glass of wine with a lady or a lord is about it for us. Sometimes potions if we're off duty, but I've seen opium habit waste the mind and the body. That shit is no good."

"I've seen Eugene both drink and indulge in opium on duty," Sofia said. It'd been a casual observation, and she hadn't meant any malice by it because she liked Eugene.

"That's because he's never *on* duty," Ignat scoffed.

"Toothless old dog, that one," Dominik said.

"But not harmless, though," Ruslan said. "I bet you both of my balls it was Eugene who poisoned the prince's ear by whispering Lady Zoya's business. Nearly got us all killed over some bullshit yesterday."

"You don't like Eugene?" Sofia grasped the common theme among sentinels as she turned to the three sitting around a table like a murder of gossiping crows. "And why would he sabotage Aleksei's plan?"

It had been Aleksei's idea to betroth Zoya to Niko. The throne needed Chartorisky silver and Zoya wanted to be queen.

"Oh, my lady doesn't know," Ignat said. "The old dog has a vendetta against the Chartorisky. He used to be a forger. He ran a group of bandits robbing the Chartorisky and counterfeiting silver coins. Got caught because the House of Silver doesn't fuck around when you forge treasury coins. Then he sold out his crew to save his skin because he's a coward, but he now blames the Chartorisky for the deaths of his friends."

"That may be human skin, my lady," Dominik said.

Sofia had been holding a leather bound, or so she thought, book and tossed it and wiped her hands on her dress. She shuddered with revulsion. It had felt odd in her hand, but she'd been too invested in the gossip to notice.

Driven by curiosity, Ignat came and picked up the book, then said, "Holy shit, it is human skin." He flipped through it. "What is this?"

"What does it say?" Ruslan asked.

"Who knows? Spell language." Ignat held out the book to Sofia, but she shook her head, afraid to touch it.

"Give it." Dominik gestured, and when Ignat handed him the book, he opened it and squinted at the pages. "To... This one is a symbol for dark, and that one for light... I think this means alchemy..."

"Come on, Doma, everyone can read it like that." Ignat laughed as he settled back into his chair, lighting his silver pipe again. "Just admit it. You're not smart enough for it. The only person alive who can read this shit is probably Lev."

"*If* he's alive," Ruslan said.

"Did you hear he died?" Ignat asked, to which Ruslan shrugged. "Too bad. That would save us the war, huh?" said Ignat.

"I hope Semyon is well," Dominik said.

"Why? He pays well or something?" Ignat asked.

"He's a friend," was Dominik's answer.

A servant came to announce they were being called for dinner, and Sofia rose with the sentinels. She'd be back to sort through the books, but as Dominik was putting back the human skin book Sofia asked him to keep it for her. She didn't want to touch it but was drawn to it. Even if she couldn't read it, she'd take it because it belonged to the Guards.

Then as they made their way to the dining hall, Ignat warned Dominik not to walk too close to Sofia, and laughed, giving him guff about approaching her in the Shield inn.

"What am I supposed to say? The prince asked," Dominik said. "You try speaking back to royalty."

"Eugene has the prince's ear. He could have said numerous things, including how the captain wouldn't find it funny," said Ruslan. "But he speaks only when it benefits him." He sneered in disgust. "Good thing the captain fell far, far, far from the Burkhard tree. He was one mad fucker."

"The duke wasn't mad. He was cruel," Ignat said. Then the sentinels hushed as though they hadn't been speaking at all because they'd arrived at the dining hall.

Six

Tea's Crown

Aleksei picked up the human skin book from the writing table. "To cast a dark... spell? No, that's not right. What does it mean when there is a symbol for light inside the one for darkness?"

"I don't know. I've never seen it written like that." They found Sofia a new room, one that didn't have a two way mirror or a secret passage through the wall, and she sat by the vanity dabbing ointment on her face. She'd returned from taking a long, hot bath and found Aleksei in the corridor. He hadn't attended dinner, none of the lords or commanders had because they'd been in a meeting. "How did the negotiations go?" she asked.

"Fought over the grain reserve the entire time." Aleksei set the book down, went to the washing table, and stood there taking off his gear before washing his face and brushing his teeth. "We're going to be fighting about it all winter and well into spring." He sighed. "The throne owes the Pulyazin three *thousand* tons of grain. It's a debt we must honor no matter what Rodion says."

"The undercroft?" she asked.

"I didn't bring up. I need to know what's happening before I decide what to do with it." He was right, of course. Aleksei grumbled like an old man as he continued, "The granaries are dry, Sofia. Harvest failed three years in a row and last year we barely scraped by. If we press the lords for more grain, we'll have a revolt, and if we don't, we'll still have a revolt, just a different kind." He tossed a cloth on the washing table.

"What did the council say?" she asked.

"The old ministers quarrel amongst themselves. Everyone wants money for their own ministry." He dragged his heels to the bed and collapsed on it. It was Sofia's bed and they hadn't shared one in a long time. Perhaps he'd forgotten where he was but she didn't point it out. "My one bright idea had been to buy grain from Elfur with Chartorisky silver but that went to shit because apparently Niko called Zoya a whore?" He sat up. "I'm not clever enough for any of this. I'd rather just build you a fire. It's going to snow tonight."

He went to the fireplace and got to stoking it. That didn't take him long and he returned to Sofia while she removed the bedwarmers and got underneath the cover. "Do you mind if I sleep on this side of the bed?" he asked. So, he did know.

"Do as you like," she said. Then requested, "Leave the light on," when he reached for the bedside lantern.

"How was your day?" He lay down fully clothed but for his boots, and occupied a tiny portion in the corner of the large bed.

"Uneventful," Sofia claimed though she felt the stranger creep in the corner where the light didn't reach.

"I have to take care of some bullshit in the morning, but in the afternoon, I can take you to the Narrow if you want to see it," he said. "The wall the mages built an eon ago still stands, as I understand, and you can see Elfur beyond it."

"I would like that," she said. "The den used to be a church?"

"Yes."

"Why don't I know that?" she wondered. They were facing each other though there was a lot of space between them.

"It's probably because the magical wall did nothing when Elfur came with black powder and steel weapons, and they butchered a bunch of mages and acolytes on this hill," he said. "The Elfurians were plain men, just soldiers, and Guards wouldn't admit to such a humiliating defeat. The archmage at the time fabricated a lore about the loss, claiming some type of dark force chewed up his mages, *then* Elfur came. That was what we were taught, anyway, that Shields are warriors and Guards are liars. That's probably not the whole truth, but this is now a Shield stronghold, not a sacred church, so…"

Sofia had never heard such a story. "Did the archmage elaborate on what kind of dark forces?"

"Shadow alchemy," he said. "The same wolf the church has been crying for eons, the soulless."

"Wolves are real, Aleksei."

"Cries the boy," he said.

"Not a boy. White Guard is the shepherd."

"Says my Lady Guard." He smiled at her, and they held each other's gaze for a long moment. "What do you think of Volg?" he asked.

"The commander?" Sofia knotted her brows. "Why?"

"Doma says Volg has the men's respect more than Rodion. Does he strike you as an ambitious man? Maybe someone who'd like to replace the duke?"

Sofia thought of the silver haired wolf with a red cape and a shoulder ornament of a slain dragon. A *lot* of darksteel on that one, he dressed like a watchman and that was intentional. "Given the chance, he'd eat Rodion," she said. "He'd also eat you, too."

"He's of common birth. He can't replace Niko," Aleksei said.

"Whereas Rodion could murder the prince and claim the throne permanently once he's regent," Sofia said.

"Right." Aleksei bit his lip, thinking. "How about Dragan? His name came up as someone who strongly opposes Rodion, and he's a legitimate heir to the duke."

"He's almost certainly a false prophet," Sofia said. "He's a puppet the duke controls, a false opposition. The archmage used to have a few of those, parsons and mages who were critical of him, but they all worked for him, and when someone approached them with a genuine concern, they'd pass on the information to the archmage. It's a trap. The church also had informants posing as necromancers. That is how they catch heretics.

"I'm wary of him," she continued. "Because by your bylaws Dragan is allowed to challenge his father's command. So either his criticism is false or he is false."

"You're very sure of yourself, Lady Sofia." Aleksei smiled. When he wrinkled his nose as he just did, it was because he found something endearing.

"Not at all," she said. "It's a guessing game, but if you're going to be risking your life, it's better to err on the side of caution."

"Volg over Dragan it is," Aleksei said. "It's selfish to say it but I'm glad you stayed. Your counsel is a breath of fresh air when I feel like I'm drowning."

Sofia slipped her hand under the pillow and patted the silk sheet between them with her other hand. "You once said I was the anchor for your mind, a memory of me in a church, but that would be gone now. Have you found a new one? I reckon you'll be using a lot of alchemy soon. Blood on the horizon, rising like a tidal wave... I feel it."

"Have I?" Soft black brows furrowed over his eyes the color rubies, warm and deep in the firelight. "The same person, a different memory, I suppose," he whispered. "You called me back in Kseniya's chamber and you still do."

"I'm sorry she hurt you," Sofia said, addressing the unspoken thing between them. "You make me wish I was powerful so I could protect you."

"You protect me plenty. The worst monsters are in here." He lifted his hand to touch his temple. "I can't run from them, can't hide, and can't slay them with a sword, either. But you make them quiet. They're afraid of you, my lady."

"Then why did you ever tell me to leave?" she asked.

"I was making you unhappy."

"The only time you make me unhappy is when you tell me to leave."

"Forgive me," he breathed.

She reached across the bed and touched him on the forehead with two fingers as a parson would, absolving his sins after he confessed. Some tears were trying to sneak up her throat, so she swallowed them down and exhaled.

"I do love you." He kissed her hand. "I'm glad every time I see you and wretched each time I miss you, and I'm so very afraid you're going to find..." He held onto her hand and needed to take a deep breath. "My shit isn't working, Sofia. I can't get hard. Whenever anyone touches me, I see Kseniya, and my skin crawls and I can't breathe. I don't know if it will ever be better. Baltar said there's a potion for it, but I feel so fucken pathetic because the men who buy such things are in their nineties... Fuck." He dropped her hand and sat up. "Fuck. First I'm sterilized, and now I feel fucken castrated."

Sofia sat up as well. She scooted over to Aleksei and rested her chin on his shoulder. Gliding her hand up his neck, she ran her fingers through his midnight curls. "Give it time, leave it be, and stop forcing it. Your bones haven't healed. Surely your soul will take longer. I'm not hanging around waiting for sex, stop it. I'm not your patron. I love you."

"I don't know why you would. I don't understand."

"That's because they lie." She touched his temple. "The monsters must be loud. But one day, you'll look in the mirror and see what I see. You are perfect, Aleksei."

"My lady is blind," he said.

Sofia shook her head. "Perfection, like beauty, is in the eye of the beholder, and I possess the eyes of someone who loves you."

"The rarest eyes in all of creation my lady has," he said, turning around to face her, "and they are the color of rolling hills, vast and full of mystery." He kissed her.

"Grass and trees, he calls my eyes," she whispered into his mouth. He tasted sweet and when their mouths parted, their foreheads remained pressed together. Her eyes closed, she let the moment linger. She stroked his crown, which she loved doing, and moaned a little to herself, sighing. Another long breath before she opened her eyes. "How about we get some sleep, Aleksei?"

"Sounds good," he said, nodding. "Let me stoke the fire first. The den is cold."

"Settled in cold," she agreed. "Sleep under the cover when you return. It's more pleasant."

"Yes, my lady." He kissed her hand and got up.

◈

"I want to see it. I want to go," the prince insisted.

"I told Sofia I'd take her, Niko," Aleksei explained as they had breakfast in the common hall. Sentinels and castleguards alike were seated along rows of long tables. They were serving porridge from a giant cauldron and men had to get up and queue for food, but it was better than nothing.

"We'll all go," Niko said.

"One of us has to stay behind and talk about the grain, Niko." Aleksei gave his piece of bread to Sofia. "It's warm and has salt. It's good."

"What is there to talk about? We don't have it." Niko had eaten with the lords already and was at the table to pester Aleksei.

"Don't say shit like that, Niko," Aleksei warned.

"We're fighting over it because they don't know we don't have it. It'll be far easier if you just tell them that."

"You can't just *not* have grain, Niko. You're the prince. You have to provide for your people." Aleksei looked over his shoulder when Ignat came up behind him. The sentinel whispered in his ear and the captain nodded.

"Your Highness. My lady." Ignat bowed, then left.

"Eugene has a plan." Niko looked into Sofia's bowl and frowned. "There's fat floating in it."

"It's lard, Niko," Sofia said.

"Do you want an apple? They have apples in the grand hall." He pointed at the exit. "Also, eggs."

"It's all right, thank you, prince," said Sofia. "Where is Eugene?"

"Asleep. He was drinking," Niko said. "We have a plan. We're going to kill the Chartorisky, take their silver, and buy grain from Elfur."

"You can't 'kill' a house of *Boyar Duma*," Aleksei hissed, his scarlet eyes flicking to scan around them. The hall was noisy and the Chartorisky retainers were seated far away.

"Why not?" the prince asked. "We're trying to kill the Guards and they are in the *Boyar Duma*."

"It's not the same, they attacked first. They assaulted Raven, if you recall. We call that high treason, but the Chartorisky are an ally, all right? Stop taking advice from Eugene. He's a drunk," Aleksei said under his breath.

"He said you'd say that because you love Zoya." Niko flinched, perhaps recalling Sofia was there, then turned to her. "Sorry. But they used to be betrothed long ago. I would have let it go had she only slept with Aleksei but she's indecent and slept with a *ton* of men."

"I was five. I didn't sleep with Zoya, and shut up," Aleksei said. "He doesn't know what he's talking about," he apologized to Sofia.

"It's... fine." She tried to stay out of it, though she hadn't known they used to be betrothed.

"You still love her. That's why you're so nice to them," Niko pointed at the Chartorisky retainers. Aleksei pushed his hand down.

"Now you're just fucking with me," Aleksei said.

"Yeah." Niko flashed a bright grin. "But don't be sad when I kill her. Now, hurry up. Let's go to the Narrow. I told our cousins I was going, and they wanted to come too."

"Ah, fuck me," Aleksei groaned. "I'm sorry," he told Sofia. "I was hoping I could spend a little time with you, but it's ruined now, I suppose."

"It's not ruined." Sofia smiled. It couldn't be. He'd made the effort, and that made her happy.

Perhaps the frigid weather at the den had to do with the altitude the fortress sat at, because though the border was less than two hours ride from the hills, it was warm like early spring.

Green moss hugged the wet black rocks under their boots, slippery as they climbed, and Aleksei held the prince ever since they'd dismounted to climb up a narrow path between boulders. Lord Vukhir gave Sofia his arm, and she clung onto him as loose soil and rock gave away under her heel and slid down.

"Careful," he said, pulling her up. Though the youngest of the duke's sons, he was the size of an armored knight and far larger than Aleksei. The rodent like face was disturbing on such a big man, and the Shield red eyes more so, but Sofia thanked him and smiled. His breath smelled of raw meat, and that was harder to ignore. She leaned away from him and toward the damp wind when he spoke to her again. "I've never met a Guard before. I thought they were supposed to be golden haired."

"Most are," said Sofia. "Lord Lev is blond, for instance."

"Perhaps it's your Elfurian father. You're the runt of the litter, then?" he asked. "Like that one." He pointed a chin toward Aleksei who was further ahead in front of them. "Did you know his mother was Durnov?"

"How is that different than your mother being a Chartorisky?"

That breath, Sofia had to lean away from him again. Then why ask him a question? Because now he was going to answer it.

"Durnov women train in alchemy. His blood isn't clean, and neither is his weapon. Duke Burkhard got cornered into the marriage, I heard. Queen Kseniya prized the Durnov."

"Because they are an invaluable ally?" She should really stop speaking to him. He turned and looked at her, breathing in her face. She considered falling down the cliff to escape him. "Do you eat the dead, Lord Vukhir?"

"Only criminals."

"That had been a joke." Sofia shuddered, disturbed.

"It wasn't funny."

"The saints have mercy," she muttered.

"There is no god."

"Then where does alchemy come from?" Sofia let go of his arm and walked ahead. If she fell, she fell. That had been an incredibly offensive thing to say to a Guard, done purposefully, she had to assume. The duke's children were insufferable, every single one. Perhaps growing up in isolation had such an effect.

"There better be a dragon's hoarded gold up there!" Niko yelled. "This is a *lot* of walking!"

Oleksandra and Dragan led the group, and Fedir and Teo, the soft boy and the brat, were behind Sofia and Vukhir. A common theme with the Shields, apparently Oleksandra and Dragan shared a bed, or so Dominik found out. Gathering information was an art, like fencing or spell casting, and Dominik had the mastery of it. Young men talked too much, Sofia supposed, when their blood drained from their brain to fill the organ between their legs.

The prince had been present when Dominik reported his findings and had said, *'That is disgusting,'* about Oleksandra and Dragan.

'Please, please, please, do not bring it up, Niko,' Aleksei had begged.

Struggling up the hill, Niko slipped and Aleksei caught him.

"You're untrained for a Shield!" Oleksandra turned to shout, and the wind distorted her laughter.

"I'm a prince! And you kiss—"

Aleksei yanked Niko and covered his mouth.

They made it to the peak, and it was worth the climb for Sofia. To one side, the grey ocean broke against the high cliffs, rolling thunder. And to the other side sat snowy mountains forever white at the top, the bottom dressed in evergreens, and a heavy fog hovered above the valley in between.

They caught a moment of calm as the gale simmered down to a gentle breeze dancing with the cloaks, and Sofia saw Elfur, home, beyond the valley. A fortress sat on a hill in the grey, a strange shape, and when Aleksei handed her his looking glass, she peered through it and saw the black dragon banner of House of Dohnan hung from the tall white walls. A chill ran through her, gathering her childhood memories like balling snow.

Her father's face came to her from the mist, a tall proud count, he used to have flowing feathers on his hat like exotic locks trailing down his neck.

"Ostrich feathers," Sofia whispered. "Imported from Paradise Islands."

"My lady dreams of faraway places," Aleksei said.

"Oh, the threat is closer than you think. I suppose you lose your bearings when you live in Krakova or anywhere else inland," Oleksandra said.

Niko was very impressed by a single tree that had managed to grow on a boulder and frightened Aleksei by peering down from the edge.

"You go where you look, Niko. You look down, you fall down." Aleksei pulled him back.

"He's like a mother hen, isn't he?" Oleksandra nudged Sofia with her elbow as though they were friends. "I guess it makes sense. The prince is such a weakling. I couldn't even shake his hand because of my gear. What the fuck is that blood illness he has? It's not a Shield ailment. Does it come from his ghost father?"

"You curtsy to a prince. When have you heard you shake hands with royalty? You're not sailors at a beerhouse," said Sofia.

"So, you're fucking my cousin or what?" she asked. "I've been told he spent the night in your bedchamber."

"You've been told correct." Sofia moved away from the duke's daughter, but the peak was crowded with the duke's other children, Vukhir and Fedir taking out their... Sofia turned away. The boys were pissing toward Elfur, and she hoped the wind changed and splashed the urine onto their trousers.

Teo stood there, sneering at Niko who didn't care she existed. The brothers laughed about something as Niko cupped his hand and whispered in Aleksei's ear. Teo had put on a gold coronet, perhaps to instigate trouble with Niko, and it angered her that he didn't care. She misunderstood why the prince had gotten ill tempered during the dinner—it was the mistreatment of Aleksei and his sentinels, not that a silly little girl was pretending to be a princess.

Oleksandra persisted by going around Sofia, facing her, and walking backward playfully. She had on more darksteel than her brothers and had thick steady legs. Sofia wouldn't know about her fighting prowess, but the lady was athletic, to say the least. Though her hair was midnight black, she reminded her of Elyena Durnova, the fiery redhead who'd raced with men, and perhaps would have placed second after Lev had the archmage not caused... well, war essentially.

"What is Lev Guard like?" Oleksandra asked, tossing up and catching a dagger.

"Loud, obnoxious, scandalous, and loved regardless," said Sofia. "He's a very gifted light user. Pity his talent must be wasted in such a brutish affair as killing."

"I've heard Guards have gold locks. You're different."

"Black sheep of the family," Sofia said. "My father comes from there." She pointed beyond the valley.

"So it's true? Was he truly a necromancer?"

"That he was."

Niko turned and frowned at 'necromancer', then returned his attention to Lord Dragan who was pointing at the stone wall running the length of the valley, and speaking. Curious about the conversation, Sofia joined the prince.

"That's the Narrow." Niko pointed at the valley. "It's a lot larger than on the map."

Dragan was talking about the money needed to renovate the wall. Though Elfur and Fedosia shared a sizable land border, the Narrow was the only place men and horses could cross. The rest was a continuous mountain range of permanent frost and unforgiving ridges.

"Why can't they invade through the water?" Sofia asked. Elfurian ships came and went through the ports of Fedosia daily. The journey was only half a month, far easier travel than through land, surely.

"It's a buoyancy problem," Fedir the soft lord answered. "Their instruments of war are metal, heavy, and archaic compared to our darksteel, Apraksin's greysteel, and even Skuratov iron. When you load those onto wooden ships, they sail low, turn slow, and get eaten by our navy. Their machines of war litter the bottom of the Zapadnoi Morye.

"We have one of their weapons in our war museum. It was captured during the Elfurian War. It's like our cannon but *much* larger. A weapon that uses black powder and the damn thing weighs nine *thousand* pounds. Imagine that!" He clearly liked the subject of war. "Our Ravagers are ten times lighter, don't need any dry powder, and a dozen of those will tear through the largest ships with the toughest hull in less time than it takes for me to fuck an Elfurian whore."

"Quickness in the bedchamber is nothing to be boastful about, Lord Fedir." Sofia would have let the last remark drop and addressed instead the hypocrisy of calling a Ravager, a Durnov machine, 'our' after having claimed Aleksei's blood unclean for having a Durnov mother, but the trouble was they were in earshot of Aleksei and he'd heard the 'Elfurian whore' comment, clearly made at Sofia.

The captain of the sentinels turned, and Fedir grinned when he strode toward him. Aleksei clocked him without a word, and the large lord dropped like a boulder. Sofia flinched because that was his injured hand. Aleksei hadn't used his hand with the exoskeleton because that would have broken the face of the mouthy boy.

A tussle broke out between Aleksei and Vukhir stepping in for his brother while Oleksandra laughed, and Dragan frowned. No one did anything to interfere. Sofia remained where she was, trying to stay out of it. Running in like an hysterical woman yelling about Aleksei's injuries would only embarrass the captain in front of his cousins.

She'd been looking right at Niko when Teo snuck up behind the prince, who'd been concerned about the fight, and placed a tiny coronet on his head. Not *her* coronet, but a pointed one made to resemble a court jester's hat. The obnoxious girl had it custom made and brought it to the Narrow for the sole purpose of annoying the prince.

Sofia had only waved and yelled because the thing had sharp teeth that might scratch Niko's scalp and bleed him. Instead, she watched as the gold turned pitch black. When she'd been told gold didn't agree with the prince, she assumed he broke out in hives as he did when he ingested honey, but that was... corruption.

She froze.

Teo retrieved her coronet and stood there stunned, soundless. Niko turned, realizing what had happened. Teo's mouth opened to scream, and Niko pushed her. The girl disappeared into the fog, and the rolling thunder of waves swallowed her thin scream.

"Did you just push her?" Oleksandra yelled.

"She fell," Niko claimed.

The fight between Aleksei and Vukhir ended in a breath, and everyone rushed to the edge to look down, Sofia too. The girl was a splatter on the jagged rocks, the tide washing her away already.

"Did you just kill my sister?" Oleksandra whispered.

"I did not! She fell!" Niko hid behind Aleksei who appeared equally stunned, but recovered in a blink, now his hand on his hilt as he backed away from the siblings while shielding his brother.

Oleksandra glowered at Sofia, the red eyes shining mad. "You saw it too. He pushed her."

Sofia had been much closer to the prince, the only one to see the change in the gold, and all eyes turned to her, including Aleksei's.

"She tripped on her hem and fell," Sofia said.

"Liar! Murderer!" Oleksandra drew her sword, but Dragan held her back. No one else had seen it.

"We can't kill the prince, sister. We'll let Father sort it out."

Sofia covered her mouth as she panted. The yelling and the screaming grew distant as a thought circled overhead like a black buzzard. Was the prince of Fedosia a soulless?

No, it couldn't be. He was a normal boy, one with many unfortunate ailments. Sofia stared at the boy clutching onto his older brother's cloak, scared and crying, then shook her head. It couldn't be. It was an unfortunate ailment. That was all. She'd never seen a true corruption of gold anyway, but she did know of potions that made metal change color. The church used it to persecute those they didn't like. The false gold would turn black when touched to warm skin.

That was all. That was all. That was all.

Seven

Duel of Honor

The grand hall of the den had a lion skin splayed on the floor and the duke and duchess were seated on a dais with the Shield red banner hanging behind them. Commanders, soldiers, and castleguards crowded the hall, and the accusatory shouting of the men made it impossible to hear what Aleksei and Vukhir were arguing about in front of the dais. Vukhir's gestures were large and aggressive while Aleksei had his hands clasped behind his back.

On one side, Niko stood like a puppy, downtrodden and his large scarlet eyes ballooned even bigger with fear. Eugene stood with his prince. On the other side were the duke's children.

Duchess Elena cried into a white handkerchief while the duke's expression remained stern.

"This is some type of dark alchemy beast?" Ignat asked.

Sofia saw he was prodding the lion's head with his boot toe, and said, "It's called a lion. They come from the southwest continent."

"Southwest of where?" Ignat asked.

"I don't know. Somewhere over the Zapadnoi Morye. A foreign emissary gifted my uncle a cub is all I know. It died in the winter." Sofia followed Zoya with her eyes as she and Daniil stepped into the half circle by the dais. "What in the necromancy hell would she have to say? She wasn't there," Sofia said.

"Neither was Eugene, was he?" Ignat said.

No, he hadn't been with the prince, which was his *only* duty. Esenov, another sentinel, had been with them, but he was left behind to watch the horses at the foot of the cliff.

"What the hell is happening?" Dominik pushed his way through the crowd. The sentinels were being made to wait outside by the castleguards so a deadly fight didn't break out in the duke's hall.

"You're a liar!" Niko's voice cut through the competing noises. "She's lying! I never said that!"

The duke lifted his hand and the chatter in the hall ceased. "Say it again, dear girl, so everyone can hear."

"The prince confided in me that he wanted Lady Teo's head because she offended him strutting around with a crown," Zoya said. She avoided looking at Aleksei who glowered at her.

"Liar! Liar!" Niko pointed and yelled while Eugene held him back.

Appalled ladies fanned themselves which included Sofia who wasn't being called to testify. They wanted Guards out of it, she supposed, but what were they doing? They couldn't kill Niko, surely.

Outraged men had begun shouting again but the voices faded as the duke spoke. "...is that your word, boy?" Sofia didn't catch what the duke said before that, but he was looking at Aleksei.

"On my honor, Your Grace," was Aleksei's answer.

"And do you stand by it, Aleksei?" boomed the duke's voice. "Not as a sentinel obligated to the prince, but as Burkhard's son who's freely choosing your words?"

"I do, Your Grace."

"And is it your word Prince Nikolas murdered Lady Teo?" He looked at Oleksandra. "Speak not as my daughter but as a lady of Shield."

"It is, Your Grace," she said.

"Duel of honor," Ignat muttered beside Sofia, and a breath later, the words were echoed by the duke.

"And who will defend Lady Oleksandra's honor?" the duke asked.

"I will fight for myself, Father."

"You will not." His tone had finality.

All three sons of the duke volunteered to fight on their sister's behalf, but the duke picked the largest man Sofia had ever seen, the captain of the castleguards who'd also stepped up along with a dozen others.

"Thank you for the honor, Your Grace." The giant bowed, his voice as deep as Sofia would have imagined from looking at the tree of a man. She was dizzy and no amount of fanning helped shuffle any air into her suffocating lungs.

"And Aleksei," the duke said, "I hope your father taught you Shield duels of honor are fought with plain swords. Your alchemy is tainted with Durnov, and your weapon is unclean. You will leave it behind."

"Yes, Your Grace."

"And it shall be to death. We are Red Shield. We don't prance around for points like Guards."

"Yes, Your Grace."

Sofia's knees folded and Ignat caught her, wrapping his arm around her waist to hold her up. "He's so large. He's so damn large. Saints have mercy," Sofia had been ranting.

"That's what she said." Ignat smiled but the humor didn't reach his eyes. The pale gaze was keen, calculating, sizing, and measuring.

The duke rose and marched out with his men. So, this was their play. They'd been looking for a reason to kill Aleksei, because without him the prince was a child with furrowed brows, crying into the cloak of Eugene, who had his arm around him. The sentinel's cold blue eye, the other white, stalked the Chartorisky siblings as they exited after the duchess. Hatred burned him and he made no effort to conceal it. Sofia didn't blame him, though. Zoya blatantly lied. The girl had found another way of clawing at the throne rather than trying to recover Niko's good grace.

"Aleksei!" Sofia fell into him and draped herself over him when he came to her. The men were filing out of the hall. The duel was *now*.

He held Sofia but spoke to his sentinel. "Doma, I need your sword, and you and Ignat will get Sofia out of here should this thing turn to shit. She is your *only* concern. The others will care for the prince. Am I understood?"

"Yes, Captain," they both said.

"It's all right, Sofia," Aleksei said, and let her go. "It'll be all right. I can handle him."

No, it would not be. Sofia remembered he wouldn't duel with Lev for points because he'd said he couldn't fight with a plain sword.

"He's a large bastard, Captain." Dominik was one of the handful of sentinels who carried two swords. The one on his back was a darksteel greatsword, but as he unbuckled the one on his hip and handed it to Aleksei, Sofia saw it was Apraksin steel. As far as plain swords went, that was the best money could purchase, and it was of *some* consolation, but not much.

"I have eyes," Aleksei said, responding to Dominik pointing out the castleguard's size.

"Better end it quick, Captain," Ignat said.

"You don't say?" Aleksei walked away.

"He's in a foul mood," Ignat said.

But who wouldn't be? The size of his opponent was astounding!

The courtyard of the soldiers' quarters was well lit with torches forming a ring around the arena. Men sat on rooftops and battlements, and crammed into every nook and cranny, including the second-floor windows. Some even sat on ledges along the wall, their feet dangling, like children trying to watch the execution at the city square.

'It's going to be an absolute shit parade trying to get out of there.' Ignat hadn't wanted Sofia in the courtyard. *'It will not make a lick of difference to him whether you are there or not, my lady. It will be better if we leave now.'*

That may be, but Sofia wouldn't abandon him. What if he got killed and this was the last time she saw him?

Niko was there with Eugene. The duke and the duchess were with their children. Commander Volg bowed to Sofia when their eyes met as though they were greeting each other at an afternoon tea. Copper changed hands and ghastly enough it was *both* sentinels and the castleguards betting on the duel.

"They would bet against their captain?" Sofia found it appalling.

"We bet on everything," said Ignat. "It's our way of dealing with death and should this be our last night on this side of the *dver*, at least we would have won some copper."

Zoya was nowhere to be seen, but Daniil stood by his aunt. They were betting as well, but the wagers of the lords were for the throne of Fedosia.

Aleksei had to swap his vambraces for plain steel, no gold or alchemy, and he stood alone buckling the leather straps as the castleguard swung with his greatsword and twisted at the waist to warm up. At least Aleksei's shield was his own, tall and almond shaped, and the weight would be familiar to him.

Sofia pulled Dominik. "The Apraksin sword, it's genuine, yes?"

"Of course, my lady."

"It's a rather expensive blade, how did it come into your possession?" She wasn't trying to be rude, but Apraksin blades were often forged. Count Gavril Illeivich had spent a fortune on one, but the saber cracked the first time he fenced.

"It was a gift from Lord Dariy Apraksin, my lady," Dominik said.

Good enough, she supposed, but she was so nervous a porcupine was rolling around in her belly. She thought she might gag, and no amount of fanning was helping though they were outside, and it was winter night.

"Give us a name."

The shadow passed by Ignat and the sentinel shivered. "Cold out here," he said.

"Go away," Sofia whispered.

The stranger didn't leave and slowly circled the castleguard now warming up his trunk like legs with squats.

"Niko, get back," Aleksei said, drawing her attention. Sofia found the prince in the ring, staring right at the stranger, his head cocked. Eugene yanked him back.

Reminded of how the prince had seen the archmage's light tentacles, Sofia frowned at the boy, but she didn't get to think too much on it as a horn blew and Aleksei picked up his shield. She turned away as the gargantuan man with a ludicrous sword charged at Aleksei, his blade swinging like a reaper's scythe.

She shut her eyes but couldn't get away from the pitiful tune of metal grating, clanking, scraping, making her skin crawl with every wretched note. She could hear the shuffling of feet on the well worn earth and the excited breaths of men.

"Give us a name," temptation whispered, but too late, she didn't know the castleguard's name. It was for the better because she would have given it, and the ensuing chaos would have swallowed them all.

A sudden roar, but she couldn't look. She folded further into herself, waiting, waiting for someone to tell her Aleksei was killed.

"Ah, fuck," she heard Ignat.

"Has he died?" she asked.

A high pitched shrill of a woman cut through the deep rumbling of men. Everyone yelled, and the chant she could hear was, "Kill! Kill! Kill!"

A complete silence. She counted, and it lasted an eternity. With every fiber of her being protesting, Sofia opened her eyes and slowly turned her head.

So much red on the ground. Aleksei dropped his shield and spat blood. Sofia tipped her head back at the sky, night but not dark, where the light of the saints shone bright.

Thank you.

She closed her eyes again and breathed. The sight of the headless castleguard sitting on his knees remained behind her lids, but only for a moment. She was too glad to be horrified.

"It appears you were mistaken, dear daughter," she heard the duke say, while a woman, probably the duchess, wailed. "The fates have spoken. I will hear no more on the matter. Now we'll feast in the honor of our prince whose innocence remains unblemished, and in the memory of Teo whose heart was pure and untouched by the world for she now shines among the stars." Every word of that was a lie. The duke was only trying to save face in front of his men. A bloodbath was coming sooner rather than later, but Aleksei lived, and in that moment, that was all that mattered.

Eight

Wolf of the Red Den

Aleksei had broken his shield arm in the exact pattern of the injury he'd sustained from the queen, couldn't make a fist with his sword hand, and had trouble putting weight on his left leg. His knee bothered him, he said.

In the conjoining room to the prince's bedchamber, Sofia helped him wash the blood off. He had no cut on him, and every injury he suffered was from the brute force of the castleguard's hits, though he'd clearly blocked them all. His darksteel shield leaning against the wall was battered to hell but the Apraksin blade which he returned to Dominik with thanks didn't have a nick. The house of true fire, they'd always claimed the flames of their forges burned hot enough to purge all impurity from steel.

Aleksei sat on a wooden stool groaning while Sofia brewed a tonic to alleviate the pain. Splinting the broken arm, changing from his blood drenched sentinel attire to a white cotton shirt and trousers, and all the other moving about had worsened the pain.

There was music downstairs from the duke's feast but every moment of it was a lie. Aleksei's scouts had already reported the duke sent riders out heading north, where he had another garrison less than fifty miles away. This would turn to shit by the morning and the tension strung the air like a band being pulled and pulled till it snapped.

The prince was in the grand hall attending the duke's feast because the sentinels had reported the drawbridge had been pulled up and if they asked to leave, the fighting would start *now*. The duke was wary of the sentinels, calling his other garrison to make certain of his victory, but time was depleting.

Ignat and Dominik were with Aleksei, but the others were dispersed throughout the den, and a handful were with the prince.

"What are we doing, Captain?" Ignat paced.

Dominik was by the door, his arms folded. "If we mean to get out of here, it must be now, Captain."

"Go where? We're still at war," Aleksei gritted through his broken bones. "We can't have the Duke of Sarostia be an enemy of the throne. It's *our* stronghold."

"What are we doing?" Ignat asked again.

"Replacing the duke," Aleksei hissed. "I need to go speak with Commander Volg."

"He won't talk to you," Sofia said. "It'll be too obvious. Let me go downstairs. Doma, please fetch my dress, and Aleksei, you drink this." The tonic was done, and she held out the cup to him. "It won't make you tired, but it will dull the pain… When is the garrison expected to arrive?"

"It's an infantry." Frowning, Aleksei drank the medicine. "They take time to move, so tomorrow evening."

"That's good. We have some time," Sofia said. "Aleksei, I don't trust Eugene. Please control Niko till then. I'll go see about Volg, and if that isn't promising, we're escaping through the undercroft to Krakova where you have more men. This isn't where you make a stand if you can't get the commander's support."

"Lady Guard speaks sense," Ignat said.

"I can't leave the den with Rodion alive," Aleksei said. "Because the next time we meet, it will be fifty thousand against four hundred. That's all the sentinels I have after adding the entirety of Krakova, four hundred. The duke must die, or Niko will lose his house, and us, our heads."

"All right, I have to go." Sofia turned. Dominik had arrived with her dress, and it was the exact one she'd thought of, too. "Ignat, you will take care of him?" she asked about Aleksei. The captain couldn't lift his sword in the condition he was in.

"With my life, as always," was the sentinel's answer.

In the grand hall where they had been accusing Niko of murder earlier, commanders and their wives drank wine and danced, soldiers carrying trays of food around instead of servants. Not a ballroom, the place still looked odd to Sofia, reminding her of the church nave it had once been. Instead of the orchestra, they had the army's marching band, drums and trumpet heavy, and the noise was too loud for the hall built for acoustics.

The duke stood in a circle with his men, Volg among them, and the conversation appeared casual though Sofia suspected they were planning tomorrow's events.

The Chartorisky, including the duchess, sat together. Daniil bowed to Sofia when he saw her but Sofia didn't pretend. They were far past pleasantries.

The duke's children were together, Niko sat surrounded by his sentinels, and people whispered in groups despite the obnoxiously loud music.

"Lady Sofia." Dragan approached her when she was taking a glass from the wine table. "Care to dance?" He gave her his arm.

"Sounds to be more of a marching tune than dancing music," she said. "But the company is good, I suppose." She downed the wine and took Dragan's offered arm.

She let him lead and they danced around the hall somewhere between graceful and not.

"I'm glad to see you here still." Dragan smiled. Because of his height, Sofia had to tip her head back to see his face. "I hope our earlier scuffle didn't frighten you. It's a Shield way of settling our differences."

"My condolences to your family. Lady Teo was very young," she said. "How is the duchess holding up?"

"Tragic accident, I'm sure. Mother will get over it."

"Couldn't fathom," Sofia said. "When is the funeral? Guards burn the pyre, is it the same here?"

"Same," Dragan said. "We've sent for the parson. The church is some miles north of here. I reckon we'll burn the pyre for her tomorrow."

"I shall pray for her."

"Thank you, Lady Guard."

They passed by the duke's entourage, and Volg shot her a look over his shoulder.

"May I be honest with you, Sofia?" Dragan asked.

"You can, but it's not recommended, Lord Dragan. I'm a Guard."

He chuckled. "My father is old fashioned. He doesn't care for the Guards..."

Then the large lord talked about how peace and cooperation among the houses was the way forward, such and such, going as far as to suggest a 'union' between Fedir and Sofia would end the conflict, while Sofia eyed Volg every time Dragan spun her.

She finally escaped him but then got trapped speaking to someone's wife. Then the prince asked for a dance, which she couldn't refuse, and the next time she looked, Volg had disappeared. This wasn't going well. She asked Eugene if he'd seen where the commander went but the sentinel didn't know which one was Volg.

A commander, not Volg, came to speak with Sofia about Aleksei's valor during the duel, kissed her hand, and left a note in her palm as he turned to speak with a young lady about her necklace.

Sofia waited a breath, went to the wine table to fetch a glass, and unfolded the palmed scrap of paper as she fixed her skirt. The note was one word: *library*.

She knew where it was. After waiting another breath, she went to Shura and whispered in his ear, "Can you make sure I'm not followed?"

"Goodnight, my lady." The sentinel bowed.

Sofia headed out of the hall and was climbing the stone steps when she realized she was being followed and turned. It was Dominik and he mouthed, "Captain's orders."

The library was in the other wing, quite a walk, and she grew glad for Dominik's company as the light turned scarce with all the candles either burned out or unlit.

The abandoned Guard library where she'd found the skin book smelled of dust and old paper, and a soldier in a red tunic closed the curtain dividing the sections and stayed on the other side as Sofia and Dominik stepped through.

Commander Volg stood by a stone globe, turning it, and lifted his pale blue eyes to Sofia. A single lantern was lit on the table, and he wasn't alone. His men moved as shadows among the shelves.

"Lady Guard, how may I help you?" He retrieved his hand from the sphere and clasped it behind his back.

"You called me," she said. Dominik stayed with his back to the wall, his keen gaze shifting, following things Sofia couldn't see.

"Let's not play games. We don't have the time. What do you want?" Volg asked.

"Rodion sent riders north," Sofia said.

"To fetch the parson for his daughter's funeral," Volg said.

"I thought we didn't have the time," Sofia said.

Volg knocked his tongue, then smiled. "Let's be brief. I'm not going to risk my men for the prince. The boy is weak. No amount of silver in my pouch or fancy title in front of my name, nothing short of an eternal salvation for my soul will make me change my mind."

"What do you want, then?" she asked.

"Nothing at this time." He smirked. He walked past her, making her wonder if the meeting had been a waste of time, but as he was leaving, he said, "If the duke was to have a tragic accident, let's say, and no son of his was left to dispute the prince's claim to the house, *then* I might have a want or two."

"Well, the head falling off the shoulder is quite a common ailment for a Shield," Sofia said. "Will you honor your word and guarantee a safe passage for the prince should such an unfortunate thing happen?"

"Guard asking for honor," he said with his back to her. "Guard honor is a liar's paradox. I knew the archmage personally. For a house of saints, your family has no grace. What I do, I do for my country. Take that however you wish." He opened the curtains and stepped through. "Rest well, Lady Guard."

"Goodnight, Commander."

Sofia looked to Dominik after Volg left and his gears were turning as well. "Long night," he said, and that was about to be true.

NINE

The Stone House of Cuckoo

ALEKSEI WAS PASSED OUT on the bed of the room with the sentinels. Ignat sat on the floor bedside and lifted his gaze from the blade he'd been cleaning when Sofia entered with Dominik. A blond brow arched, asking, waiting.

"How's Aleksei?" Sofia went to check on him and found him frowning in his sleep. He also ground his teeth and mumbled, nursing a bit of fever.

"Not well," Ignat said. "But if there is a fight, he'll get up. He always does. So, what's happening?"

Dominik closed the door. "Volg wants us to kill the duke."

"That shouldn't be too hard," Ignat said.

"If there is fighting and the commander backs out, we'll be trapped," Sofia said. She felt Aleksei's crown. His body frail and still healing, he was drenched from cold sweat.

"Again, what are we doing?" Ignat asked.

"How good of a forger is Eugene?" Sofia asked.

The two sentinels turned to her, not liking Eugene being involved, but she had a plan that didn't involve fighting or Aleksei getting hurt again. At the end of the day, his well-being was more important than having a sense of honor, and there was her Guard showing. Sometimes, it paid off to have been the archmage's niece, though the thing she was going to do, she learned from Baltar. She was his protégé, or so the old physician would claim.

***

It was snowing outside. The winds were calm, and the large snowflakes were feathers floating in the air.

"Sofia," Aleksei said.

She blinked, her eyes coming into focus. The large arched window was behind him, and she'd been watching the snow over his shoulder. "The saints must be having a pillow fight," she said.

He twisted in his seat to see, then returned with a smile. "My lady is a poet at heart."

"What lines of poetry have I said?"

"You find beauty in things a poet might. I see the coming snowstorm and the travel difficulties, but my lady thinks of feathers falling from heaven."

She reached across the table and tucked a loose strand of curl behind Aleksei's ear. His locks were getting longer and wilder. His hair was fairly straight when the length was short, but beyond a certain point they'd decided to curl like Niko's, or just their father's, she supposed.

"Love birds." Oleksandra snapped her fingers in front of Aleksei's face. They weren't alone. The duke, duchess, their children, Volg, and a handful of other commanders were in the den's sunroom, though not very sunny at the moment. The weather outside was silver and the fireplace crackled behind Sofia, warming her back. "She's rather old for you, no?" Pretending to nudge Aleksei, she struck him in the shoulder of his injured arm.

Aleksei didn't flinch and swung his scarlet gaze to Oleksandra. She was sitting beside him. "He's rather related to you, no?" He looked at Dragan who was speaking with his father.

Oleksandra cleared her throat and brought the gold cup to her lips. They were waiting for the prince and drinking in the meantime. It was sometime after ten in the morning.

"Good clean fight yesterday, Captain," Volg said from down the table where he sat with four other commanders.

"Is there a general?" Sofia asked. "I don't know how Shield forces are organized."

"We're organized in tens," Volg said. "The smallest unit is made of ten soldiers, a *desyet*. Ten *desyet* a hundred, the next a thousand, and once you lead ten thousand, you are called a commander. Below that, you are called by the number you have. A soldier in charge of a ten is a *desyetniik* for instance."

"So, there are five commanders?" Sofia asked.

"Not at the den, but in total, yes." Volg smiled. "Antev is a commander." He draped his arm over the broad shoulders of a sour man next to him. His mouth had a downward curve. Then he gestured at the rest of them. "They are *tisachniik*. They each lead a thousand."

"They are Volg's unit," Commander Antev clarified, unhappy about something, and slurped wine. "His Highness must sleep well."

"We all used to at that age, Antev," Volg said. "Before blood and politics kept us awake."

"You don't drink enough," Vukhir said, his shoulder leaning into Sofia.

"A Guard has never been accused of such." She emptied her cup.

The Chartorisky were leaving and Zoya and Daniil came in to bid their aunt goodbye, and the duchess got up to see them out.

"Bye, Aleksei," Daniil said.

"Careful out there, bad weather coming," the captain said.

Daniil nodded at Sofia, but she didn't bother getting up. "Best you get going before the prince arrives," she said.

After the Chartorisky left, Dragan, who'd been at the head of the table speaking with his father, came and sat down next to Sofia. "What did I miss?"

"Not much." Sofia turned to him and smiled.

"Cousin, you're a sentinel," Dragan said to Aleksei.

"Yes." Aleksei frowned.

"You can have neither title nor family. How about we marry Sofia to Fedir? She's too old for Vukhir, but Fedir is due for a wife. I think that will bring peace with the Guards. What say you?" Dragan asked.

Aleksei smiled. "Best you ask Lev Guard and see how that goes."

"Never met the man but I assume he's reasonable," Dragan said. "We're offering peace."

"All right," was all Aleksei said, hardly containing his laughter because Sofia had gone 'pfff' at the mention of her brother being 'reasonable'.

"That is what we're doing," Dragan said, not keen on being laughed at. "I'm just letting you know."

"It won't bother me when you die. I'm just letting you know," Aleksei said.

"They say Burkhard was mad. Is it true?" Oleksandra asked.

"He wasn't mad," Aleksei said.

"But he did kill your mother?" Oleksandra was instigating.

"He did," Aleksei said, pretending to be unbothered though his jugular pulsed.

"Must be tough growing up with so many brothers and mattering less to your father," Sofia said. "Always having something to prove, it appears exhausting."

"Fuck you," Oleksandra said.

"Foul language doesn't make you tough, only crude," Sofia said.

"Heard your cousin is a cocksucker." Oleksandra sneered.

"So what? Are you not?" Sofia cocked her head.

"Woah, too much wine, ladies," Dragan said. "We're all friends here."

"Friends don't marry friends to your brother," Sofia said. "He smells bad *and* is rude."

"That, we don't deny," Vukhir said.

"Where is that little shit anyway? Has he fallen down a hole?" Oleksandra looked to the door. The brown oak door was closed and there were two castleguards outside it, for now.

"Where is the parson you sent for? Has he fallen down a hole?" Sofia asked.

Oleksandra was confused because they never sent for a parson and there wasn't a church north of the den. Dragan was such a good liar Sofia had almost believed him. The duke's children were being belligerent because they expected Aleksei to be killed before the evening, and Sofia was speaking her mind because she expected the lot to drop dead any moment.

She excused herself and got up when the duke coughed. He'd been clearing his throat for a while. She went to stand by the window and Aleksei came up behind her. She turned and checked his forehead. The fever had subsided.

He draped his cloak over her. "Are you sure you don't want to step out?"

Behind them, the Shields were having a coughing fit. Fedir collapsed. Dragan looked at his hands and saw he'd coughed blood. The duchess screamed because the duke toppled over. Everyone sprung up from the table, Volg spitting his wine out.

"Simmer down. It's not the wine, Commander," Sofia said, flicking a look at Volg. No one was armed, all the swords were left by the door at the duke's request, which was good because hysteria took hold. She touched Aleksei's splinted arm, wondering if he was going to be using it in a moment.

The castleguards weren't bursting in despite the screams, most probably because they were dead. Not the poison, though, just sentinels. They were using the hollow in the wall to move around. Guards liked secret passages, which was why Raven had them too. Fedosia was built by Guards.

"I wonder how Lev is doing. It gets cold at Usolya," she said.

"We'll send an envoy once we're back in Krakova," Aleksei said. "Hopefully, it will go better this time."

"I'll go. The train is running?"

"It is," he said.

Vukhir had found a sword and screaming, frothing blood from the mouth and eyes, he swung at Aleksei. The captain twisted out of the way, caught the lord's hand, and put his blade through his throat.

Another man who'd had a hidden blade up his sleeve was Volg, and he'd stuck his in Commander Antev's eye socket. He'd calmed down, and sat there with his men, drinking the rest of his wine. Chaos was about to ensue as the sentinels dealt with the castleguards to bring the den under control. The rest of it, Volg would take care of. That had been the deal. He'd just been surprised because Sofia hadn't told him she'd be poisoning the duke's family.

It was their cups. Gold would corrupt with the touch of poison, but she'd had Niko steal them because he didn't need light to see, and *no* one ever heard the prince sneak around. Eugene forged the gold and Sofia poisoned it. Though elixirs, poisons, and tonics weren't alchemy, she finally found something she was good at. At the moment, she didn't feel proud because with her talent she'd killed people, but she did feel useful, and that was a start, she supposed.

The wind outside whistled in varying pitches from a shrill scream to a coarse hiss and reminded Sofia in part of a wobbling metal plate. Night had claimed Fedosia hours ago, and the men were getting to eat only now as Niko hosted dinner in the Hall of Grace—Sofia had been calling it that because of the church like structure—that Aleksei hadn't been allowed in their first night at the den.

Aleksei had lost a few men, Volg too, ridding the den of the hundreds of castleguards who were all loyal to Rodion, but the keep was quiet now. The northern garrison had arrived, and they bent the knee for their prince.

Antev was dead, but the four other commanders, including Volg, were at the prince's table. A number of key sentinels, Dominik, Ignat, Shura, Ruslan, and Eugene shared the table as well, but the others ate in the common hall, boar and not porridge.

Aleksei had cleaned up before the midnight dinner, but Ignat had red in his white hair. Volg had blood on him too, as did most of the men, and the dead were being taken to the undercroft to be burned in the incinerator, because a snowstorm was passing through where Fedosia bordered Elfur and the pyre couldn't be lit outside. The necromancers were sending their bad weather, the soldiers had been joking.

Food was good but Sofia was so tired she'd been yawning with tears. Aleksei was no better and he'd nodded off a couple of times beside her.

Niko sat at the head of the table with his commanders and cheerily discussed matters going forward, promising them lands and estate from the bit of conversation Sofia caught. She hardly cared about the topic and had been turned to Aleksei, adjusting the straps on his vambrace because they were interfering with his splint, when he said, "Niko, you can't do that."

"Why not?" the prince's voice came.

"The Chartorisky are a house of *Boyar Duma*," Aleksei said. "You can't just kill them and take their lands because Zoya lied."

"Well, I'm the prince and I say I can. Commander Volg agrees," the prince said. "I also asked you to kill them, Zoya and Daniil, but you let them leave. Why?"

"This morning?" Aleksei asked. "I didn't know they were leaving till they were, and I can't have a fight with both the castleguards and the Chartorisky retainers."

"I don't think that's the real reason. I think it's because you love Zoya. You disobeyed me and let her escape though she committed high treason."

Sofia let go of Aleksei's arm and turned to Niko, frowning, because it wasn't a way to speak to Aleksei in front of other sentinels. They had fallen silent, the sentinels, their gazes swinging between their captain and the prince. Volg smirked and decided to stay out of it, literally pushing his chair away from the table as he was seated between the captain and the prince.

Aleksei didn't respond, probably because the commanders were watching, but he tossed his fork on the table, apparently done with the dinner. Sofia thought he should eat more but she wouldn't say that in front of other men and minded her food and wine instead.

"Anyway," Niko said. "The silver mines the throne keeps but the land and the castles, I'm distributing to my men and my allies. All land of Fedosia belongs to the throne."

Aleksei let it be and took Sofia's hand and held it on his lap, finding a smile as he gazed down.

"Aleksei," Niko called.

"Yeah?" Aleksei shot him a look.

"I've been thinking," Niko began crisply but lost his nerve and played with the napkin on the table, making everyone wait. After a long pause, he murmured, "You're the queen's captain. You served my mother well, but I think it's time I pick my own."

"Niko," Aleksei's pitch dropped to a growl. "You're at war. Don't do that."

"Lev will die soon. Perhaps he's already dead. I don't need you anymore. Especially that you don't obey me when you like women. Lev of Guard, Zoya of Chartorisky both are guilty of high treason. I want them dead, but I don't think you agree with me, and I can't have a captain of the sentinels whom I can't trust."

"What are you doing, Your Highness?" Sofia whispered, eyeing the amused commanders. Behind her, the sentinels had fallen dead silent. "Your Highness?"

Niko folded and unfolded the white napkin on the table and didn't look at her. "I pardon you because of your helpfulness but Lev must die."

"His Highness was seeking peace once. What happened?" Sofia asked.

"I never was." Niko blinked, then stared at the table and didn't say more.

"We'll discuss this another time. Everyone has had a long day," Sofia said.

"His Highness has spoken, please turn in your gear and leave, Aleksei," Eugene said.

For a moment, nothing but the wind sounded in the Hall of Grace. Aleksei scowled, the chair screeched as he pushed back from the table and got up. The sentinels rose with him.

Aleksei gestured them down. "Your duty remains the same, protect the prince." He turned on his heels and strode out.

Sofia excused herself and got up. She took a good look at Eugene, because this underhandedness to dismiss Aleksei in front of the commanders so the sentinels didn't throw a fit came from him and not Niko.

"Perhaps His Highness will reconsider when he has rested." She curtsied.

"I told you it'd be awful," she heard Niko mumble as she turned her back on the prince and strutted out.

Upstairs in the room with the blue ceiling, she found Aleksei packing his saddlebags.

"You're leaving *now*?" She stood by the door with her arms folded.

"Yeah." He strode past her, collecting his things from here and there. "I'll tell them to protect you. They'll obey me that much."

"If you're leaving, I'm leaving with you, Aleksei."

"Sofia, there's a blizzard." He stopped and looked at her.

"You will wait for me, and you will take me with you." Sofia turned. "Let me change and bring my things. I won't be long."

"Sofia, there's a blizzard."

"I have eyes and ears, Aleksei. You *will* wait." She'd hoped for sleep but there would be none if she let him leave alone, so she was riding through the snowstorm, she supposed.

TEN

Save Me

NO ONE FOLLOWED THEM as they slipped out of the den, and Sofia thought it was because they hadn't expected Aleksei to leave that night. He didn't hand his duty over or speak to his brother. He was just pissed.

They rode through the wailing storm moaning and moaning about the world it hurled itself upon. The wind was on their backs, adding speed to their mounts, and the snow didn't lash onto their faces, but under the moonless, starless sky, the night was blind.

As the dawn silvered and the blizzard passed, the whole earth had turned white. They'd veered off the road and had no idea where they were.

"I'm sorry," said Aleksei, his breath steaming and his lashes frozen over the scarlet eyes. "I shouldn't have left the den in anger. Are you cold?"

"I'm all right." Sofia pulled down the scarf iced from her breath. As far as they could see, it was bare white terrain, nothing like the evergreen hills she was used to. "But the horses probably need a rest." As soon as she said 'horses', Charger gave her the side eye. She could swear that creature understood language more than a horse should.

"Yeah," Aleksei said, twisting in his saddle to look around. "We're supposed to be heading southeast, so let's just go that way and hope we get back on the road."

Now that the weather allowed it, she talked while she rode alongside Aleksei, though Charger was compelled to lead even if by a few inches and kept pulling ahead. The snow crunched and the tack on both horses jingled in the eerily still morning as the sun rose red and deep purple in front of them. The sky hadn't cleared and hung heavy. If they didn't find shelter before nightfall, they'd be caught in the snow again. No wonder the harvest failed. They were getting too much wet weather both in the cold and the warm. Also, the winterkill was causing wildlife to starve when the snow was too deep for the creatures to find grass underneath to graze. It'd been years since Sofia had seen a deer when they used to be everywhere when she was a girl. The starving wolves grew more aggressive, attacking stables and venturing into the city... It was as if Fedosia had been bewitched the last four years.

She asked Aleksei about his arm, and if the cold hurt it because the splint was steel, and he said, "It could be worse." Then he continued, "Thank you for saving us in the den, but I guess you'll get nothing for your bravery and wit because you're saddled to me."

"Well, that's not nothing," she said. "My life is far better riding through the storm with you than sitting by the fireplace at the Illeivich estate."

"The count?" Aleksei looked back because Charger was pulling forward and trying to leave Sofia behind. "I'm glad he's dead."

"I killed him," Sofia said because he wouldn't remember that.

"Then he deserved to die." He tightened his reins to slow down the ill tempered gelding.

"Probably not. He had daughters," she said.

"Oh, well, it's Fedosia," was his answer.

"Why did Niko turn on you? Just over the Chartorisky? I'm afraid he's been influenced by Eugene. I hear he has a grudge against the House of Silver."

"I'd say Niko's ego is being inflated because now commanders are kneeling to him, but he's done things like this before, blindsiding me with decisions that seem to come from nowhere. It's as though he gets possessed sometimes... I think he killed our father. Burkhard was very powerful was the reason I doubted, but if he could kill Kseniya and a dozen watchmen, he could kill Burkhard too. There was no one else. I was on duty that night, and the only one to go in and out of the duke's quarters was Niko."

"Aleksei." Sofia kicked her horse and caught up to him. "How *did* Niko manage to do that? The queen, I mean. Not saying it was a bad thing because he saved you, but I don't understand."

"I'd rather not say it because you're a Guard. Forgive me."

"That doesn't sound very trusting, Aleksei."

"It'll frighten you, Sofia."

"Something to do with dark magic, then," she said. "That would explain the corruption of gold. Dark magic leaves residue and taints your blood for a long time, or so my uncle used to say. It's hard to separate the truth from the politics when dealing with the church... They'd take something true and twist it into complete horse manure. People had a way of turning into necromancers and heretics when they had a dispute with the synod. I wonder how many innocents the archmage convicted with his way of... questioning."

"He hadn't been terrible. At least there had been order," Aleksei said.

"You only say that because you don't remember he tortured you."

"Maybe," said Aleksei, and they rode on.

The blizzard was wicked, worsened after sundown, and they only realized they were riding through a town because a man had opened his door, to go piss perhaps, and they saw the light. All windows had been boarded.

The villager had no room in his house and no stables for their horses but was kind enough to lead them on foot through the storm to the church which had both. A silver coin helped, as it always did.

The church was wooden, and the keeper was a brown cloaked parson. Sofia didn't drop her Guard name because that would have invited too many questions. Instead, she put silver coins on the collection plate to get warm stables, feed for the horses, and permission to stay the night in the church.

The nave had a bare wooden floor, faded smooth and bent inward where the aisle was, and the boards were fresher where the benches would normally be. They were stacked and stowed against the wall tonight.

The parson brought them a clay pot of hot soup and a brazier like a cauldron with iron legs. Guard churches had tall spiraling roofs with an upward draft and the smoke wouldn't bother them, but the coal would remain warm for hours.

Sofia showed her gratitude with more silver and the old parson's grin widened. He lived right next door, he said, and to knock if they needed anything else. Then Sofia sat with Aleksei in the dark red glow of the coal burning brazier, eating much needed warm food even if that was potato soup. The wind howled around them, and the wooden church groaned and creaked.

Afterward, Aleksei made a bed for them on the floor with cloaks and walked to the altar with his hands clasped behind him, his face tipped to the painted saints above the dais. "Do you suppose they are real?" he asked.

"They were once people like you and me." Sofia sat on the cloak and searched her saddlebag for the wool stockings she knew she packed. "But whether they still live, only *dver* knows."

"The first time I'd been to a church, I was twelve and I'd run away from home because I drowned Niko. He was five. It was the Church of All Saints in Krakova, and I begged and begged the saints to return my brother.

"Then, Niko returned. The reasonable part of me wants to believe Niko survived and found his way home, but I *know* I killed him. He was dead. They answered my prayers." He held up his broken hand to the saints. "Now they forsake me for breaking my promise. I swore to be good but paid their mercy and grace with Pyotr Guard's blood. They are angry with me, I sense it. Kseniya going off on me, I believe that was my atonement, and I'd be thankful if that was all, but now I worry they're going to take you from me."

"No one is taking me away from you," Sofia said. She'd found her wool stockings and was putting them on. "You have more faith than any Guard I know, and that includes the archmage. More than likely, they are just dead men. Otherwise, there wouldn't be so much misery in the world with the blessing of so many saints."

"Hush, Sofia. Maybe they do hear."

If he truly believed the prince returned from the dead, that wasn't the saints but quite the opposite. He knew so, and so did she, and this unsaid thing hung between them like a wet cloak.

"Come, Aleksei." She held out her hand. "Let's go to sleep and hope the weather is better tomorrow."

"My lady." He came to her, kissed her hand, and allowed her to pull him down.

Now that Sofia had dry stockings on, she'd sleep wearing her spare boots. It was too cold otherwise. She hiked a leg over him as he lay down beside her.

"If you want to make another promise to the saints, I'd accept it as a lady of Guard." Sofia laid her head on his chest, feeling his warmth and strength through the layers of wool and cotton between them. "So as long as you don't break this one promise, you're absolved from all your past transgressions." Blasphemy really, but she hoped to be forgiven because her intentions were good.

"What is it, Sofia?" he whispered, his voice barely audible over the crying winds.

"You will not harm Lev. I realize there may arise situations where you have no control," she said. "I'm not speaking of other men's actions if you have no say, but you, Aleksei, shall not put steel in my brother or order others to do it for you. I'm not certain I can get over that, so that may be the only thing to take me away from you."

"Is that all?" he asked.

"That's all."

"Then, I swear it, Sofia, and I'd die before I break it."

"Thank you." She gave him a quick touch on his lips, but he held her nape and it turned into a slow, sweet, pining, and longing type of kiss.

"I see." He sighed afterward. "That's how that is." He lay on his back looking up at the painted saints. "You save me from despair, Sofia. The sun on your crest, it's hope. Had you not been here, I would have nothing. Yet I have everything. You are the difference between nothing and everything."

She could say the same about him, and feeling mighty wealthy was part of loving and being loved, she was learning, and happily, she'd been falling asleep when the presence of the stranger startled her out of the pleasantness.

"What's wrong?" Aleksei asked because she'd jolted.

"Nothing. Just had a falling dream." She closed her eyes though very aware of the shadow circling them.

She had invited darkness onto hallowed ground when she cursed the archmage, and this thing was growing more brazen by the day. She had to figure out what he was and get rid of him. His growing menace made her skin crawl like the sound of metal grating on glass.

"Are you cold?" Aleksei asked, embracing her tighter.

She shivered, she supposed. "Yeah... But I'm all right now."

Listening to Aleksei sleep, she stayed up for a while and only closed her eyes when she was certain the stranger had left.

Eleven

God

Through the window of his ivory hall, Fedya frowned at the grey sky—more snow, wicked winter, hard times for Bone Country made worse by the failures of the boy tsar. He still didn't know what to make of the carnage of the House of Menshikov. Hoping to find his sister who'd been married to Lord Menshikov, he'd sifted through the bodies, and they'd been... grotesque. A two-headed man he'd found, the charred skeleton joined at the ribs sprouting two necks. Every intact remains they found had been marked by darkness. The death of the archmage and the fall of his synod had woken evil in Fedosia that had been asleep for centuries.

Saints have mercy and watch over your children in these dark times.

Naming the saints, Fedya thumbed the beads of his rosary. Carved from the bones of an elephant, a great beast from a faraway land, the rosary had been a gift from the archmage.

"Lord Pulyazin, what say you to the prince's offer?"

Fedya tore his gaze from the heavy sky, suspended low like a summer fog—bad omen—and turned to the prince's envoy sitting on the wooden chair with his legs crossed under the long white robe. The red baldric certainly caught the eye, and the longsword he carried as well.

"It sounds like blackmail, Grigori." His hands clasped behind his back, and the rosary dangling, Fedya crossed the ivory hall. No reason, he was simply pacing. The leather soles of his fur boots softly tapped the wooden floor, and the eyes of the two druzhina standing guard by the door shifted to Grigori when the wooden chair creaked. But the tall man was only changing the cross of his long legs.

Long black hair, long black beard, and pale blue eyes as though haunted, Fedya had never cared for the appearance of the throne's alchemy advisor. It was hard to call him a mage for Grigori had never been ordained by the church.

"It is your duty to answer when the throne calls, Lord Pulyazin," Grigori said.

"Have I not answered enough of Her Majesty's calls?" Fedya cocked his head. "My people cut wood for Her Majesty through the sowing and harvesting seasons because we are promised grain in return for our timber. The House of Pulyazin has never sent Her Majesty's train empty, if you recall, but now that we ask what is *owed* to us, instead of honoring the queen's deal, your prince makes demands, holding our grain hostage. This displeases me greatly, Grigori, I'm not going to lie."

"His Highness will honor the trade, of course," Grigori said. "He's simply saying it will be expedited greatly if this conflict with the Guards... ceased. The prince must now move his forces from the border in winter to defend Krakova, a costly affair as you can imagine."

"Lev Guard's head by my blade is what you're asking." Fedya walked back to the windows. His wife and children were playing in the courtyard. Today was Day Solis and instead of going to church, he was being burdened by this unholy negotiation. He peeled back the white mink trim of his sleeve to touch the gold cuffs underneath, his alchemy pulsing through his veins as he did so.

Lev was a drunk and a degenerate, a disgrace to his family name. The boy's life was nothing to Fedya if it meant food for his people, but dirtying one's hand with Guard blood was surely a sin. The saints were watching.

"I'll discuss it with my people," Fedya said. "You'll have my answer tomorrow... How will you be returning to the capital?"

"I'll manage." He smiled.

After Grigori followed the steward out to find a hot bath and warm bed, Isidor, the captain of Pulyazin druzhina, came into the ivory hall. Fedya was still by the window, his face tipped to the thickening clouds signaling bad weather.

The tall druzhina with leather armor and fur cloak brought Fedya a cup of hot tea.

"Thank you, Isidor," said Fedya, taking the cup and enjoying the warmth between his hands. "It's going to be a tough winter."

"It's Bone Country, my lord. Every winter is tough but we're tougher." The young man had a bright grin Fedya found pleasing. "Lady Anfisa is asking if my lord will be going to church with his family."

"I am." Fedya crossed the hall and set the cup on a small wooden table where Grigori had been sitting. "Dark magic, it leaves a stench." He ran a hand over the crest of the carved chair and rubbed his fingers. There was nothing there, but it still *felt* like soot and grime. "I don't like this mage. What do you make of him?"

"If nothing else, he's a liar, my lord."

Mmm, Fedya remembered. When Grigori first appeared in the Fedosian court, having suddenly gained the queen's favor, the archmage had asked Fedya to confirm Grigori's identity because the mage had claimed to be from a ghost town wiped by the plague decades ago and buried under snow. Though Fedya couldn't name the inhabitants of the small settlement, he was more than certain no grand mage had been born of it. He would have heard had there been a light user in Bone Country.

"May I speak honestly, my lord?" Isidor asked.

"You always should," Fedya said.

"I'm not an educated man, my lord, but I don't think we should be slaying the last of the White Guards. They say the House of Sun is the guardian of light. Darkness may befall Fedosia should we commit such a sin."

"People can't eat faith and lore, Isidor."

"Neither can they negotiate their way to the stars with grain, my lord."

Somberly, Fedya considered the truth of the young man's words. He shook off the unease and headed for the door to join his family in the courtyard, and made it down the hall with Isidor behind him before another druzhina strode toward them, bringing a message from The Church of All Saints in Krakova.

The archmage's death had plummeted the church into disarray and courier pigeons hadn't been flown for months. Fedya took the small scrap of paper carrying the archmage's seal, though he hadn't been notified he'd been succeeded, opened it, and saw what the urgency had been.

The Chartorisky Port burns. The House of Silver is no more. The Boyar Duma are hereby notified Daniil Chartorisky has made an attempt on the crown prince's life. He is wanted for high treason. If found, kill on sight.

It was signed, Luminary Matvey. Fedya knew Matvey, a man of common birth but of honest heart. The difference between a mage and a plain parson was the mastery of the light alchemy and not the strength of their faith.

"Pigeon flew here?" Fedya clarified.

"The post came with a rider from Usolya," the druzhina answered. That made more sense.

"The throne has broken the treaty with its lords." Fedya knocked his tongue, displeased, then said, "Let Lady Anfisa take the children to church. Another business has come up for me."

"Yes, my lord." The druzhina rushed off.

"What is the business, my lord?" Isidor asked.

"I need solitude. I must think."

Fedya left Isidor in the corridor and headed to his study.

What am I to do, Mother?

She used to say, *'Listen to the saints, they will guide you',* but the only voice speaking in Bone Country was the howling of the winter winds.

Fedosia was a wide expanse. The further east you went, the further north you'd also be, and everything northeast of the Black Ore Hills of the Skuratov was considered Bone Country for it was frozen white most of the year. Mountainous terrain for hundreds and hundreds of miles, the north bred tough, but even the strongest still must eat.

The Pulyazin castle covered in snow was indistinguishable from the jagged grey peak it perched upon, and Fedya was skating on the frozen lake in the valley, trying to remember the freedom he felt as a boy, when he saw Isidor riding along the bank. The druzhina dismounted, then skated toward him, his alchemy seamless as the ice forming under his boots propelled him across the lake without effort.

"Lady Anfisa sends word she'd like to stay overnight at the church," Isidor said, gliding alongside Fedya. "She heard of the Chartorisky's misfortune and would like to pray for Lady Zoya and Lord Daniil."

Fedya nodded. Anfisa was his second wife and many years younger than him. Daughter of Lord Vietinghoff, she grew up in Krakova and would have known the Chartorisky well. The loss saddened her, no doubt. Though he'd loved his first wife, she bore him no heirs and went to the stars a decade ago. Before his Anfisa blessed him with three young ones, Fedya had considered calling Ignat back, though the boy was a harlot and nothing but trouble.

"Also, word from the Apraksin, my lord," Isidor said.

Lake Saikhan was a mile and a half deep, but the ice was so clear they could see the bottom as they skated over it. On a sunny blue day, the below would mirror the above, but today, it was just endless grey and white, sky and earth.

"Which Apraksin?" asked Fedya.

"Dariy, my lord. He would like to try again to arrange a meeting between my lord and Lev of Guard."

The Guard had been requesting to meet with Fedya and the last time he'd sent Isidor in his place.

"You've met Lev. What was your impression of the boy?" asked Fedya.

"I don't know, my lord." Confusion shaded Isidor's face. "Lord Lev wore a woman's dress and appeared drunk. I couldn't tell if he was insulting the Pulyazin or if that was the way he was. I don't know much about court or courtiers and didn't know if his demeanor was considered... acceptable."

"He's probably mocking me." Fedya grimaced. That helped him decide. "Tell Dariy I'll take the meeting. Usolya is a formidable fortress. If we're invited to it, it saves us the trouble of breaching it when I take the boy's head."

"Yes, my lord," said Isidor but didn't leave and followed Fedya as he skated around an ice boulder.

"What is it?" Fedya asked.

"Will we not anger the saints, my lord?"

"The Shields have murdered the archmage yet they haven't been stuck dead," Fedya said.

"They have, though, my lord. Their queen is dead, and their heir is mad. Breaking their treaty with the nobility of Fedosia, the Shield reign appears to be at its end." He had a point, as he always did.

"Accept the meeting, nonetheless," said Fedya. He'd assess the boy for himself. Bend the knee or take his head, he'd decide then.

※

The evening brought welcome news. A Durnov train with a hundred tons of grain had rolled into Khenter. A far cry from the three *thousand* tons owed, but it had been a good faith gesture from the prince, much appreciated, while Fedya happily ordered half the grain to be distributed to the people. Half would go to the granary of his Ivory Fortress.

The prince had sent him a chest of silver along with a letter carrying the throne's seal. It must have been dictated by a child, for the message simply read: *Thank you for your support in these dark times. I shall honor my mother's trade and more trains will follow. I was saddened to hear of your sister's passing. Also, relay to the eastern houses I have no plans of aggression toward the Boyar Duma so long as they do not pick up arms against their throne.*

Signed, *Prince Nikolas of Red Shield, Heir Apparent of Fedosia, Commander of the Imperial Army.*

Commander, Fedya sounded and tasted the word. Duke Rodion must be dead for the prince to claim command of the Shield forces. The boy was making a name for himself, commendable in Fedya's opinion. Then the dilemma returned with a heavy sigh. What should he do about Lev Guard? The fate of his house hinged on this single decision.

A new ball of trouble falling into his lap as soon as he tossed one up for tomorrow, Fedya walked his halls tired of the juggling act.

The Ivory Fortress was designed with many smaller rooms meant to trap and manage heat, and the dining room was no different. It had a modest table, wall to wall wool carpet, and the fireplace was larger than the window. His only guest was Grigori and the prince's envoy sat at the other end of the table from the lord, all the chairs between them vacant.

Fedya enjoyed a slice of pickled watermelon with his wine, a splendid burst of taste in his mouth after a long day, while his guest had potato salad with bread. The roast duck remained untouched between them. It had been frozen for months and brought out because of the special guest.

"Will the lady not be joining us?" Grigori asked.

"Anfisa went to church. Today is Day Solis," Fedya said. Through the one small window, he frowned at the dying light, trying to recall how many druzhina accompanied his wife and children. Wolves were large and ferocious in the north, unlike the small and downtrodden ones of the west. Anfisa would forget that and venture out after dark, sometimes even taking the small ones for a 'walk'.

"Tell me, Grigori, why does the prince wish for Lev Guard's head? Though uncustomary to eradicate a great house, such as the Chartorisky, without the Boyar Duma, it's Fedosia." Fedya shrugged with a single shoulder. "The Chartorisky may have allies in the west, but in Bone Country where a man can't eat silver coins, no one cares for the house of do nothings except for my soft hearted wife.

"The same can't be said for the Guards. Bone Country is built on old faith. Evil roams these hills after dark, and the church, which is inseparable from the Guards in my mind, keeps the light on through the long winter nights. The fate of the Menshikov bears witness to how darkness never leaves, not truly, and only waits for the retreat of daylight. So, produce for me, Grigori, a compelling reason to soil my hands with Guard blood other than grain. Death comes whether you're full fed or starved.

"The Menshikov had been stocked for the winter, sitting smugly on the grain they'd hoarded, but did that save them, I wonder, or if the grain burned with their defiled bodies." Realizing he was tired of juggling, Fedya let the balls drop on the floor. The warm embrace of a beautiful wife and worry for his young children had made him soft, but this was Bone Country where faith and hardship defined a man.

"Wolf, wolf, cries the church." Grigori pushed his plate and loaded herbs into a wooden pipe with a silver bite. "Yet no one has seen one in centuries. Lev burned the Menshikov in their sleep and arranged some black bones to frighten fools like you, Fedya. Not even an honest day's work, fusing corpses with alchemy, since much of the remains were eviscerated by the fury of the black powder."

"You call me a fool in my own house, zapadnik?" *Westerner,* Fedya sneered at Grigori. "What do you know of faith? Pleasant weather makes for wise cracking cowards and heathens."

"If your answer is no, simply say so, Fedya. No need to preach. Though it may be Day Solis, this is hardly a church. You don't have the gold to be a mage, the title has been bought and sold like cows on the market for centuries. It is meaningless."

Then Grigori mumbled in a foreign tongue and Fedya pitched a chalice at the mage's mouth because it had sounded like the language of spells.

Grigori touched his split lips, then grinned with bloody teeth. "It's not a curse, you fool. It's just Elfurian. 'Your saints are dead,' I was saying."

"And that wasn't a chalice, you fool, only a distraction," Fedya said.

The commotion called the druzhina and they burst through the door. Fedya, who was at the head of his table and facing the door, gestured them down. Blood spurted from the mage's mouth, a vomit of red frozen slush running down the front of his white cloak. His breath steamed.

"That's death fever," explained Fedya, finding another chalice to sip wine from. "It's the body's reaction to being stabbed with Pulyazin ice."

Underneath the table, the floor and the legs of the chairs were frozen, and ice spears like grotesque crystals painted in blood protruded around and through Grigori. The mage's haunted eyes widened before his head slumped over.

"Well, that's one way to answer, my lord." Isidor strode by the mage, grimacing as he passed. His eyes fell on the duck, and Fedya gave him the nod.

The druzhina slid the plate of duck along the long table and away from the blood and sat down beside Fedya to eat.

Andrei, another druzhina, pulled Grigori's head back by the hair. No one would ever survive Fedya's alchemy, but the man was going to make certain and cut the mage's head off. Andrei twisted and reached for his saber with his free hand, the other holding up Grigori's head. For a fraction of a beat, Fedya *thought* he saw the mage's eyes pop open, but in the exact instance, Isidor obstructed his view by getting up and reaching for a piece of cheese across the table.

Isidor sat back down, and Grigori was gone. The red ice remained. Andrei held his neck, blood gushing through his fingers. Silently, he pointed at the door, then collapsed.

Fedya sprung up and his chair fell back with a great noise.

"Find him." Fedya shoved Isidor. "FIND HIM!"

They locked down and upturned the Ivory Fortress, spent too much time only to find the remains of two young women, Anfisa's maids, dead. The bodies were hideous and unrecognizable but for the clothes. Their hair turned white and their flesh dried and peeled back to reveal the teeth, their death looked old, though Fedya had seen them alive this morning.

"What devilry is this, my lord?" the men whispered. Those who wore protection amulets of the saints pulled them out and kissed them, tipping their eyes to the star beyond the stone roof, beyond the storm clouds.

"I don't know. Some dark art," Fedya muttered for he'd never seen such a thing.

Druzhina yelled from down the corridor, "His horse is gone, my lord! And the stable master is slain!"

Cursing, Fedya gathered his men. He wouldn't have chased a dark practitioner at night had his wife and children been safe at home. But they weren't.

The blizzard had swallowed Grigori's tracks, but Fedya had a sinking feeling, a knot in his gut. *No one* could weather through a northern blizzard out in the elements, and there was only a single shelter for miles.

"The Church of Light," he whispered. If he was wrong, he didn't care, but if he was right...

Anfisa, I'm coming. Don't let the darkness in.

Moonless, starless night with nothing but the dark, howling wind. Fedya encased his lantern in ice to amplify the light. The wet barrage of snow in his face made it impossible to open his eyes. Squinting, he'd been riding against winter when his horse put his leg in something and sent him over the saddle.

He'd been galloping at full speed and had lost his druzhina behind. His horse wasn't getting up and he didn't want to leave the loyal creature to the wolves and ended its fear before picking up the lantern, forging forward on foot through snow so deep that his leg sank to the knee with every step. He'd also ridden off the trail, he realized.

He looked back but there were no lanterns behind him. He had no idea where his men were, but he had to continue. He formed a shield from clear ice and held it in front of him to be able to see but in his haste leaving the fortress, he hadn't worn gloves, and now the ice burned his skin.

A rider blew by him. Thinking it was one of his druzhina, Fedya yelled. The wind tore his voice inches from his mouth, but the rider turned, and it was an Apraksin retainer. A voice at the back of his head cautioned Fedya the man had been riding without light, but he wanted that damn horse.

"Come here, boy! I need that horse!" Flailing, Fedya screamed but he couldn't even hear himself over the wind. "Horse!" He pointed.

The rider whipped his horse and came for him, holding out his hand, as though two grown men were supposed to saddle the sad looking mount he had. Meaning to yank him down, Fedya reached for his hand, then froze. The Apraksin wore their alchemy on their gauntlet and his was... The gold was ruined and black.

Then he realized the horse was missing flesh in parts, and its naked ribs were showing. An ice spear formed in his hand, and he thrust through the rider's neck. It turned and screamed at him, the jaw dislocating like a snake.

Fedya didn't think himself a coward, but the thing had startled him, and he ran. Trekking through deep snow, he was being run down by a soulless devil on a dead horse when a druzhina plowed into the rider and wiped him from God's earth.

"My lord!" Isidor jumped down and surrendered his horse to Fedya. His druzhina had finally caught up.

"What the hell was that!" Fedya yelled.

"The devil, my lord!" Isidor boosted Fedya up the saddle.

As many as the trees the damned soulless were everywhere. Fedya had been torn from the world of the sane and plunged into a horrid tale told to scare children. Had he not seen them with his own eyes, he wouldn't have believed it. But as sure as the naked blade in his hand and steaming breaths of the galloping horse, the *dver* was wide open, hell on the other side, and the soulless crawled his lands.

In his peripheral, he was losing men left and right, but when one of these bastards pulled Isidor down, Fedya circled and charged with a spear. He nailed the bastard, through and through, but something grabbed his horse from under the snow, tearing its guts out. Then he was in the fray, fighting alongside his men, not a death he would regret had his wife and children not been on his mind.

Heaving, his breath steaming, Fedya thrashed. His blade got stuck on Apraksin armor, and he lost it, so he used an alchemy weapon. Apraksin greysteel would *always* bite into Pulyazin ice. They were famous for their forges after all. So he had to use a spear and find flesh because it wouldn't go through armor and the fighting had become futile... A losing battle trying to fend them off.

The man beside him fell, and when Fedya picked up his sword, a wolf leaped from the dark and bit his arm. The snarling creature got a mouthful of fur cloak, no flesh, but the blood and the fighting were drawing starved wolves.

Something shoved him. Another pulled him down. Anfisa had been carrying and he'd been hoping for another daughter. A waking dream of his wife came to him, the woman humming carelessly in the sun, on green grass, and among wildflowers, while he stabbed up with a dagger and warm blood spilled on his face.

"My lord! My lord!" Isidor screamed somewhere. The wind wouldn't tell him where.

On his back, Fedya was being dragged through the darkness by a horse or a man, he couldn't say. He'd gotten stabbed and felt his life draining. Anfisa, Anfisa, the only thing on his mind, when a sudden daylight blinded him. As bright as heaven, the sun rose over Bone Country at night.

His hand on his wound, Fedya rose first to his knees, then got up and stood in awe. The forest on fire, the soulless burned, and rolling on snow didn't appear to help them. He'd been so close. He could see the Church of Light. The damnedest thing, the sky above them was still black and the light was coming from the church.

God, he thought, *I see God.*

Twelve

Lover's Heart

Lev staggered down the hall in his mother's red dress, high, high, high, and flying through the clouds while he laughed. Life was shit in the east. What was there to do but to get fucked? The marble statues of twenty-foot saints holding their favored relics wrapped around the pillars, and the clatter of Lev dropping his gold cup on the stone floor when he fell echoed through the grand hall. Twelve fireplaces burned, and the hall was still freezing. The ceiling was too high, and the windows were too tall was Lev's guess. He crawled onto the dais and sat up on the gold crested chair, hiking one leg over the gilded armrest—all of it cold.

He peered into his cup but sadly he'd spilled his wine. "Steward, wine!" he yelled, and his voice echoed, wine, wine, wine.

While the frigid old man with a flourished cloak fulfilled Lev's request, Lev squinted at the shapes waiting for him. He was supposed to meet people, but he'd forgotten who.

Apraksin retainers with the crest of a silver dagger on their leather armor, all right. Their lords Vasily and Dariy, all right. Vasily Apraksin had been with him when Lev and his entourage rode up to the Menshikov and found them... dead. Vasily was a good fighter, a young but proud northern lord, and Lev had known him since childhood. His humor was stupid but he was a friend.

Dariy, Vasily's older brother, was a loser, however. He gifted his heirloom Apraksin steel to win the favor of a sentinel whore named Dominik. Lev sincerely hoped Dariy got his money's worth, but the man was the butt of a sad joke.

Who else? Skuratov retainers, of course, and Semyon. Handsome in his iron cuirass, the emerald of his cape made the blond hair shine. Lev smiled at him.

Then he found a face he didn't recognize and frowned. He pointed. "Who are you?"

"Captain of Lord Fedya's druzhina, Isidor of Pulyazin, my lord," Konstantin answered and startled Lev. He hadn't seen the tall knight because he blended in so well with the saints.

"You are late, my lord," Isidor said.

"Oh, it speaks," Lev said.

"You *are* late, my lord," Erlan bent and whispered and scared Lev. Another knight he hadn't seen, and the giant bastard was on the dais, right by his chair too. This hall, like all other halls at Usolya Fortress, had too many statues and they were hard to tell from people when the sun was glaring in his eyes through the arched windows.

"You said morning." Lev pointed at the sun. "It is morning."

"That's the west, my lord," Erlan whispered again.

"Morning, evening, same difference for the sun never sets on the Guards," Lev proclaimed. "You say I'm late, but it appears your lord never arrived, Izda of Pulyazin."

"Isidor, Lord Lev," the druzhina corrected.

"Whatever. What do you want?" Lev blinked, then gulped wine to clear his head. It did not help.

The druzhina turned to Vasily, confused, then returned his attention to Lev. "Did *you* not request a meeting with the House of Pulyazin, Lord Lev?"

"With Fedya, yes, but you're not him." Lev stumbled on his hem as soon as he got up and Erlan caught him.

He thanked the knight and had been walking away when he heard Isidor grumble, "You're surely joking. I rode for two straight days to come here because you called, Lord Lev."

"I'll tell you a joke." Lev turned. "Once there was a duck whose name was Quack-Quack. All Quack-Quack did was fuck, fuck. There also was a red fox whose name was simply Fox. Then Fox ate Quack, the end. The moral of the story is life isn't funny. It's stupid nonsense, then you die. Don't be a duck, but if you're going to be one, be Quack and not the hens he fucked."

"Goodbye, Isidor of Pulyazin." Lev threw up his arm. "Best get going, a two-day ride you said."

"I can't tell if this is outrageous or you're simply odd," said Isidor.

"That's the charm," Lev said, walking out. "I'm a jester. Laughing is the correct response."

Lev lounged pleasantly warm in his bed, the logs cracking in the fireplace, and with a lantern by his bedside. He was reading *not* in his mother's dress but in cotton sleep trousers and shirt. Wool socks and felt slippers, legs crossed at the ankle, he flipped the page when the door opened, and Semyon came in.

He hid his face behind the book. "I'm sorry."

"Yeah," sighed Semyon. He hung his cloak and crossed the room to sit at Lev's table, helping himself to the cold dinner Lev hadn't touched.

"Were you just outside? You brought the winter in." Lev rolled out of bed, took his book, and went to sit by Semyon. "You're upset."

"No," he said while being upset.

Lev lay his head on his folded arms on the table and sighed. Both the Apraksin boys, Vasily and Dariy, were the runts of the litter of seven brothers and didn't have the authority to promise Lev a single goat. They had their personal retainers which put together amounted to a few dozen. Semyon's family disowned him for just being here, Lord Skuratov making it very clear he would not be taking sides in the conflict, meaning he'd already chosen the Shields. There was too much profit to be made from the queen's railway which was still being laid with Skuratov iron.

Chartorisky, Durnov, Vietinghoff, those were Shield allies already and Lev didn't have a chance in hell with them, but he'd hoped the eastern lords would support his claim. All had gone to shit following the Menshikov incident, which he still didn't understand. Sometimes he wondered if he'd just been high and imagined Bogdan had two heads. Had he been alone, he would think so, but to this day, everyone who'd been with him swore by what they'd seen, including Semyon, but he was slowly losing his faith in Lev.

You're a fool for having one in the first place. What made you think I could pull this off?

In the spring when the earth thawed and the Bone Country stopped being absolute misery, the Shields would take their train and come for Lev. The only reason they hadn't done so already was they didn't want to lay siege to Usolya in the winter. He was a realist and knew this to be the truth. He wanted to live a little the last year of his life but people like Semyon got disappointed he wasn't better and didn't try.

"You actually think I can win, don't you?" Lev turned his head and propped his chin on his arms.

"Not this way, you won't," Semyon said, chewing some measly bread and wiping his nose with the back of his hand. Everyone sniveled all the time, their noses running. It was so cold that the blade stuck, and the soul wept while the tears froze on the face.

"You should go home, Syoma. Apraksin too."

"Lev, you realize they'll kill you?" Blond brows furrowed, so serious when he was angry. But Semyon didn't have any menace. His hair was the same tone as his skin and from a few paces back, you couldn't tell if he was moving his brows, or if he even had them.

"Yes. Which is why you shouldn't be here," Lev said.

Shoulders hunched, Semyon sat somberly and quietly while Lev spilled some salt on the table and fiddled by tracing symbols on it.

"Look," Semyon said after a while. "I'm not leaving you. So if we're dying, I suppose we're doing it together. But it *would* be nice to have a few more men."

"No one I don't know by their first name is going to fight for a brat from Krakova, Syoma. It's a dream. Leave it be. It's annoying."

"You just need to convince a couple of people." Semyon reached across and put his hand on Lev's shoulder. "Then a couple more, then a couple more. It will get easier each time, and once you have enough people, others will come to you without you asking. That's how it is. You can do this. You're charming when you want to be. Out here, people have had nothing but hardship all their lives, and especially the last four years. Their kin are dead. Men are eating their dogs and parents are burying their children. They are *starving*, Lev. All you need to do is tell them it's the prince's fault, you hear?

"People love the church. Promise them hope. Promise them a spot among the stars. Promise them the queen's granary. Tell them there's food in Krakova. Say anything and they'll believe you, Lev. If you're losing, it's only because you want to.

"You'll bring a golden age to Fedosia. The throne is yours, take it. The Shields are burning this country. Tell *us* you'll save us." He pounded his chest. "It's true whether you believe it or not."

Lev wished he wouldn't say things like that, wouldn't look at him the way he did... It made him feel guilty for wanting to lie down and die, and it ruined his peace of mind. He stared at the salt.

"You're not alone." Semyon cupped Lev's nape as though he meant to be tender, but then just shook him by the neck till Lev laughed. Then he noisily slurped cold soup and spoke while chewing. "Light inside dark? The times we live in?"

Lev blinked, sat up, then realized Semyon was talking about the symbols Lev doodled in the salt. "Oh, it's a soul encased in shadow. It means darkling."

"What's that?" Semyon pushed away the empty bowl and reached for the plate of smoked herring.

"A children's tale for one," said Lev. "But according to Soful, Uncle said it on the day he died. So, I've been looking into it. From what I gather, it's a vengeful spirit caught in shadow alchemy. The soul is energy, light as we call it, yeah?" Lev illustrated writing it in the salt because Semyon looked puzzled. "Once you lose the physical vessel that sustains your energy..." Lev realized he was overcomplicating it when Semyon arched a brow. "When your body dies, your soul goes to the *dver* and crosses over, hopefully to a good place, yeah? But this thing, darkling, is a person who died very angry, and his soul got absorbed by shadows. He doesn't cross over because though he has no body, he has a shadow and exists inside it..." Lev rolled his eyes and grunted when Semyon made a shadow dog on the wall with his hand. "Oh, never you mind."

"No, I'm listening. A haunted shadow killed the archmage. How, though? Where did it come from?"

"The most common cause of death among mages isn't murder or old age," Lev said. "It's fucking with magic beyond their ability. Whether that's someone testing a poison on himself, an incendiary spell blowing up in his face, or summoning a haunted shadow he can't control, that's how most mages die. They're always looking to immortalize their name in the light codex. Three miracles to sainthood and don't forget a new spell counts as a miracle."

"You think the archmage caused his own death?" Semyon asked.

"I think so. Unless he'd been fucking with it, why would he know such an obscure thing? As far as I can tell, it's only been cast once before, ever. I always thought it wasn't the Shields, but Father just... He hadn't been simple minded. He just made an unfortunate call, which we all do from time to time." Lev bit his lip. "This conflict is meaningless. Father died for nothing. He caused others to die over nothing. And now I'll die as nothing. How's that for good news?"

"It may have started over nothing," said Semyon. "But it won't be fought over nothing. People want a Guard tsar. It's fate." He took his hand. "It's *your* destiny. I'll fight for you, Lev, preferably with a few more men at my side."

"Ah, you're a fool."

"That's because you're so bright. Everyone is a fool compared to you."

"Get out of here with that." Lev pulled his hand and got up. He would get Semyon killed and he couldn't stand it. "Please find something better to die for."

He'd left his wine bedside and was fetching it when he heard, "Is this the darkling book, then?"

"No." Lev filled his cup and touched the wine to his lips. "It's the life chronicle of a mage who lived five centuries ago. The 'darkling book' appears to have been lost during the Elfurian War. Pity. It was written by the acolyte who summoned it, or cast it, depending on the mechanics of it. She went mad and wrote on her own skin. That would have made an interesting read."

"So, it's a diary?" Semyon was flipping through the pages when Lev turned. "Why is it in the language of spells, then?"

"Because we're pompous assholes."

"It's amazing you can read this. It's just shapes." Semyon put the book aside.

"It's just symbols of alchemy, like the one you have on your armor. We've assigned sound to it. That's all."

"You can speak and understand alchemy?" Semyon looked bewildered.

"Come on, Syoma, that's what spells are. You knew that." Lev sat on his lap facing him and put his arms over his broad shoulders. "Instead of writing it, we're just saying it, because some spells take hundreds of symbols. When you speak it whole, it's incantation, but you can shorthand it to a single word if you understand all the alchemy it contains. You do it in here." Lev tapped his temple with his free hand. The other holding his drink. "Dragon's Breath, for instance, contains fifty-seven symbols. No one's got time for that." He hooked his elbow around Semyon's neck. "Recently, I've found the longest spell I've ever seen. The fucker is an entire codex with three thousand four hundred and one symbols. I'm calling it Illuminate."

"What does it do?" Semyon took Lev's cup and set it aside, pulling him closer and bringing their hips to touch.

"It's gold expressed as light." Lev liked to talk with his hand and demonstrated a bloom, but instead of going through the convoluted explanation of what a soulless was, why they corrupted gold, and how the gold being light altered the interaction, he simply said, "It vanquishes evil," and freed his chattering mouth for a kiss.

"Sounds like a useful thing," Semyon said.

Yeah, Lev had thought so too. But the spell would just collect imaginary dust in his mind as one more worthless shit he knew. When they said alchemy couldn't create gold, they meant the cost was exorbitant and couldn't be settled by more gold.

"May I see it?" Semyon whispered, his strong hand callused by years of sword practice, the steel kind, stroking Lev's gold locks. His other hand found another kind of swordplay.

"What?" Lev muttered, suffering the peril of the blood draining from the brain.

"The illumination, may I see it?"

"Not unless you want to die. The spell costs a lover's heart, and I ever only had one of those."

Thirteen
Charlatans and Buffoons

Was it still the same night or another night? Had Lev slept too little or a whole day? He turned and Semyon wasn't there, so he really didn't know. The fire had been stoked and the room was warm for a change as he swung his legs over the bed and stepped on the—

"What the fuck!" Lev leaped up and clung onto the bedpost like a flailing cat, sliding down due to not possessing claws. He looked at the floor and there was a bearskin. It hadn't been there before.

It hideously clashed with the rest of the décor, but he didn't mind it because bearskins were warm, and he could always use warm. Now that he knew it was there, the fur was a pleasant texture under his bare feet.

Semyon burst in with a great purpose. It was either too early or too late for so much energy—Lev felt tired putting on his slippers.

"The next time you bring a dead thing into my bedchamber, please tell me." Lev yawned.

Semyon opened the curtains and afternoon sunlight blasted Lev. So, it hadn't been night. The bed creaked with the weight as a blond bear in full armor plunged onto it. "Are you awake, Lev? We have some bad news."

"Isn't that just news at this point?" Lev rubbed his eyes. "So, tell me what terrible new thing happened?"

"Apraksin scouts spotted Grigori. The trail he was on, he was headed to the Ivory Fortress."

Semyon and Vasily had this theory Grigori might be responsible for the deaths of Menshikov since he'd been seen in Bone Country around the time. They'd been 'spotting' him for months and had been on a goose chase with the elusive one.

"Leave it alone," Lev grumbled. "He's a charlatan who tricked the mad queen into believing he is a mage. He's not one. He studied under no one. None of the real mages knew him and no one has seen him cast a single spell." Lev blew a raspberry. "His patron monarch is dead. He's probably looking for another fool to leech off for another decade." He looked at the cold porridge on the table, looked at his warm bed, and chose the bed.

"You don't think he's carrying a message from the prince to the Pulyazin?" Semyon asked. "I think we should capture and question him."

"Don't join Lev Guard, or you'll starve this winter. There, I saved you time." Lev laid his head on the pillow. "He's a straggler. Leave him be, Syoma."

"*Something* happened to the Menshikov. Maybe he knows."

"Leave it be," Lev whispered as he closed his eyes. "We have enough trouble on this side of the *dver*. Don't poke darkness with a stick. Maybe it bites."

"But you're the guardian of light."

Lev scoffed. "That was the archmage and he's dead."

Semyon stepped out. Lev went back to sleep and by the time he was staggering about—just tired, not drunk—looking for food, dinner had already been served.

He sat alone at the long table for fifty and composed another letter for Soful which she'd never get. The servants lit the candles as the day fell, darkness coming earlier with each passing day, and the cook reheated some mutton for him. They'd been saving him food because he never ate when it was being served.

Hello, Soful.

How have you been? I miss you much. Father, too. It's the darndest thing, the memories that stay with us the brightest. With you, it's always us hiding under the covers during the lightning storm. They're so loud, thunder, I mean. The cover didn't help at all, but you did.

With Uncle, it's when he got me a miniature pony. And Father...

Lev set the quill down and held his face in his hands. Lord Pyotr had not been all right for so long that Lev struggled to find a memory in which he wasn't sad. Soful would tell Lev how his father used to sing for his mother, how they used to be happy together, but as far as he could remember, Mother was always sick and Father always sad. When she passed, Pyotr Guard's soul died. Father knew the Shield *couldn't* have killed the archmage, he must have, he wasn't stupid. Instigating a conflict with the House of Steel, he was looking for a way to go to his wife.

Father, did you think it was dignified, the way you went out? It was not. You killed yourself and left me holding the bag of shit. I hate you.

He hated the archmage too. His ego was too big and caused his demise. There was a running theme with the men in his family—suicide.

"My lord."

Lev looked up. "Yes, Konstantin."

"They shouldn't be out after dark. Do you want us to search for them?"

"Who's they?" Lev frowned. He thought Dariy had been called back home.

"Vasily Apraksin and Lord Skuratov, my lord," said the knight, then perhaps seeing Lev's confusion, he asked, "Did you not send them to find Mage Grigori?"

"No," groaned Lev. "Matter of fact, I said the opposite." He got up and marched to the window. It was so dark he couldn't even see the courtyard. "They're going to get lost and freeze to death, aren't they? Fucken buffoons." His shoulders slumped and he pressed his forehead against the cold glass. "Please take the hounds and go find them."

"It's Usolya, my lord. We didn't bring the hounds." He had to clarify things like this because when Lev was inebriated he'd forget where he was and ask for his father. "But their tracks are still fresh. It shouldn't be too hard," said Konstantin.

"Yeah, do that. Thank you."

"How many should I take?" Konstantin wasn't used to being the captain and would run all his decisions by Lev. Good old Clodt, the kind giant who'd captained the knights for three decades, was another casualty of Father's suicide stand at White Palace.

How many should I take, the man asked as though Lev had hundreds of knights. He did not. They all died at the White Palace. *Father, you killed them.*

"Saints," Lev breathed. "All eleven of you, I suppose, or is that too many? Do you think we'll disturb the wildlife unfairly with the thundering of our hooves?"

"I'd rather not leave the fortress unguarded, my lord... Will six men suffice?"

"They *all* left?" Lev threw up his arms. "For a single old man?"

"They wanted to comb the area and not miss the mage. Lord Skuratov seemed to believe it was important they captured the mage."

"Stop calling him a mage, Konstantin. Uncle was a mage. Father could have been a mage. *I* am a mage. Grigori is a charlatan. I only care that Skuratov is going to freeze his balls off and get eaten by the mountain. It's unforgiving out here, and the boy from Black Ore doesn't seem to understand that. Take your men, all of them, and go find Semyon. The Apraksin are from here. This is their terrain. They'll manage."

"Yes, my lord," he said but hesitated.

"We have a drawbridge, Konstantin," Lev said. "I'll pull it up after you leave. Besides, who the fuck is going to come here in *this* weather?"

"Yes, my lord."

"And Captain, take more gold than you need. Whatever ate the Menshikov is still out there. Gold, I can spare. Knights, I cannot."

"Yes, my lord."

Lev stood at the gate and watched his knights ride off into the dark void. Their torches, like fireflies, vanished once entering the trees. He told the men to raise the bridge, waited to see that it was done, and strode through the gatehouse.

"Lock up," he told the gatekeepers. "And you do *not* open the gate for *anyone* without telling me first. Understood? I don't care if it's your mother or a naked whore. You do not let anyone in without me here, yes?"

"Yes, my lord."

Then for good measure, because plain men were superstitious, he said, "There are spirits out there. Evil lurks in the darkness and takes the form familiar to you. That," he pointed at the Guard crest above the door, "protects you. Evil can't cross it and must use trickery to be invited in. Understood?"

"Yes, my lord."

Then he scared them with the tale of two-headed Bogdan, which was purposefully botched alchemy and not an evil spirit, but it seemed to do the job as men pulled out their protection amulets and wore them over their cloaks.

He climbed the never ending stairs to the battlement and stood there with the men, thankful for the calm weather. Later, he walked the allure which didn't have to be manned too heavily because Usolya sat on a small island inside a grand lake, the drawbridge connecting to the narrow strip of land stretching from the bank like the reaching arm of a friend. The lake was frozen now, but a few vials of Wrath would break the ice easily and dunk anyone foolish enough to try to cross it that way.

He joined a card game with the soldiers, purposefully lost a few coppers which seemed to make them *so* happy, realized that was infectious—happiness—and smiled as he continued his wall walk.

The difference between a soldier and a knight was the use of alchemy, not birthright. Having access to gold helped, having a father who could teach you alchemy helped, of course, and most Guard knights were legacy, but that didn't stop the plain soldiers from fiddling with the light codex, trying to unravel the thing, thinking it would better their lives. In theory, anyone could make a knight, but life was just a little different.

But Lev thought to award their effort and helped a group of soldiers when he found them with a page of a codex, trying to learn basic alchemy. Half alchemy, really, they were just trying to start a fire with an alchemy flint. Drawing with a stick on the snow in the courtyard as a crowd gathered around him, he explained what a complete transmutation was, which was necessary to understand half-alchemy. Some stared blankly, some nodded, and Lev gave everyone who wanted one a gold coin so they could practice alchemy.

Gold was rare, sure, but the perceived value only came from its use in magic. One couldn't eat it, clearly, and couldn't even make potato with it. Living alchemy was a trade in time. You couldn't create a potato, but you could make the plant grow faster—time, and for that, the *dver* only accepted time in return, meaning it shortened your life by the equivalent number of months or years.

It was illegal for commoners to possess gold, and though curious, the men were wary at first, but Lev said to return it to him after they were done practicing, and they left better. A little girl tried reaching for the thing glittering in the firelight, and her mother slapped her hand, so Lev gave them silver instead.

"Buy something good when we get out of here, yeah?" he said.

"Are you going to be the tsar, Lord Lev?" the girl asked while her mother bowed, profusely apologizing.

The whole of the Guard household had been lost during the fall of the White Palace, and the servants here were from the Bone Country. When he first arrived, they'd flocked to him like pigeons to a handful of grain. Many had come to pray because they thought a Guard meant a saint, and Lev had hired more people than he needed because they appeared to be starving and he had food. Not enough to feed the Pulyazin, but enough to sustain Usolya for the winter even stuffed to the brim, which it wasn't.

So he did that, killed time without getting trashed because he was worried for Semyon, and didn't want to be drunk in case he had to go look for him in the dark.

When dawn neared and the men hadn't returned, Lev played cards with the soldiers in the watchtower. Any shouting in the courtyard, real or imagined, made him pop up and rush to the arrow slits. Soldiers talked about whores a lot, even the ones with families, and one asked Lev about the courtesans at court.

'*I don't pay for sex,*' he wanted to say but didn't want to sound condescending because they'd been talking about just that, and went instead with, "They're all right. Not worth the money, though, especially sentinels."

"Aren't sentinels... men, my lord?" asked one, and his friend elbowed him. They cleared their throats.

"I was courting Zoya Chartorisky," Lev said.

"Ah." They nodded.

Lev had been with Zoya. So had Semyon. They were just high. Raven balls, good times, Lev sighed.

"Oy, a pigeon." The soldier pointed behind Lev.

Lev didn't understand why that was noteworthy and drew a card.

"Oy, another pigeon."

Yes, he could hear the cooing as though they were having a flock gathering out there, but—

"They don't live here, do they?" It finally occurred to him, and he got up.

They were church homing pigeons, he realized at once, couriers, but there were so many! They flocked to the tower and crowded the railings and the ledges. Lev reached out through the arrow slit and caught a pigeon. Because they were used to being handled, the bird let him hold it and pet it.

"It's freezing outside," Lev mumbled. "Do we have a birdkeeper?" he asked, knowing they didn't. Usolya hadn't been used in years and he'd seen the empty aviary when he first arrived.

Yet these pigeons must have been raised here and they were returning home because someone let them out.

"Oh, holy fuck," he realized, once he saw they were carrying message capsules.

He took the one from the pigeon he held, releasing the bird afterward. Running a finger over the archmage's seal, for a brief moment he was a boy receiving a miniature pony from his uncle. He let that go with a long exhale and opened the scroll which wasn't from the archmage... and it was addressed to a count he'd never heard of.

Then he got another pigeon, the same message and not addressed to him, either.

The Chartorisky port burns. The House of Silver is no more. The Boyar Duma are hereby notified Daniil Chartorisky has made an attempt on the prince's life. He is wanted for high treason. If found, kill on sight.

It took him a while because the exceeding stupidity made it harder to understand, but after twelve pigeons or so, Lev realized some brilliant mind at the church must have put all the birds in the same aviary following the archmage's death. Now they didn't know which bird was homed where and just released them all. Except they didn't even know how church couriers worked. There was no need to be addressing little lords and wasting parchment. You notified the church overseeing the area and the local parsons sent couriers, people this time, out to the lords if they found it relevant. Besides, there were only eleven or twelve places in the whole of Fedosia the pigeons were homed to, and all of them were churches and Guard estates.

Twenty pigeons later, Lev even found one addressed to Gavril Illeivich, Sofia's dead husband.

Luminary Matvey, the donkey who'd signed these, was a charlatan, a failed acolyte parading around as a man of deep faith. He'd assumed control, Lev guessed, because all the mages and acolytes worth their salt were dead, and no Guard was around to call him on his bullshit. He couldn't even direct pigeons. How was he running the church? Such a thing boiled Lev's blood because the buffoon was pissing on his family legacy by using the archmage's seal.

It took him hours to home the pigeons in the aviary, find suitable caretakers, assign people to repair the aviary so the birds didn't freeze in the winter, and sort through the hundreds of scrolls, making a pile for people close enough he could send riders to.

Then he burned the rest because how was he to deliver the message to House Durnov, a damn Shield ally, not to mention their estate was at the other, the western, end of Fedosia?

The irony of it was that in the *hundreds* of messages, not a single one was addressed to Lev. *Suck my cock, old shriveled fuck.*

While he fumed, the Skuratov and the Guard knights arrived safe by the saints' grace.

"We didn't find him," said Semyon, disappointed, when Lev went to the gatehouse to allow them in.

"You shouldn't have stayed out through the night, Syoma," Lev scolded the blond bear on a tall horse.

"Yeah. We got separated from the Apraksin and got lost." He hung his head in shame as he dismounted. "It turned out we were just circling our tail."

Lev had known they'd get lost too, a foot of snow hid the roads. But he was just glad they'd returned.

"Do you want us to look for the Apraksin, my lord?" Konstantin asked on the bridge.

"Never you mind," Lev said. The Apraksin lived less than a day's ride from Usolya. They could manage. "I need your advice on something, come on in."

"What the fuck is this?" was Semyon's response to the hundreds of tiny scrolls laid out on the long table of the dining hall.

"Here, this one is for your father." Lev gave him one scrap. "These are for your brothers and cousins." Lev handed him a bunch.

"What *are* these?" he mumbled as he opened them, growing more bewildered about the multitude of scrolls sent to the same household rather than the content of the message.

The knights frowned at the sheer number of messages. Erlan took one, held it open, and scoffed, "You don't say?"

No one other than Matvey was surprised Duke Rodion would eat the Chartorisky as his first meal after his claim to power. The Chartorisky were rich, played too many games, and depended too greatly on the Shields to protect them, hardly keeping any soldiers. Lev didn't believe for a single beat that Daniil would have the balls to try assassination.

The Vietinghoff were the same and they were next was Lev's guess. After the Guards were banished from Krakova, Lev realized the *Boyar Duma* was a farce.

The other knights read the scrolls as well, and Konstantin remarked, "I thought Duchess Elena was Chartorisky?" He looked at Lev as though he was supposed to know who that was, then clarified, "Duke Rodion's wife."

"Oh, the Chartorisky are backstabbing bitches," said Lev, recalling how Zoya blamed him for cheating at the Royal Cup. "The duchess probably doesn't care about her house now she's going to be queen, and her children tsars. Next, they're going to eat Prince Nikolas, too. I hope Aleksei knows that."

"But this is good news, my lord," said Konstantin. "If you'd allow us, my lord, we'd like to deliver some of these messages and make a case for my lord's cause. Those who were blind to the Shield's tyranny will perhaps now see the House of Steel will swallow them all. Once the throne starts seizing the lands of its nobles, it will never end. We'll stop by the churches as well. Rallying the common folks always helps sway their lords."

"That's not a bad idea," Semyon chimed in.

Lev let the knights discuss their plan and divide their tasks and sat at the head of the table, drinking his third bottle of wine. He relaxed after Semyon returned and was making up for the lost time.

Five bottles of wine, and he blew a raspberry hearing Konstantin assign Pulyazin to a knight. "Fuck Fedya. Send a simpleton. Don't waste your time with him. He's already knelt, prepared to suck Rodion's cock."

Semyon came and snatched the wine away from Lev. "You had enough."

"Breathe, Syoma. Your corset is wound up too tight."

"Quit it and go to sleep."

Lev got kicked out of his own dining hall because men were 'working' but he didn't go to sleep, and strolled to the music room to bang on the piano just so he could be a nuisance. He was happy, though, finding his first sliver of hope since his father's death. Maybe the knights could corral people to his cause; not Pulyazin, that house was bought and sold, but the east was vast, and they'd been starving long enough. It was time to get up and march on the capital.

He stayed up all night in the music room. No longer trying to be obnoxious, he just played waltz, the music his parents danced to.

Konstantin knocked on the door frame to announce the knights were leaving. Some of them would be gone for months since they meant to travel far and wide, and Lev got up to bid them a safe journey and prayed because his men had asked him to. It didn't mean shit to him, but it did to them, and if it helped them believe the saints would watch over their journey, it was worth something.

Then he and Semyon fell asleep together, their limbs sprawled and tangled with one another. Lev loved him. He'd been in love since he was thirteen and Semyon eleven, since the blond boy kissed him in the woods behind the White Palace. If life was a circle beginning and ending at the same point, sailed on a small boat in the open waters, Semyon was Lev's anchor that tethered him to his path, kept him from drifting out into oblivion, and he was the center point Lev circled, the meaning of life when there was none.

"My lord." A voice called Lev from his dream of warm waters and sunshine into the freezing bedchamber in Usolya where the fire had gone out. "My lord."

"Stoke the fire." Lev groaned and sat up.

"Right away," the servant said, but there was a soldier with him, staring at Semyon sleeping in Lev's bed.

"What is it?" asked Lev.

"Ah." The soldier blinked, minding his manners suddenly. "The Apraksin party returned, my lord. Should we open the gate?"

Fourteen

Sunshine

The hangover banged in his skull, the earth swayed under him, and the smoke of burning fat from the kitchen nauseated him. Taking his time, Lev walked through the courtyard and labored the length of the fortress ground to arrive at the gate.

"Lower the bridge." He squinted at the sunlight. Why was the day so bright when his hangover was the worst? He meant to brew himself a cure once he returned to his chamber. For now, he shivered in a thin cloak as the many pullies and chains clanked, the long drawbridge slowly bowing till the tip touched the narrow strip of raised earth.

The Apraksin were on the other side, and as they crossed the bridge Lev went out to meet them halfway. They'd brought bodies wrapped in cloaks draped over saddles, and Vasily looked as though someone had sapped the life out of him.

The morning was calm but the chill from the frozen lake seeped under Lev's cloak and penetrated his bone marrow. Yet people lived out here, little children too. He was just a whiny bitch, he supposed, but couldn't help wrinkling his nose at the Apraksin men, who'd apparently rolled around in manure since they left. Lev was tempted to plunge the men into the frozen water to wash them before they entered what was essentially his home. Had it been warm, he'd think the stench was from the dead, but it was freezing.

"For the saints, Vasily, even your horse smells," Lev hissed under his breath, frowning at the ooze running down the mount's side. "Please keep that horse out of the stables until the veterinarian looks at it. I don't want the other horses catching whatever that one has caught," he said, then realized he didn't have a veterinarian at Usolya, just the stable hands. "Never mind, I'll look at it." Later, later, he'd do everything else but needed to fix the wretched headache first.

"So what happened?" Lev grimaced at Vasily, but the Apraksin only blinked. Sometimes, he acted as though not all right in the head. "Your men, Vasily, what happened to your men?"

"Wolves." Vasily shrugged.

"Wolves?"

"Wolves."

Lev sighed and dragged his heels to a horse with a body draped over the saddle and pried open the cloak. The retainer's throat was ripped out by a wild creature. Bear or wolf, who knew, but it certainly wasn't a blade.

Heading back to the gate, Lev passed by Vasily. "Burn the pyre for them before it gets dark, and please keep that fucken horse away from the stables till I can look at it, yeah?"

Lev made it all the way to the gatehouse, realized the Apraksin were still on the bridge, sighed, and went back. He'd ask them about their troubles, of course, but he'd hoped to do it inside, after he cured his hangover and put on a fur cloak. But it was what it was.

"I'm sorry for your loss, Vasily." Lev searched deep into his patience to produce a spoonful of empathy. "Do you want to tell me what happened? Is there anything I can do for them? I'd say send them home, but they need to be burned before dark, yeah?" said Lev. Vasily didn't answer. He sat like a doll on his pus oozing horse. "I'll make sure their families are compensated," Lev managed though he'd *clearly* told them not to go. And how Vasily managed to lose half his men to wolves was beyond him.

"What is that?" Vasily whispered, only audible because the morning was still and no one else was speaking.

Lev looked over the shoulder at what Vasily was asking about. It was the Guard crest. The Apraksin were so odd. When they were children, Vasily's twin sister had passed and the prick frightened Lev by telling him how he'd killed her and had her stuffed like a hunting trophy. It wasn't true. His sister was thrown from a horse and broke her back, but at the time Lev hadn't known that and was scared of Vasily.

Then there was the time he lied about how Apraksin forges were for incinerating bodies and how Apraksin steel was forged with the ashes of the dead. Not only it wasn't true, but his father beat him for the lie. Vasily liked grotesque things, assumed others would enjoy them as well, and when he joked, it was just weird.

Lev had fallen down the rabbit hole of his childhood memories and frowned at how Vasily once chased him around with a ladle of shit. It was exactly as it sounded. He put human feces on a wooden ladle and chased Lev threatening to fling it at him. He couldn't recall how old he'd been, only that he was small enough Sofia could pick him up.

They were at the White Palace, and she came out and yelled at Vasily because Lev had been screaming and crying.

'That's disgusting. Stop it!' she scolded Vasily. *'Where did you get it anyway?'*

It turned out Vasily had climbed down the outhouse in the servants' quarters. Why!? No one knew, and Soful had washed him out in the yard like a dog and burned his clothes in a pit.

"Why is it so bright?"

"What?" Lev realized he was still out on the bridge, his balls frozen solid. He flicked a look at the Guard crest Vasily was squinting at, and said, "Because it's a sun made of gold. What the fuck is your problem?"

"It hurts," he whispered. "It's hurting me."

"Then stop looking at it." There was a marble ball in a tin cup rattling inside Lev's head. It did hurt. "For the saint's sake, go in!"

"You haven't said we could come in," Vasily murmured.

Lev wanted to punch him but restrained himself because he'd lost many men. Perhaps stupid humor was how Vasily dealt with distress.

"Come on in," Lev said and turned, this time the Apraksin following him. They'd been out in the cold for two days. He'd go make sure they had warm food, but hangover cure first. That was killing him.

They used to have a proper veterinary surgeon at the White Palace who took care of Rhytsar, and the other expensive racehorses Lev had. But he was dead now. Usolya only had a few villagers pretending to be stable hands. They didn't have a physician, only an old woman who knew the names of some common herbs and could bandage wounds. Anything a bit more sophisticated had to be Lev and it said more about the shambled state of the fortress than him. He was terrible. He knew was. Even then, he'd gathered his shit including a set of surgical knives, a veterinary book of common communicable diseases, bandages, some ointments he had, and had troubled himself with dragging them to the courtyard only to find someone, probably Vasily, had struck the horse in the head with an axe and left the creature on the snow—a while ago from how the blood had coagulated already.

He found Vasily by the well and punched him in the face.

"It's a living thing, no?" Lev stood over him and hissed, "Why did you kill your horse?"

"You said it was diseased." He got up, wiping his mouth, then flinched as if Lev beat him all the time.

"I said I'd look at it! I hope you treat your men better than your mount. It doesn't seem like being loyal to you pays off very well." Lev was furious about the horse, and the men Vasily brought back dead, and the Apraksin's nonchalant attitude wasn't helping.

He'd been so upset when he lost Rhytsar and seeing the dead horse had reminded him of that, somehow, and he'd been sitting in the stables and crying like a boy at everything that just had to go to shit, when Semyon found him.

"What happened?" he asked.

"Nothing." Lev got up. "I just need more wine. Sobriety sucks."

"Do you know what will make you feel better?" Semyon asked.

"Dying?" That would solve all his problems.

"Draw your sword, Guard." Semyon smiled. "Your form has fallen to shit because you're drunk all the time."

"Says a fat boy to the fencing champ—" Lev twisted to evade Semyon's thrust, the steel hissing by his face. "That better be a training sword!"

"Nope. It's got two sharp edges."

"I'm not in the mood." Lev took his empty wine cup and strolled past Semyon, and the bastard struck him in the ass with the flat of his sword. It stung.

"Point," said Semyon.

The House of Iron bred large men who carried heavy armor and thick steel. Lev finished his wine and drew his saber. Unlike Skuratov's two-handed longsword, Lev's curved saber was single-edged and single-handed. He used his free hand to hold onto his favorite wine cup while they fenced as though they were children and chased each other around the courtyard.

Lev kicked snow into Semyon's face and slapped him with the flat of his blade. Semyon narrowed his eyes at him, and Lev pitched his cup and ran. Blond bear had been right. He wasn't only his lover but his childhood friend, and sparring like stupid boys running around the fortress did brighten his soul like sunshine... till Lev had to pray for the fallen before they burned the pyre.

"How did you lose your men?" Lev tried being respectful and not judgmental because the Apraksin were here for him when they had a home they could go to, but he'd cleaned the bodies to prepare them for the ritual and couldn't help but notice the oddity. A man had his armor on, Lev cut the leather laces, removed the cuirass, and found the side of his ribs missing, eaten by scavengers.

"Wolves," said Vasily, somber faced. But that wasn't an answer.

"How?" Lev frowned.

From the wounds, it appeared as though the men had died, were left in the elements *without* their armor, got scavenged on, then were dressed again. Were they sleeping when they were attacked? But then, why not have their gear on?

Vasily grumbled and stared at the dead. It'd been a hard day, Lev supposed, said a word of prayer in Fedosian rather than in spells, and lit the pyres with a Dragon's Breath. It was an expensive spell costing three ounces of gold.

Before the conflict began, he used to wear a five-ounce gold bracelet, but since then, he'd been wearing fifteen-ounce cuffs, just in case. Any heavier than that and it became clunky, got in his way, and bothered his wrists to always have them on.

"Why don't you have a shadow?" Vasily whispered, or at least Lev thought that was what he said.

"What?"

"You don't cast a shadow." Vasily was staring at the ground where earlier snow had melted from the pyre and turned to slush.

It made Lev look at his own shadow, dark in the bright of the fire. "What the fuck are you talking about?"

"You have no shadow." Vasily looked up at him and stared.

"You're so odd." Lev grimaced. Then it occurred to him Vasily was making a light alchemy joke. It was clever, perhaps something a mage would have said, and the answer would be, "Because we're godlier than thou."

Guards being considered the source of light shouldn't cast a shadow, except they did, and Lev's shadow was long and behind him because the pyres were in front of him. He placed his hand on Vasily's shoulder, trying to comfort him, and tipped his head at the darkening sky. They went from night to night, it felt like, the daylight shortening till it was just one long night over the frozen wasteland they called the Bone Country.

"Dinner, Lev." Semyon stepped into the lanternlight.

"Not hungry." Lev was on a ladder in the library. It was an entire wing in the fortress, and the rooms didn't have candelabras or any such fixture where you could leave an open flame unwatched. From childhood, he'd been taught to bring a single lantern and leave with it. Anyone who left a candle burning at the library would be whipped to the bone.

His lantern was on the table where he'd been reading, and he was using a bit of alchemy, a little ball of light on his palm, no fire, to look through centuries of Guard writing. The good thing about the mages was they presumed every single thought they had, each little thing they did, even the number of times they farted in a day, were important enough to memorialize, because ego, but that was also the bad thing about mages. There were shelves, and shelves, and shelves, and shelves of useless shit, making it harder for anyone to find anything.

Instead of having a section for unusual spells, for instance, it was sorted by the mages' names, so Lev had been reading everything every mage wrote around the time frame he was looking for—five centuries ago, the one and only occurrence of the darkling before the archmage's death. Since then, the incident had only been referenced, and the recounting was conflicting, to say the least. So, he was looking for records contemporary to the incident. So far, nothing.

"It's as if they destroyed the records," Lev muttered.

"What are you mumbling about?" Semyon came and groped him.

"Nothing, don't worry about it. I'm not hungry." Lev frowned at the illegible scrap of parchment. *'Hire a fucken scribe!'* he wanted to yell at these people beyond the *dver*.

"Did you hear they didn't even find Grigori?" Semyon asked. "They got lost, camped in the wood for the night, and got attacked by a pack of wolves."

"Is this your attempt at washing the fact *you* got lost?"

"Well, the Apraksin got lost and this is their terrain. At least I didn't lose men."

"Is this because Konstantin found you?" Lev sneezed from the dust. He thought to organize and clean the library wing while he waited for his knights. There wasn't much to do, anyway.

"Maybe." Though Semyon was behind Lev and he didn't see his face, he imagined the blond bear smiling and scratching his head.

"I think the Apraksin were doing each other," Lev remarked. "Why else would they have their armor off in the middle of the night in the woods?"

"Unless their cocks are on the chest, there's no need to be stripping the gambeson. That *was* weird," said Semyon. "What do you think they were *really* doing?"

"Dancing nude and sacrificing virgins," Lev said. "Fuck if I know. They're an odd bunch."

"What are you looking for? Can I help you?"

"Can you bring the lantern and hold it here for me? I don't want to keep wasting alchemy." Lev flicked off his light.

"Sure." Semyon stood behind Lev, holding the light while Lev shook an imaginary fist at the dead mages. "You're so smart," Semyon said.

"Oh, shut up. Can you move the ladder that way?"

"Sure. Tell me when. Here?"

"When."

"So, what are you looking for?" Semyon asked after a long silence where Lev just flipped through pages. "Am I distracting you?"

"Ah, no, sorry." Lev slid a scroll back into the narrow columns of wood holding them. "It's the darkling thing. It's bothering me. It was first cast by an acolyte, which means she was a Guard…"

"All right," Semyon said after waiting for a while.

"Sorry." Lev flipped through a nonsensical codex someone had written as a joke. The Apraksin weren't the only ones guilty of a shit sense of humor. "Vasily mentioned something and made me think of another thing… Anyway, the darkling, I realize, sounds more like shadow alchemy than dark alchemy. If that's the case, it's not something Uncle could cast, so I was…" He found an interesting looking scroll, but it was blank. Not that the letters were faded, just blank.

"What's the difference?" Semyon asked.

"What?"

"What's the difference between shadow and dark alchemy?"

"One is not dark, and the other is not alchemy." Lev turned and smiled at Semyon. "Don't worry about it."

"No, tell me. I want to learn. Maybe I can't be as smart as you, but I can't always not have a clue what you're talking about. Eventually, I want to be able to hold a conversation with you."

"All right," Lev said. He didn't want to be like his uncle who always sneered when he asked him a question. *'Don't worry about it, boy. It's beyond you.'*

"The term 'dark alchemy' comes from the symbol 'dark', which in the language of spells also means 'forbidden'. So, it really means forbidden alchemy, which is necromancy. Not only it's wrong and horrible, fusing creatures together, it's also profane because the ultimate goal of necromancy is to create life without conception. You put some ingredients together, like clay and earth, and voila, a man. Do you see how that's blasphemous?"

"You're trying to be God," said Semyon.

"Yes, necromancers are trying to be God. But most of the time, it ends up being hideous cruelty because they fail and make things like a butterfly with one wing and a two-headed sheep that lives for three days and dies. That's three days of suffering and fear that didn't need to be. It's cruelty to God's creatures. Necromancy can't create life, period. Not human, not donkey, not even a seed that sprouts into a plant.

"But what they *can* do, is take the body of the deceased, and animate it with alchemy. It's like Durnov machines, but instead of darksteel, they are using flesh. The dead do *not* come back because their essence, light, soul, whatever you want to call it, passes through the *dver* and becomes a star in the sky, yeah?

"So, these 'dolls' let's call them, have varying degrees of sentience depending on how much magic was used, but they do not have light. That's where the term soulless comes from, because the symbol for a man is light inside life, and the symbol for a soulless is just life, without the light.

"Because *all* alchemy even the so called 'dark' alchemy uses light, a soulless cannot perform *any* alchemy. However, it has been recorded they can... Manipulate shadows, is the best way to explain it, I suppose. It goes into dark alchemy lore and what a shadow is. Basically, a shadow is your reflection onto the world beyond this one, and a soulless has, let's call it 'art' because alchemy is the wrong term, *art* which can affect you in a different dimension.

"It kills your shadow, and you die is what it is," Lev said, realizing he was rambling. "So, dark alchemy is necromancy. Shadow alchemy is a creepy thing that exists in scripts but I've never seen. Anyway, I thought the darkling thing might be a part of shadow *art,* but if so, there isn't a way for Uncle to cast it because he wasn't a soulless. Am I making sense?"

Frowning, Semyon thought for a while, then said, "You're looking to see if that acolyte was a soulless. Then it would confirm it was shadow *art,* and if that's the case, we still don't know who killed the archmage."

"Yes!" Lev was so proud of Semyon.

"But why would there be a soulless acolyte?"

"She was an acolyte first, then died, and was brought back," said Lev.

"Then that story also has a necromancer," said Semyon.

"This is true." Lev chewed his lip.

"Quit doing that."

"What, this?" Lev bit his lower lip.

"Do you want to be fucked?" Semyon mouthed, a crooked smirk on his face.

"Why so crude? I was going to say you're my sun—"

Lev felt a breath on his neck, turned around, and threw a punch. "You gutter crawling whore!" he yelled.

He'd struck Vasily in the face because the freak had come out of nowhere in the dark, making him nearly wet his trousers. Semyon hadn't heard Vasily either and lunged with his sword drawn before he laughed his ass off.

Lev had to take a moment, a panting and heaving moment, to calm down, and once he did, he said, "All right, let's get out of here before we slice each other's bits off swinging sharp objects in the dark. I'll try tomorrow when there's light."

"You didn't eat," said Vasily, walking behind Lev and Semyon as they headed out of the library.

"Wasn't hungry," said Lev. "Have you eaten, Syoma?" He didn't like Vasily behind him because he felt his presence but couldn't hear him at all and it was making his skin tingle and the hair at the back of his neck stand on end. "Vasily, walk ahead of Semyon, please."

When Vasily didn't reply, Lev stopped and let him pass. "Are you all right?" Lev asked because Vasily was grimacing and rubbing his temples.

"It's just so bright," he whispered.

"Sure is." Lev bumped into a fucken statue. The moving light stretched their shadows, and their stone faces flickered.

"What's with the knife, Apraksin?" Semyon asked.

They were walking ahead, and Lev flicked at look at Vasily and saw a plain cleaver tucked into his belt. Then he noticed the Apraksin didn't have any of his gear.

"What's bright, Vasily?" Lev asked, slowing his pace and falling back. It crossed his mind that Apraksin blades had gold on the pommel. They'd been acting strange since they returned—the retainers not saying a single word, and Vasily sulking all day. They were grieving, Lev had thought, but there was a stench in the air, like invisible soot that he could no longer ignore. "What's bright, Vasily?"

"It's his attempt at a joke, Lev," Semyon said. He stopped and turned, and now Vasily was in front of him.

"Didn't ask you, Syoma." Lev looked from Semyon to Vasily. "What's bright, Vasily? Maybe it's making your head hurt. I'll turn it down if I can."

Semyon made a face because he thought Lev was ridiculing Vasily. "Drop it, Lev."

"Asked you a question, Vasily." Lev's hand glided down to his hilt. He was standing in the dark, they had the lantern, Semyon didn't see Lev reach, but Vasily's dark eyes followed Lev's hand.

Lev couldn't toss Dragan's Breath down the corridor because Semyon was in the way, and he gauged the distance between himself and Vasily. "Don't lose the light, Syoma. He can see in the dark."

"Lev?" Semyon frowned.

"But it's not dark," Vasily muttered. "That thing above the gate is so bright."

"You mean the crest of my house?" Lev pursed his lips. "It's cast with Saint Aleksandar's gold. It's a sacred relic. We like doing that, blessing our own shit."

"Oh." Vasily looked down. "It hurts to be here. I want to leave."

Vasily reached for the cleaver, Semyon slammed him into the wall, stepped back, and grabbed the hilt of his sword, but it looked as though his blade stuck, because he froze that way, took a beat too long, and Vasily's cleaver bit into his side.

A shadow of a man grabbed the shadow Semyon cast, and it fucked with Lev's mind making him think there was another person in the corridor though there wasn't. He'd never seen shadow alchemy, and though he deduced this was probably that, he'd reacted by leaping back and drawing his saber when the shadow on the wall turned and ran toward him.

The mind kept searching for the thing casting the shadow rather than... Lev didn't know what to do. Was he supposed to make his shadow stab the thing? He tried when it pounced on him, hacking and hacking at his shadow, but nothing happened to Lev, which was more confusing.

"Why won't you die?" Vasily whined.

It made Lev look that way. He had to stop freaking out about the shadow because it didn't do anything. But Vasily's real cleaver had struck real Semyon who was still frozen as though he'd turned into a statue. Lev threw a dagger and it hit Vasily's shoulder. Vasily twisted and fell, and the lantern rolled on the floor, making the corridor strobe. Lev got to Semyon, but Vasily was nowhere to be found.

"Are you all right?" Lev inspected Semyon's wound. Though the red gash was nasty, and the iron might have fractured a rib, the blade hadn't gotten any further than that. "It's not too bad."

"What the hell was that?" Semyon was bewildered. He wasn't too worried about the cut but was startled by the shadow.

"I think the Apraksin may have died." The 'may' was unnecessary. Lev knew they had died and returned soulless. It was a hard thing to believe, though, because it turned from a thing that happened to the Menshikov, to a thing that was *happening* to them.

Fifteen

It Belongs to You

The candles had burned out since they died, slumped over the tables in their chairs, and retched blood on their food and on the floor. Red Carnation, Lev recognized the poison, but it was such a difficult thing to brew, how did Vasily manage? Did turning soulless come with intrinsic talents? Lev covered his nose and mouth with his sleeve because the stench was rancid.

The whole fortress had fallen silent. Was it the well? Was it the food? Something had been tainted.

Semyon threw up in the corner. A thing clambered in the dark and all the candelabras and every stick of candle in the holders and on the stands in the grand hall burst alive with Dragon's Breath. There were rats on the table rattling the plates and cups, nibbling the poisoned food and some of them were already dead. Yet they kept eating.

"We have to get out here, Syoma," Lev whispered, slowly backing away and reaching for Semyon who was behind him.

"Give me a moment," Semyon strained.

"Can't. No time," Lev said.

There weren't any statues in the dining hall. Those were Apraksin retainers, and they all turned at once to stare at Lev and Semyon.

A dragon breathed, lighting the grand hall in an instant yellow glare. Lev grabbed Semyon and fled as the armored Apraksin began coming through the wall of fire. A tall one burst through the flame, screeched, and sprinted toward them. Another breath of fire, and the whole place caught, the woodwork on the wall and the floor cracking and snapping in the intense heat. Wine cups burst, stained glass windows shattered, and the fire took a heaving breath with the fresh draft rushing in.

Lev took Semyon and retreated. He couldn't control the fire, only cause it—he wasn't an Apraksin. Mercifully, the soulless were no longer from the House of Fire and had lost their alchemy.

Lev tossed his room looking for his trunk before finding it by his bed. A damned candleholder had been on top, and he'd mistaken it for a dresser.

"Lev!"

Semyon was in his iron armor, swinging by the door to keep the soulless out. He'd sent a few back to the necromancy hell they'd crawled out of but there were more. Through the grace of the saints, it appeared only Vasily had shadow alchemy. The other *things* had no speech, barely any mind, and just trashed at them with steel without any technique. Lev had to wonder if they understood they were holding the most expensive sword in Fedosia or if they'd trade it for a stick if it had a longer reach.

"Lev!"

"Duck, Syoma!"

Lev found what he was looking for, a chest of gold cuffs he'd had cast, because the one he had on was about to be spent. *Dragon's Breath!* He was burning down his own house a section at the time, the last of the Guard heritage homes after the fall of the White Palace.

Bright blaze breathed, engulfing the soulless along with the furniture in the room. His bed caught aflame. Lev collected all the gold he could find into a satchel and grabbed their cloaks as Semyon broke the window and the frame, then they climbed down. They had to get to a tower, somewhere with a single entrance and spiraling steps Lev could rain fire down like breathing into a tube.

Semyon had to shed his iron plates to follow Lev along a railing of the keep, and he dropped the rest of the weight as they climbed the steel ladders of the tower, going up, around, and around, and around. Up inside the bartizan, the soldiers on watch were dead, their throats slit as they were playing cards.

"I'm stupid," Lev muttered. He'd let Vasily in, though it had felt wrong. "Syoma, are you all right?"

He'd turned ashen. Lev carried the fallen soldiers to one side of the circular space and sat Semyon leaning against the wall. Dark blood had soiled his white armor tunic, but Lev couldn't inspect his injury because footsteps rushed up the steel ladders. Unlike Vasily, the speechless ones were loud, clumsy, and ran senseless when set on fire.

He roasted them, returned, heard a ruckus outside, found more of them trying to climb the tower from the outside, unsuccessfully, but he had to keep an eye on them, and so the night was spent.

"Is there water?" Semyon asked.

"There's plenty outside," Lev said. "I'm waiting for the day to turn a bit brighter, and we'll go to…" The town's name escaped him, but he knew it was less than twenty miles. "Soon, Syoma. We'll get out of here soon."

Lev cleaned and bandaged Semyon's wound with a part of his shirt, but Vasily's weapon had been laced with poison and now it was corrupting the blond bear's flesh, pus oozing at the onset of gangrene. It wasn't something Lev could figure out an antidote to, and he needed a real physician.

The soulless fell silent after the sun rose, but daylight was so short, and Lev didn't dare waste any of it. He went to the stables. The Apraksin had taken their own horses, and everyone else's was… dead. The well was poisoned as well, he realized. The horses had died from drinking water.

He found a workhorse outside the granary. The poor creature was tied to a hitching post and probably had been outside all night. The driver was dead in the servant's quarters along with all the help Lev had, and the cooks had died in the kitchen. One had fallen onto the open firepit and had roasted. Lev would scorch it all, but he couldn't afford the alchemy, and hoped the crest of his family was strong enough to keep the necromancer—he had to accept the truth there was a necromancer—from entering uninvited. Guard knights would bury them once they returned.

Lev would rather wait for them than wander in the open, but Semyon's situation was urgent. They had to get to the town before dark, and he ran up the stairs of the watchtower after he hitched the lightest sleigh he could find to the workhorse. He put hay down for him in the meantime, but the watering would have to wait.

Semyon looked like shit. The baby blue eyes had turned murky, and he was flushed with fever.

"Come on, Syoma. Get up."

Letting him walk down the steps was taking too long so Lev carried him on his back, complaining about his weight.

"Woah, you hitched the sleigh?" Semyon smiled weakly. "Didn't think you'd know how."

"Shut up, you heavy bastard." Lev set him down on the open sleigh, threw his cloak over him, and learned to drive which wasn't hard, but it was maddening how slow it went. He couldn't whip the horse though, it was the only one they had.

※

The road to the town was a slog, Lev had to get off and push the sleigh more than once because the horse was too weak. Judging by the light it took them nearly three hours to get there, and all of it had been a waste. The cluster of cottages along the road, the town hall, the brothel, the inn, all of it was empty, not a single soul, not even a dog, and unless these people abandoned what little grain they had and left their homes in the middle of the bone cracking winter, they were all dead, and now Lev had *thousands* of soulless to account for.

He could return to Usolya and just *not* invite any more dead in, drink wine, and wait for Konstantin to come with light magic and proper mounts, but he wasn't alone, and Semyon needed help. The Menshikov gone, Apraksin was the closest but for all he knew Vasily was at home right now, spinning lies to have them killed on sight.

"Syoma, we have to go to Pulyazin. Hang in there, all right?" Lev knew the vicinity of the Ivory Fortress on a map, but he'd never been there.

"I'm not going anywhere," Semyon whispered, his lips blue.

Lev would head northeast. That was all he got with the roads buried under snow. Pulyazin was the largest house in the east, and Lev hoped the fortress was obvious and easy to find. The word 'ivory' worried him though, making him think the fucken thing might be white in all this snow.

He found live horses in the town stables for visitors, which further confirmed the people were all dead. Travelers didn't leave their horses behind. Lev saddled a lively one for himself, but Semyon wasn't in riding shape. They still needed the sleigh and would have to travel at the speed of it.

On an even terrain, Lev managed a steady trot, but the Ivory Fortress was nearly a hundred miles from Usolya. He didn't expect untrained horses to trot all the way. The traveler's horse maybe, but not the workhorse, not a chance, so the distance was fifteen hours at least, if the calm weather held.

"We're getting there, Syoma, just hold on." Lev twisted in his saddle and looked back when Semyon didn't respond. He looked to be sleeping.

White Palace had a physician, Eva, second only to the old bastard Baltar, but she died when Father decided to defend the palace without sending out any of his people. Resentment stewed but for the first time, Lev tried to let it go. Anger for the dead was a chain he needed to be free from, to be able to think, act, and drum up the courage needed, heading toward the darkening horizon.

Lev rode through the night, stopping only to piss and get water for Semyon—not in that order, though. The morning came later than yesterday, and tomorrow it would be even later. The way Fedosia lay on the map, you went further north as you traveled east, and the daylight hours grew shorter with the miles. The northern terrain was made of monstrous mountains and evergreen forests cloaked in snow as far as the eyes could see. All of the tsardom's timber came from here and in return, they got grain for they had very little land they could farm.

The only good thing the Shield ever did was when the red queen had laid steel tracks across the country during her reign. Lev had never seen a train before because they ran between Seniya, Shield city northeast of Krakova, to Pulyazin province, and he hadn't been to either. The archmage hadn't allowed the queen to lay her tracks over Guard lands, the machine went around them.

But he saw one today. Winter having swallowed the roads, he got lost, but he found the steel tracks and had been following them hoping there would be a town at the end of it.

The train was loud, frightened him at first when he saw the white steam over the tree line and didn't know what it was, and as it passed, it rattled, shook the forest, created a draft, and hurled snow.

He stood in amazement at the angry machine, puffing and huffing, and hauling carts the size of cottages behind, and smiled at having seen the thing.

After it passed and the sound faded in the winter winds, he turned to Semyon. "Syoma, did you see that?"

He didn't answer, so Lev dismounted to check on him. The hot breath had frosted his blond lashes, and his clothes were drenched in cold sweat, then frozen.

"Syoma." Lev shook him. "Get up and change your clothes. The cold will ease your fever a bit too."

"It's all right." The white of his eyes were yellow when he opened them. "Do you remember the spell to vanquish evil?"

"Illuminate, yes." Lev went to his horse and dug through his saddlebag for a dry shirt.

"When I die, take my heart, Lev. You're the last of the guardians now. You'll need it."

"Shut up, Syoma. No one is taking your heart. Come on." He helped the blond bear up and changed his shirt, stupid tight on him because Lev was much smaller. He didn't inspect the wound. He could smell it, and it was way beyond anything he could do. They needed a real physician. "We'll be at the Ivory Fortress before nightfall."

They *had* to reach the Pulyazin today because Semyon wasn't making it another day. If wills could move fortresses, Lev had enough of it to pull the tower and the mountain it sat upon closer.

"No one's taking my heart, says you." Semyon strained to lift his hand and touch Lev's face. "You already have it, don't you know? Take it. It belongs to you anyway."

"Shut up." Lev got peeved. Who needed to be crying out here, tears stupid and frozen on his face? Fuck, he was wasting time. They had to go. He tucked in Semyon and mounted his horse, which he'd named Star because the bay horse had a star shaped white patch on his forehead.

Feeling incredibly alone in the white forest, nothing but the wind whistling through the treetops, Lev rode after the train. There had to be a town—had to. Snow crunched, the tack jingled, and Star's breath steamed.

"Lev, what is that song you sing?" Semyon asked from the back, not sounding too ill just then. A fool's hope sprung eternal, and Lev was a fool.

"Which one, Syoma? I sing many songs. I'm quite talented."

"I don't know. Any, I guess. Will you sing a tune?"

"So the soulless can find us faster?" Lev asked.

"Please."

"Well, since you said please, I guess I'll be pretty."

Lev knew which song he was talking about. It was a lewd song his mother used to sing, about spring maidens inviting men into the woods. When they were boys, Lev had been singing it to make Semyon laugh, but they were in the woods, and the blond bear misunderstood him and kissed him. They were eleven and thirteen. Lev was older but shorter.

They were in the woods again, and though it wasn't spring, Lev sang as he rode along steel tracks. He thought Semyon was humming along but it could have also been in his mind where it was spring and warm with the White Palace just beyond the bend.

Sixteen

Illuminate

The sun glittered on the snow, incredibly bright for a breath before dipping behind the storm clouds. Blizzard tonight, Lev knew that. For two days he'd been singing, and he'd been walking since he lost his horse. He didn't know where the tracks were and that was all right. He was no longer in the trees and saw a church. It was Day Solis after all, and he tipped his face up at the silent saints.

Semyon held on for as long as he could, but he just slept now. Awake among the saints perhaps but he wouldn't wake up in this world again. Something, though Lev had a pretty good guess what, was scaring all the creatures out of the forest, and he'd run into wolves last night. They got his workhorse. It was just Star and him now. Semyon draped over the saddle, Lev walked beside him with the lead in his hand. Beside and not in front because he didn't know where he was going and let the horse decide.

"You found a church, Star." Lev petted his muzzle. "I hope you have coins for the collection plate because I got nothing."

The horse snorted. He gave him a bit of sugar, the last of what he had. He had nothing in his world now. No fortress, no parents, no house, no lover. Just his cock, his hand, and this one horse which he'd stolen.

Laughing at me now, aren't you, Syoma?

Life down here must be pretty stupid once you're in the sky, eternal peace among your beloveds.

It was a typical country church made of wood after having blown the entire budget on the gilded dome. The wooden gate was open, and Lev tied Star to the hitching post. The snow was trampled and melted around it. They'd had a crowd earlier, the tracks leading away to where he assumed the illusory town was, but the nave was empty when he entered.

"Parson!" Lev called, and after some moments, an old man in a brown robe holding a piece of bread appeared from behind the vestry. Brown cassock signified clergy without alchemy. "Is there a mage?" Lev asked.

The old man finished chewing his bread, swallowed it dry without water, then answered, "There was a great tragedy in Murmia a season ago. The archmage and his synod gather with the saints now. How may I help you, my boy?"

"Surely, they are not *all* dead," Lev said.

"Some remain, yes." The parson nodded. "But Luminary Matvey has called them to Murmia. He's to bring order to the church in these dark times, and now we wait. What brings you to Bone Country, young man? You're not in my congregation."

"Well, my friend is outside. Will you read the rite for him proper? I need to do the last thing he asked, then burn him before dark."

"I see." The parson wiped crumbs from his beard. "Let me get the codex." He turned and hobbled away. "What was his last wish?" He stopped and twisted back because Lev hadn't answered. "I must know because it's part of the rite, so his soul may be at rest."

"I'm going to cut his heart out."

The parson grimaced in distaste. "We're not heathens. You may not do that here, and if that is the intent, you may also leave." Gesturing at the door, he marched back toward Lev.

"I need it, Parson. I'm going to kill a necromancer."

"Nonsense, boy. No one can kill a necromancer. You must be a Guard for it."

"So what if I am?"

The parson pointed at the painted ceiling. "Saints hear you, boy. Don't blaspheme in the hall of prayers."

"They hear nothing for a necromancer walks these lands and they do nothing. But I am Lev of White Guard."

The man with a tall nose squinted at him, studying him, then unconvinced, his grimace returned. He was going send Lev out, so Lev closed his fist with the cuff glowing and opened his hand holding an orb of sunlight. Once, he didn't like playing with light because too much of it would turn him impotent like the archmage, but what did he care now? His lover was gone, he had no need for a cock.

The parson dropped to his knees with his hands in prayer. "Guardian of light!"

"Get up, old man. I'm not God, but a brat with a lot of hate in his heart."

The sky threw down some snow, a handful of flakes before it unleashed the storm. A large fluffy snowflake caught on Semyon's lashes—they were always so long and curved up naturally. Women had been jealous.

The country church didn't have an incinerator, so Lev built his lover a pyre and ran his hand through the soft blond locks one last time. He'd cut out his heart and put it in a glass jar which he held now. Semyon may have left his heart but had taken Lev's with him. Equivalent exchange, that was fair.

"Bye for now, Syoma." Lev kissed his forehead. "I'll see you again someday." But not before he killed the necromancer.

Dragon's Breath, my love. Let your light rise with the flames and sit amongst the stars where the saints live.

The vestry room was small with a single bed and a single writing desk. It also had a coffin the parson was keeping for himself, which he offered to remove when he gave his room to Lev. *'The warm bed is enough, thank you, Parson,'* Lev had said. *'But the rites need to be the old way now. Burn the dead, at least for a while.'*

Then, as they sat in the church kitchen around a modest table, Lev told him about the necromancer and the soulless, so the parson didn't get blindsided. The necromancer didn't have a name because Lev wasn't certain yet. Grigori was his best guess, but if he was wrong, he didn't want to confuse the parson.

Lev had been holding a hot cup of tea with both hands and enjoying it much when he heard hooves and sprung up, thinking the Apraksin had come, but the party turned out to be Lady Pulyazin and her young children along with some druzhina. With carrot colored hair, the lady was actually someone he knew—kind of.

"You're Erik Vietinghoff's cousin," Lev said because he'd forgotten her name.

"Lev Guard!" She greeted him, kissing him on the cheeks though his name made the druzhina uneasy.

The children knew the parson and wanted some type of oat biscuits he made so they disappeared into the kitchen. The druzhina pretended to secure the tiny church while eyeing Lev with their hands on their hilts.

The lady was carrying, so Lev pulled up a chair for her and they sat together in the nave, facing the altar of saints. Lev had put the jar with Semyon's heart in the hemp satchel the parson gave him. He wore the strap across his body, and he kept the satchel on his lap, clutching, afraid to set it down lest he lose it.

"What are you doing out here? I heard you were in Usolya." The lady stroked her swollen belly as she spoke.

"I could ask you the same," Lev said. "What the fuck did you marry a Pulyazin for? Do you enjoy snow that much?"

"Language, Lev!" She flicked him. "Lord Fedya is a good man."

"If you say so."

"I do say so! Where are Semyon and Vasily? I thought you were with them."

"It's complicated," was Lev's answer. "If your lord is such a fine man, what are you doing sleeping in a shi—" Lev swallowed his word when one of the children came running to give him a biscuit. "Thank you." He smiled at the little one. They had Pulyazin silver hair and didn't look anything like their mother.

The child dashed back into the kitchen, laughing. One of them had probably dared the other to touch the stranger because the boy had also poked him. He didn't love children but didn't dislike them either.

"What am I doing in a church and not in my lord's bed? Was that your question?" The lady had a dimple when she smiled. "It's complicated."

"Fair," Lev said.

"What happened to Erik? Who killed him? You boys could never get along."

"Syoma."

"What for?" she asked.

"Erik betrayed us then tried to kill me in my own house, in front of my father, nonetheless."

"Fair." She nodded.

The winds battered the wooden shutters over the windows and a druzhina came to tell the lady a couple of them would be stepping out to keep watch, and then, Lev remembered her name because the druzhina had addressed her by it—Anfisa.

"Your lord got his grain from the Shields, Anfisa?" Lev asked.

"You know what occurs to me, Lev?" Anfisa tapped her chin. "It's none of your darn business."

"Of course it's my business if your husband is going to be sucking Shield cock."

"Language!"

"None of those are bad words. Sucking. Shield. Cock. Well, I suppose one could argue saying Shield in church is blasphemous."

"You haven't changed a bit. You're still nine years old."

"Say, Anfisa, those train machines, they bring grain to Bone, but they must return to Seniya, right?"

"What is it to you?"

"Seems they are a lot faster than horses and don't die in the frost. I would like to ride it to Seniya. Can you ask your benevolent lord?"

"They are run by Durnov. Why would they let you live?" she asked. "And have you lost your mind? Seniya is a Shield city."

That, he knew, but *if* Grigori was the necromancer, his work in the Bone Country was done because Usolya was no longer, so the dog might be returning to his master.

"What did I do? They attacked us," said Lev about the Durnov, recalling how their Crawlers chewed through the living wall his father had erected with his life.

"Haven't you heard? Lord Durnov and a slew of puppeteers are dead. Pyotr Guard killed them, people say."

"From beyond the grave? My father is dead."

"I heard. My condolences. But Lord Durnov turned into a mummy. Pyotr Guard's curse, they said."

Lev laughed till he fell off his chair, then some more while his cackles echoed through the church.

"It's not funny, Lev. I heard it was terrible, dehydrating alive. Also, Elyena died because you cheated in a steeplechase. It's Lady Durnov in charge now, and she's a Shield, just so you know. So, there's *no* chance of you boarding a train."

"We'll see."

They talked about being children, about Lev's miniature pony everyone had been jealous of. About the archmage, about Semyon who would visit every summer. Wanted to see the pony he would say, and Lev wondered why he didn't just get his own, but it wasn't the horse he'd wanted to see.

Lord Skuratov had disowned Semyon for supporting Lev, but he was a father nonetheless and deserved to know his son had gone to the stars.

"Semyon passed," Lev said. "Perhaps you can let the Skuratov know. I don't suppose I'll be returning from Seniya."

"Oh... So much death." She caressed her belly. "I hope it ends soon. What are you going to Seniya for?"

The more he gnawed on it, the more certain he grew Grigori was the necromancer. In that case, this was all Shield's doing. They were mad, that whole house had redlined bringing darkness into Fedosia. Lev would do one good thing with his life and end the Shield reign. Seniya wasn't the final stop, Krakova was. He was going to kill Prince Nikolas.

But he wouldn't say that to Anfisa, though, and smiled. "Sightseeing. I've never been to Seniya."

"Oh, never you mind."

Anfisa pursed her lips and furrowed her orange brows. She was having an internal debate, probably about Lev. She put her hand over his, and took a long inhale, perhaps to tell him something, but a druzhina announced, "Vasily Apraksin, my lady."

Lev turned and saw Vasily was at the door. Because Lev had been sitting, Vasily hadn't seen him and his blue eyes widened, meeting his. The soulless couldn't enter a church without permission, so Lev could have just stayed inside and told the druzhina not to let him in, but fury blinded him.

A small voice at the back of his mind reminded him there were children here, but not nearly loud enough. The only reason he took the fight outside rather than unleash the dragon in the wooden church was he didn't want the druzhina to misinterpret his intent and get in his way. He'd never seen Pulyazin alchemy and didn't wish to learn it just then.

Not caring about the poisoned blade, Lev was out in the blizzard bashing Vasily's face in, his teeth lodged into knuckles, when he realized it wasn't Vasily but some plain villager. A soulless, though, and he tried biting Lev with his naked gums. Lev put a dragger in his skull, and it twitched still, trying to get up, so he twisted the neck till the head came off. That did it.

In a snowstorm, Dragon's Breath wouldn't catch. He really should have let Vasily in and burned him in the church. Now he couldn't see shit with the weather lashing at his eyes and screaming in his ears.

"What happened!" Anfisa screamed when Lev barged back in.

"Parson!" Lev yelled. "Soulless are at your door, don't let them in!"

"What?" Anfisa was afraid. Her children ran to her, and the druzhina couldn't decide who the threat was. Vasily was an eastern boy, but Lev was what they called zapadnik around here, an outsider. Perhaps it was the parson coming out from the vestry with a torch and a blade, but

Anfisa finally said, "Don't let the Apraksin in unless your lord comes and says so."

The druzhina would obey their lady.

Lev had left the door open when he charged at Vasily, and the church was so small the gust had blown out the candles at the altar. Shadows moved on the wall from the torches the druzhina lit, and the parson had turned to attend to his altar, when Vasily appeared at the door again and his shadow cast long into the nave.

His sword drawn, Lev marched toward him, sneering, when Vasily's shadow turned and stabbed the shadow of a druzhina. The soldier had been inside the church, Vasily was still outside and hadn't produced a sword or turned, but blood sprayed from the druzhina, halting Lev dead in his tracks. Because this thing was so novel, Lev couldn't calculate for it.

The only thing he could think of was to disrupt the shadow, and blasted light directly at Vasily, casting his shadow behind him and outside the church, not but before Vasily had cut another man's head off.

A druzhina used the bright flash from Lev to kick the Apraksin and push the door closed. His head jerked back, and a spear slid out through the back of his skull, smooth steel slick with blood. The druzhina fell against the door, managing to close it as he died.

The parson ran with a gilded icon of a saint, probably the only relic the tiny church had, and placed it against the door, mumbling prayers to ward off evil.

The two remaining druzhina huddled with their lady and the children, trying to protect them while scared shitless themselves. They were hardened warriors, no doubt, but they were superstitious out here, and the shadow alchemy was tripping them, clearly, because they were praying instead of drawing their blades or doing whatever it was the Pulyazin did. Water alchemy, Lev knew, but he could never understand why anyone would spend gold freezing water in the Bone Country where everything was frozen anyway.

The stained glass window shattered, and a slew of vials like red crystals were thrown in and rolled on the wooden floor.

"Wrath!" Lev shoved the parson out the door and both fell on the snow while the church behind them erupted into a towering flame.

The old man got pulled from Lev and was dragged away by the soulless into the night as Lev tried to grab him. If the man screamed, the storm ate it, and Lev was left holding a torn scrap of brown cloak. He got up, wiping the snow off, and saw in the light of the burning church the blank faces staring at him.

A baker with his apron, a brothel girl with a feather in hair, the stableboy, the farmhand, the reaper, an old woman, a little boy... Here was the missing town, and yes, he was surrounded by the soulless as far as the light could see.

Then he caught a familiar face, not a soulless, but a necromancer in a blood drenched robe, a broad smile on his bony face.

"And here I've seen the end of the White Guard," Grigori said in Elfurian.

"That's what you are, then," Lev answered in Elfurian. "Your alchemy is shit, old man. The soulless you made are simple beasts."

"Sadly, the artistry gets sacrificed when you're dealing with so many." He gestured around. "So falls the mighty White Guards of Fedosia. Any last words, boy?"

"Run, I suppose."

Lev would have gone for the necromancer, maybe he would have succeeded, more likely he would have failed, but he resisted the urge to scratch the flaming itch of vengeance because Anfisa and her three small children had escaped the fire and were crying behind him. No druzhina left, it was just Lev now, and letting a pregnant woman and little kids die so he could grieve seemed like the wrong thing to do. It was just an inkling.

Anyway, he reached into the hemp satchel. The glass jar had broken from his falling on it, and Lev cut his hand on the shard, but Semyon's heart was still there. For a thing that fit the whole world, the flesh hardly weighed anything sitting on Lev's palm.

Grigori frowned, he didn't know what it was, but he guessed at Lev's intent and the soulless charged like a rush of black floodwater. In the back, Lev could faintly hear Anfisa screaming, but his gaze was on his lover's heart as he shorthanded three thousand four hundred and one symbols, each signifying a separate step of alchemy, into a single word: Illuminate.

The sun rose at midnight over a wooden church in Bone Country, and it was so grand it could have only come from Semyon. That was why a lover's heart, Lev thought, because nothing else could bear the cost of such an inordinate amount of magic—not enough gold in the world.

In his mind, Lev ran through the trees behind White Palace, thirteen years old, and singing about the spring maidens. It was going to rain, and mist had rolled in from the hills, blanketing the forest floor like soft cotton.

'*Lev,*' Semyon had called.

Lev turned and was kissed. It wasn't like the time he'd kissed Zoya, and in his memory, *this* would stay as his first, where they would remain forever young.

Seventeen
House of Silver

The Chartorisky port was a smaller Krakova, with a handful of grand structures and the rest a cluster of wooden huts with mucky streets running through them. Though the ocean brought a warm draft, it was still winter in Fedosia, and people sitting at the harbor in thin shirts, some barefoot even, was a harrowing sight. Like vultures, they were waiting for something dead and fat to wash ashore. Those who had a boat or even a raft were already in the grey waters circling the dying Chartorisky ships. They'd been running away with their wealth and these people were going to try their fortune diving after the sinking ships.

The setting sun refracted with the colors of the rainbow over the ocean and the soft pillow clouds, but the port was grey, the water cold, as the House of Chartorisky took its last breath before drowning at the bottom of the Zapadnoi Morye.

Sofia had seen sailing ships, grand up close with tall sails, sure, but a wooden ladle tied to a puff of cloud from the distance. Yet she'd never seen the Durnov Defender before, a floating iron monstrosity with funnels like the crooked teeth of a comb, spewing heavy black smoke that hung around it rather than dissipate in the air. Like a diseased thing, it dropped iron worms into the water, gold tipped but darksteel otherwise, and they were ravaging the wooden hulls of the Chartorisky ships.

It was loud at the pier. Dying ships groaned, the wood popping and the cables snapping. As Sofia stood on the wooden pier, troubled by the sight, Aleksei was beside her.

"Can she swim?" she asked.

"Not very well," he said.

Aleksei had been looking for Zoya. The soldiers Niko had brought inland from the border, the duke's men, were acting like animals, like foreign invaders rather than imperial soldiers, and the prince did nothing to correct them. With each passing day, Niko looked less like his brother and more like his mother, and Sofia could see the hope Aleksei once had for Fedosia's future fading like a memory of a dream after you wake up.

Scavengers circling, cannons firing from the dying ships as well as from the port, and with people in the water, the ocean looked like a bustling market with only misery for sale. It was cold to stand on the dry pier draped in a fur lined cloak, so Sofia couldn't imagine swimming in the ocean. Come morning, the beach would be littered with corpses and debris.

"Aleksei." Dominik had come up behind them. He was one of the few sentinels Sofia recognized by the voice. "His Highness grants you the audience you sought."

"Yeah," Aleksei said. "Give us a moment."

"I'll take you to the prince when you're ready." Dominik left.

At first, the sentinels had trouble addressing Aleksei by his name, but it'd been a while, and Ignat was jailed because he wouldn't call Eugene 'Captain', and that was the color of the banner Niko raised.

A crewman washed ashore, and a few people immediately fought over his boots. They were behaving like rats. The seagulls were loud overhead and bird droppings covered the deck. Sofia turned away. She had been curious about the Defender but now regretted having seen it.

"Sofia." Aleksei frowned. "I've been carrying around bad news all day. I didn't know how to tell you, I'm sorry. But I suppose it's better you hear it from me than from Nikolas." He took a long pause, his eyes on the horizon where the sun set orange and red. "A train returned from Bone Country twenty days ago. Dariy Apraksin sent a message along, and it came with a rider this morning. Seniya is a few hundred miles from here." He was stalling and Sofia's dread grew. "Vasily is dead and Usolya has fallen. After his arrangement with the Menshikov fell through, Lev couldn't garner any real support in the east, and there appears to have been infighting in Usolya."

"Lev?" Sofia whispered.

"Usolya has fallen," he repeated.

"And what does the Pulyazin say? Apraksin isn't the only house near Usolya, and such significant news would be reported more than once, surely?"

"I don't know," said Aleksei. "I believe there's another train leaving soon. I'll ride to Seniya and deliver any letter you want to send to Pulyazin."

She shook her head. She wouldn't believe Lev died, but the thought of her brother stuck in the frozen wasteland with dwindling allies hurt her heart.

"Niko won't hear of peace, I suppose. But will you speak to him, anyway? This is wasteful." She gestured at the ocean. "Lord Durnov, my papa, Erik Vietinghoff, the Menshikov, the Chartorisky, and now Vasily... Enough dying. No one is winning, and I don't even know what we're fighting over. Do you?"

"I can try," Aleksei said. The sadness weighed the corners of his eyes, and it made him look older, more tired. He seemed to be dragging his heels and barely getting by. The last interaction she caught between the brothers, Niko turned and walked away when Aleksei was speaking, and now Aleksei had to seek an audience through the steward just to see Niko.

The prince didn't even speak to Sofia now because she'd yelled at him to do something about the behavior of the soldiers. They were assaulting women out in the streets.

Only a day after her falling out with Niko, soldiers attacked the inn Sofia and Aleksei had been staying at, killed the innkeeper for nothing, beat young women and old men, dragged Sofia by the hair, tore her dress, and she survived with a few bruises and nothing more only because Aleksei had forgotten something and returned. It was hard to believe such men had mothers and sisters, and now Sofia couldn't even go to the washroom by herself, but they were still at Chartorisky port because Aleksei had been waiting to speak with Niko and there was no one to take Sofia to Krakova. Ignat had said he would, but he was in the dungeon now, and that was how this was going.

"Go see your brother, and let's go home, Aleksei." Sofia took his hand. The fractured bones were mended but Niko had broken his brother's heart. What for, Sofia didn't understand. Perhaps such was the effect of power... Perhaps Fedosia would have been better with Rodion at the helm. Every time she did something, it appeared, chaos of unintended consequences followed.

The prince sat on a red velvet bergère chair, dressed in all black with his legs crossed, in the drawing room of what used to be the Chartorisky manor. The Shield red banner was hung behind him, but they hadn't taken down the paintings of the Chartorisky, giving the space an air of oddity. The prince was in the middle of the room, as though on display, and Eugene was on a settee by the window, ankle across the knee, and thin white smoke curling from his mouth with the smell of burning poppy.

There were others in the room. Sofia recognized Lady Durnova, and a man in a brown robe seated next to her introduced himself as Luminary Matvey. He was a somber looking man with a long black beard.

"Lady Guard," Matvey said. "It's a blessing to meet you."

"Likewise, Parson." Sofia didn't know how to address him because 'Luminary' was not a real title in the church.

Aleksei stood beside her with his hands clasped at the back. There weren't any vacant chairs in the room, and it felt awkward as though they were servants.

"Zoya has been captured," the prince said. "Her execution will be tomorrow. I've been advised burning at the stake is the most merciful I can be to a traitor. So, that's what I went with. I thought you might want to know."

"The girl has no alchemy. There is no need, Prince," said Aleksei. "I'll find and bring you Daniil. Just strip Zoya of land and title. That is the most common punishment for a *female* member of the family."

"Well, her execution will be tomorrow. It's been talked over and decided, unfortunately. I wasn't asking for your opinion on the matter," said Niko.

Aleksei stared down at the floor. Since this was the tone Niko was taking with his brother, Sofia should have kept her mouth shut, but she asked, "I hear a train will be leaving for Bone Country. May I go with it?" She'd surprised Aleksei and he turned to her.

"Why?" Niko frowned.

"I'd like to go speak with Lev. I'm certain peace can be negotiated between our houses," she said.

"No," Niko said. "No peace. I want his head."

"Oh, I see. Good luck, then," Sofia snapped. The thick red curtains swayed at the hem as a draft passed through the room though there hadn't been an open window.

"Give us a name."

Niko's scarlet eyes ballooned, and he twisted, slowly, in his chair and looked back. There was nothing to see. Sofia kept the stranger at bay, convinced it would be another chaos she introduced to the world should she give him another name. The pond wasn't done rippling from the last rock she'd tossed.

Since the day the prince pushed Teo off the cliff, Sofia was becoming convinced, little by little, that Aleksei had really killed his brother, and the boy sitting on the red chair was an imposter. Soulless, the Guards would call him, but it was such a difficult thing to believe, blurring the line between lore and life, and she kept it to herself. What new carnage would she bring to Fedosia by claiming such a thing? Was it a bad omen even to suspect the sitting monarch of Fedosia of being a debauched creature?

Who would she tell, anyway? Aleksei? That would be a fine way to get him killed.

"Nikolas!" Aleksei barked because he'd said something, and Niko was still eyeing the curtains.

The prince turned, taken aback by Aleksei's tone.

"Give Zoya a lesser sentence. Cruelty is unbecoming of you," Aleksei said.

"I can't," the prince said.

"Then I suppose we are done," Aleksei said. "You've turned into Burkhard, you're worse than your mother, and I'm done with you. And Eugene, if you can't tell Niko what he's doing is wrong, you're exactly what they say you are, a coward, a traitor, a bitter old man, and a conniving bootlicker. Don't fucken call me when Krakova starves this winter because you sent all our grain trying to win Fedya over and you can't control the mob rushing Raven, and don't call me especially when Lev cuts your throat in your sleep because city patrol is bought and sold by the Guards."

"Lev is dead!" Niko yelled. "Fedya will bring me his head when I send him the grain Mother *owes* him."

"Fedya Pulyazin is coming to Krakova on the train to bring you Lev Guard's head," said Aleksei. "*Every* part of that sentence is false, and if you don't understand that, it's because you're stupid and the captain of your sentinels is stupid, and you two together don't listen to anyone who might know better."

"Why would he lie?" Niko frowned.

"Ask someone who cares." Aleksei turned on his heels and marched out.

Niko mouthed something after Aleksei, and she thought he said, *'I'm sorry.'*

"Well, that went well," Eugene said.

Sofia remained a moment longer, not knowing what to make of it. The two houses of the Bone Country both claimed Lev had passed. Was it true?

"If Lord Fedya brings you anything, may I see it?" she asked, her voice barely audible even to herself.

"Sure." Niko just looked sad now, pursing his lips and holding back tears. "I suppose he hates me now."

"He doesn't hate you," she said. "But he's angry with you… Niko, he doesn't ask you for much and he's the *only* person," her eyes narrowed at Eugene, "who genuinely cares for your wellbeing. Perhaps consider being merciful to Zoya Chartorisky, not because she's deserving, but because Aleksei had asked you to be." She curtsied. "Something to consider, Your Highness."

She backed out of the room, then sat on the marble stairs with silver railings because she couldn't breathe. Had Lev died alone in the wretched Bone Country? Was her whole family gone now?

She sobbed as quietly as she could manage but couldn't catch her breath and had been heaving with her hand over her mouth when a white handkerchief dropped in front of her face.

Looking up, she saw Dominik. "Thank you."

He sat down beside her and tossed a casual look over his shoulder. "May I give you something and you won't tell Lord Lev you got it from me, should he ask?"

Sofia sighed, crumpling the handkerchief in her hand. "I suppose."

"Here." He reached into his vambrace and pulled out a white rose.

Sofia took it and studied it, trying to understand the significance of it.

"I stole it from Semyon Skuratov because he turned me down and that *never* happens with young lords of a certain persuasion," he said. "I've had it for three years now, and it doesn't wilt. I believe it's Lord Lev's enchantment, like the evergreen garden of the archmage, but that garden died when the archmage passed, yet this rose remains untouched by time."

Sofia embraced him. "Thank you."

"But don't tell Lord Lev. He may get the wrong impression because men gift me extraordinary things all the time, and I don't mean to cause trouble for Lord Semyon. He has a golden heart, and I've taken the rose as a token to remember good men exist. I meant no harm, and at the time

I hadn't known the significance of the rose, only that Lord Semyon kept it on his person."

"I won't." Sofia cried, but now for a different reason. "And thank you so much."

Lev's living alchemy was graceful. He took after Papa in that regard, and now Sofia had this thing, a white rose, that would tell her if her brother lived, and he did.

Eighteen
Something Nice

LEAVING THE RED GLOW of the burning port behind, Sofia and Aleksei rode toward Krakova for seven days, and were halfway to the capital when they came upon a town of scribes and crafters and Sofia begged to stay in an inn for the night. She wanted a hot bath and a warm bed was the excuse, but she wanted to speak with Aleksei. He wasn't all right, hadn't been since they left Chartorisky port.

Before they rode out of the port he left with Dominik, disappeared for the whole night, and hadn't said much since he returned, and that was eight days ago. He was back to hurting himself and Sofia wondered if Niko understood how frail his brother's mind was.

In the inn, on the second floor, they rented a neat little room with a single bed. From the dresser shaped like a music box to the lantern with ivory paper parasols that softened the glow and dissipated the light evenly, every detail of the room said they were in a town of crafters. The wooden floor was stained with a mahogany hue and the rug was beautiful. Sofia took off her boots by the door and walked around in her wool socks. The floor was warm because the kitchen was below them, and the smell of bread baking seeped up through the boards. The fireplace was already lit, and the innkeeper went to heat water for Sofia because she'd ordered a hot bath.

Aleksei carried in their saddlebags and left them on the floor by the door, shed his cloak and weapons, and hung them from a hook by the bed. "The stables are warm. Charger will be happy." He sat on a tiny stool and rubbed his face.

"How's your arm?"

"It's fine." He picked up the lantern and turned it, inspecting the contained flame. He would appear as though he was doing things, but his eyes were blank. The light had gone out of them.

Sofia ran her hand along the carved edge of the writing table, left her cloak draped over the chair, went to Aleksei, pulled the rug to where she wanted, and sat down on it. Her skirt rustled.

She put her hand on his knee. "How's this?"

He blinked. "Sure."

"How's your knee, I asked."

"It's fine."

She didn't ask, *'What's wrong?'* Because then the answer would be, *'Nothing.'* The numerous times he'd hurt himself she didn't mention, because he would take it as her barraging him. Aleksei was delicate, difficult at times, but he was the man she chose, so she was learning him as she would anything else important to her. She made small talk, then told him about the rose Dominik gave her, and showed it to him.

"It's beautiful," he said, feeling the petals. "I hope they are well. Semyon is a good man."

"And Lev?" Sofia looked up at Aleksei and flicked a brow.

"I can't say there's love lost between us." He returned the rose to her. "But I do believe he's courageous when he wishes to be and graceful when he's not wasted."

"How did Dominik come to have an Apraksin sword?" Sofia put her chin on Aleksei's knee. "Lev has one, and it's rather expensive."

"You don't say?" Aleksei pretended to be taken aback. "Doma just has nice things. I suppose people find him pretty."

"He *is* pretty."

Aleksei narrowed his eyes, cracking his knuckles. Then the playfulness dropped out of him, and he was bothered again, his jugular pulsing as he clenched his jaw. "Grigori's back, I heard," he said casually, running away from the thing bothering him.

"Doing what?" Sofia asked. After their rather peculiar interaction the night the queen died, he'd been gone for… Well, ever since then. She wouldn't say he'd been missing because no one cared to look for him. "He knew my mother, I think. He asked if I was Yelizaveta."

"Yeah, you look a lot like her. Not that I'd know but just from that painting… Your aunt was kind. Lord Pyotr, too. I wish I could have met your mother. I'm sure she was as pleasant as you."

"I had a dream about my father the other day. I saw his face. Well, I mean, I remembered his face. Do you know who he reminded me of?"

"How would I know, Sofia?"

"That's true. You wouldn't. In my dream, which I'm not sure how accurate it was, he looked like Grigori."

"I'm glad you look like your mother, then." Aleksei frowned. "Please don't say such things. I have enough nightmares."

"What? You don't like Grigori?"

"He's freakishly tall, Sofia. The man looks like a walking tree."

"I believe he's of average height for a male." Sofia buried her face against the inside of his leg and hid her smile.

"The joke is on you, woman. You chose me. Your brother is shorter than me, by the way. You're calling him minuscule, then."

"Lev is *not* shorter than you, Aleksei." Sofia reached up and nudged his shoulder.

"Skuratov and I are the same height, and Lev is shorter than Semyon."

"Aleksei, Aleksei," she laughed, "Semyon is a bear!"

"What am I, then?"

"A moody stallion," said Sofia. "And Lev is a macaw, a brightly feathered little bird that goes yap, yap, and yap. Not so little, Uncle was a peacock."

"What are you?" he asked.

"A cat."

"That's not so good for macaw Lev," Aleksei said. "Do you know what I would do if I were him?"

"Macaw Lev?"

"I'd blow up the railroad, kill Fedya, and wreak havoc in Bone Country, so Niko has come deal with me. I'd make the Shield army march the length of Fedosia, where the supply line is going to choke around Black Ore. It'll be an expensive campaign the throne can't afford, and come winter the Shields will *have* to retreat or find out how darksteel fares in the freezing weather. We're on the brink of a bloody revolution. All he needs to do is give a little shove, and the throne, the houses, and the lords will come tumbling down. We eat so well we forget the country is starving. Do you know how much it costs to stable our four horses for the night? Ten coppers. Do you know how much a reaper earns during harvest? Fifteen coppers a month. Serfdom was never abolished. They just gave it another name, Treasury.

"Niko and I used to talk and talk about this. Alchemy enforces serfdom, it keeps the wealthy in power, and I thought a prince who can't do alchemy would understand the inborn unfairness. Fedosia is dying and I hoped he'd save her, but he's the same as everyone before him, unworthy." He closed his eyes and slow tears trailed down the length of his face. "I killed her, Sofia. Lord Chartorisky drowned with his ship. Daniil fled to Elfur. Zoya didn't have anyone else because we killed her aunt. She didn't want to burn because it would have made her ugly, she'd said. I killed her because she asked me to. Why do I break my back for him if he's going to act *exactly* like Burkhard the first chance he gets?" Aleksei crinkled his nose and the large scarlet eyes glistened with tears.

"The archmage wasn't wrong," he continued. "We're the worst house in Fedosia. Just fucken dogs foaming at the mouth, mad from eating each other. I wish Viktor was alive. He had a way of putting people in their place. He wasn't wrong about us either. I'm not good enough for you." He wiped his face.

"You say that because you didn't know my uncle," said Sofia. "And if you really believe alchemy is serfdom, the archmage was the tyrant of it all. Alchemy belongs to the Guards, we only allow you to use it, his words."

"He was a cocky bastard, wasn't he?" he remarked.

"Uncle was arrogant, yes." Sofia got up and tapped Aleksei's leg. Now that he'd told her what was hurting him—Zoya's death, the rest was just venting—he looked relieved. "Will you go get us food? I suppose my bath is ready now, and I'd like to eat something before we go to sleep."

"Sure." Slowly, Aleksei rose. "I'll go get us more firewood as well." He pointed at the window. Sofia turned and saw it was snowing.

"Can we stay a few more days and rest the horses?" she asked. "They have beautiful things here. I saw a shop of rare ingredients when we rode in. I want to visit it tomorrow. There was also crystal... Do we have money?"

"Only bags full of silver coins."

"What?" Sofia eyed the saddlebags. Those were a lot of bags, and she didn't recall having that many clothes.

"Well, it doesn't belong to Niko, either," Aleksei said. "I served him for all fifteen years of his life. I'm due my pay. I thought to get you something nice, which I reckon I never have."

That was a lot of nice things. Sofia tore her eyes from the bags and smiled at Aleksei. "You're my something nice."

Aleksei turned to her and held her face with both of his hands, as she was looking up at him. All right, he was taller. The space between them gradually depleted. Their noses touched and they looked at each other's lips as though they'd never kissed before, as though they didn't know where a mouth was on a face, as though they'd never seen each other. Aleksei went for it first and Sofia closed her eyes.

She tasted him. His tongue was in her mouth. He breathed a small sigh, a soft moan, then picked her up, her wool socks dangling in the air, carried her, and sat her on the dresser shaped like a music box. The fancy alchemy lamp fell on the rug and rolled when she felt for a place to put her hand. She gave her neck to him, her hand on his crown as he kissed down the side of her neck.

The winter whistled outside, the logs crackled in the fireplace, and a muffled chatter came from the kitchen downstairs, but the loudest was his breathing, turning sharp. He pulled her to him and their hips met.

"You're so beautiful." His hand in her hair, he pulled her head back and down, exposing the front of her neck. Then his other hand closed around her throat. "Sometimes I want to fucken kill you, so you won't leave me."

"Do it, then," Sofia whispered.

"How about I fuck you?" he hissed.

"No, I don't want you."

He sobered from the haze he'd been in and released her hair. The soft brows furrowed, confused, and he cocked his head, asking. Dear saints, she'd escalated it wrong. Because he was still Aleksei, sometimes it escaped her mind he didn't remember how they used to play these games.

"Oh, never you mind." She grabbed his shirt and pulled him, and her legs wrapped around him.

"Are you sure?" Now, he was just confused.

"Yeah, sorry."

Then there was no longer any confusion as her hand slipped inside his trousers and he took a sharp inhale. The troubles he'd been having had taken the night off. His want was pronounced, fully erect.

"This feels warm," he said about her stockings before he tore it. She liked that stocking. It had been wool, and it *had* been warm. But they had money to buy another one, she supposed.

The innkeeper found the most unfortunate time to enter without knocking to tell Sofia about her bath, then fled, and the door slammed behind her. Sofia didn't care, but Aleksei's eyes flicked to make sure it wasn't someone dangerous, it wasn't, and returned to her.

Their lips had been locked together when he pushed into her and she moaned into his mouth.

"God," he whispered.

"Blasphemy, Aleksei."

"He understands."

The dresser shaped like a music box played a strange type of tune, knocking into the wall behind it, and sounding as though they were assembling furniture with hammers. Apparently, very sad furniture or a murderous one because not long after, Sofia was either crying or being killed. She wouldn't say she healed him, but they'd come a long way since they left Krakova, and not just in miles. His desire for her was gone, he'd said, but it appeared he'd had a change of mind, fully and wonderfully.

"Aleksei! Aleksei!" she yelled at him, clawed into his back, wheezed with her hair stuck to her face, and turned unpretty before she cried, stuttered, and erupted.

"Aleksei..." She pressed her forehead on his shoulder and quivered with a long winding sigh.

He just breathed and held her.

A moment passed, then he carried her to the bed and lay her down. *Bath,* she thought, then she pulled the cover over her. She was too spent for anything else.

He cleaned up at the washing table, then said, "We need more firewood, and I'll see what food they have."

"Yeah." Sofia was racing toward sleep as though into the arms of a long lost friend on the beach. "You do that."

"*Yelizaveta.*"

Screaming, she sat up. Her whole body shivered. Aleksei had been by the door and stared at her as though she'd lost her mind.

"What's wrong?" He came and knelt by her bed and took her hand. "Bad dream?"

"He touched me, Aleksei." Sofia scanned around the room, inspecting the shadow cast from every stick of furniture. "I felt him touch me."

"There's no one here, Sofia."

"There is. There is. I need to see Lev. He's the only one who can help. Will you take me to see him?" For decades, the stranger had been as benign as the stuffed macaw she used to talk to, but it had been growing stronger since the archmage's death. It was her fault, and she knew so.

"Of course," said Aleksei, though he was still confused. "Krakova is on the way, anyway. Let me go home and find out where Lev is, and when the next train is leaving..." He thought for a moment because they wouldn't be allowed on it. "Yeah, I'll figure it out." He nodded and got up. "Let me go get firewood for now. Then we'll figure out the rest, yeah?"

"Wait, I want to go with you." She got up and grabbed her cloak. The craft town was ruined now. The damn thing had frightened her. She clutched Lev's rose and took it with her as though her brother's light would protect her from thousands of miles away.

Then as she descended the steps with her arm looped through Aleksei's, she reconsidered her decision. Though he hadn't hesitated, they had no way of boarding the train or staying on it. Aleksei had no resources in the Bone Country, should they manage to get there, and not only Lev hated Aleksei, she hadn't taken into account a vital thing: Aleksei killed Papa. Lev might or might not know it was Aleksei who killed his father, but he certainly knew the Shields burned his home and slaughtered the Guard household.

"I had a bad dream," Sofia said. "Don't worry about the Bone Country." She'd figure it out on her own.

"Are you sure?" he asked.

"Yes, I'm sure. But you won't mind if I put Guard sacred relics in the Red Manor, would you?"

"Of course not, you do as you wish. Everything I have belongs to you, and if I don't have it, I'll get it for you."

Nineteen
An Old Fool

The Custodian was waist high and hummed, engraved with gold. Eugene had seen a setup like this when they attacked the White Palace. It was Guard alchemy that kept the indoor garden evergreen. The marble fountain babbled, and they were on top of a tower. It must be nice to have so much money. The light filtering through the ivory windows had the soft shine of pearls—more money.

Eugene lifted Zoya's head, the girl's blonde locks staying perfectly in place, held with butterfly shaped pins, even after death. A wound to her temple the size of a pinprick, clean, small, through and through. Zoya Chartorisky had looked as though she was sitting on a bench in the pearl light, turned away from him, when he came in.

"Why was she in her tower and not the dungeon?" Eugene let go of her head and the body slumped back onto the bench. Even that thing was beautiful with engravings of winged saints.

"The captain." A soldier who'd been on duty shrugged. He chewed tobacco while he spoke.

By 'the captain', the soldiers meant Aleksei. They'd come from the den and remembered Aleksei dueling the giant bastard on the prince's behalf. It never got through their thick skulls Eugene was now 'the captain' and the demeanor of his sentinels didn't help either, referring to Aleksei as 'the captain'.

Ignat for one had been openly talking shit and Eugene had to put him in a different box before the mold spread through the whole batch. It had been the right call relieving Aleksei, because if he couldn't obey the prince about the Chartorisky, he certainly wouldn't about the Guards. Eugene had nothing against Sofia, but the woman had her claws sunk too deep into Aleksei. He wanted to be a lover boy and not the keeper of his brother.

"Dismantle this shit. Take whatever you want, careful about that Custodian though, I hear they are sometimes cursed, and toss the bitch out the window."

Fuck the Chartorisky and their money. Eugene loathed the House of Silver. He descended the spiraling steps and spilled out into the filth they called the Chartorisky port. The streets stunk of literal shit as he rode through them, and the houses were crooked and collapsed as though built of sodden paper. The place was diseased. They'd burn it all down.

He washed his boots with a bucket of water and wiped the soles before entering the manor house. Going upstairs, he found two sentinels he hadn't posted at the prince's door. "Where's Dominik?" he asked.

They both stared at him as though he'd spoken a foreign tongue, then one shrugged. "On a break." That one was mouthy too, Ruslan, but Eugene couldn't jail everyone. He needed the fuckers to kill Lev Guard. Nothing else mattered. Not his life, not theirs, nothing mattered but the prince.

The tall bastard Grigori was sprawled on the cushioned chair when Eugene stepped into the room. He closed the door behind him. The boy was lying on a settee, crying as he often did these days, and sat up seeing Eugene.

"Well, she's certainly dead." Eugene crossed the room and opened a drawer of a stand where he left his opium. His body ached.

"That's sad," said Niko. "Aleksei?"

"Left, I hear. Probably headed back to Krakova."

"And the girl?" Grigori's voice had the quality of a smiling snake right before it bit your damn head off. The necromancer indulged in opium too and held out his hand when Eugene produced a pouch. He had his pipe, so Eugene put a few pinches of herb on the bony palm of the tall man and settled on the settee by his prince.

He took off his darksteel gear before ruffling Niko's hair and the boy smiled with puffy eyes and a red nose. He was always like this, and when he was a child, he would light up like a fool whenever he saw him, and would follow him around, saying, *'Do you want to be my father? I don't have one.'*

Nothing else mattered but this boy.

"Yeah, yeah, I'll bring her to you," said Eugene about the 'girl'. "Lev first, Grigori, because once I take Sofia from Aleksei, all hell will break loose." He took a heaving sigh, then lit his pipe. He needed the shit with the amount of bullshit on his shoulders. "Why do you want that girl? There are a thousand others more beautiful than her and a thousand-fold less trouble."

"Aleksei will be sad." Niko's head dropped, becoming sad himself and folding. Then he lay back down.

No, boy, Aleksei will be murderous, thought Eugene. He'd cross that bridge when he came to it.

Eugene wasn't a smart man. He had no misgivings about that. He knew nothing of light or dark alchemy but understood the Guards held the key to the prince's freedom. The prince born of the red queen had died as a child, and *this* prince, *his* prince was made by Grigori from the dead prince. Made from the heart of a child, the prince retained his innocence through the years, and though his body grew, he was a child still.

The boy killed Burkhard because the duke had been making Eugene's life hell, and had said at the time, *'You're my father. Burkhard is just a man.'*

But as perfect as his child was, he didn't have free will. The snake smoking Eugene's opium had made him that way. Whatever Grigori said, the prince *had* to obey, and that was no way to live. Lev Guard dead, Sofia Guard alive, and the necromancer had sworn a blood oath to cut his marionette strings from the prince.

'I'd be like a real person, then,' the prince had said.

But the boy *was* a real person. No one could convince Eugene otherwise. He kept his hand on the prince's dark crown to comfort the boy because he was crying again. It was Aleksei, it was always about Aleksei. Because he was a child still, a little boy, the approval of his older brother was paramount.

"Why *that* woman in particular, Grigori?" asked Eugene, rolling the sweetness of the opium on his tongue before releasing the thin white smoke. "I don't think you understand how much trouble that will be."

"If I tell you, I'd have to kill you." Grigori appeared warm when he smiled, it was part of his charm, but that was false like everything else about him, even his name. Ten years of serving this fool and Eugene didn't know the necromancer's name. Only that it *wasn't* Grigori, because that was a Fedosian name, and the fucker was Elfurian. "But it *must* be that girl, and her alone, and alive and well. I must warn you that if she's harmed, I will turn you inside out. And the boy too."

"Easier said than done," Eugene muttered, then inhaled opium. His trouble was he couldn't kill Aleksei. Niko wouldn't allow it. Otherwise, he'd put a bolt in the boy while he slept and take Sofia—done. But priorities. Sofia, he would deal with later, but the bigger trouble must come first. "Tell me about Lev," he said, getting up to fetch wine because his mouth had grown dry. He could taste the stench of the city too.

"Except for his little trick with fire, the boy doesn't have magic that could hurt *you*. The real danger is to the prince, should he find out." Grigori changed the cross of his long limbs. "I had a small misfortune in the east, I must say, a miscalculation on my part, and the Guard has the Pulyazin by the balls now. We're going to send the train Fedya asked, full of grain, as he'd asked. But what's really happening is, on the return trip, the train will be full of druzhina and one Lev Guard.

"They know I left for Seniya because there are only two train stations in Bone Country and I was seen by many boarding at one. They're coming for me, and you're going to go to them. Take whatever forces you can muster and wait at Seniya, and when the train comes, kill the druzhina and Lev Guard. You'd have the upper hand, I should hope, because it's a limited number a train will fit, but you have tens of thousands at your disposal. A simple ambush shouldn't be too hard to set up, since they won't be expecting you, not at Seniya, correct?"

"What if I just blow up the train as it rolls in?" Eugene asked. He didn't want to get into a scuffle with druzhina, lose Lev, and scour the country for a single boy.

"So as long as you can *confirm* Lev Guard's death, do it however you please."

"Why Lev? Other than he's a Guard?" Eugene asked.

"It's because he's a Guard," Niko whispered. Eugene had thought he'd fallen asleep. "The last of the White Guards, when Lev dies, so does light alchemy. Then no one can stop him. Isn't that right, Grigori? You want the whole of Fedosia to fall. You don't like my country. I've become the enemy of my people."

"Child," Grigori smiled, "you have no country, you have no people, you're not a prince, you're not even a boy. You belong to me like a doll to his master, that's all. Don't get big ideas. Matter of fact, tell your dog to kill Aleksei. You have no brother."

Niko sat up, his eyes dark. "Kill Aleksei, Eugene." He laid back down, turned his back, and didn't speak again. It was shit like this Eugene had to put an end to. He could hear the boy crying softly.

For a decade Grigori had stayed put like a coiled snake, waiting, hiding from the archmage and his synod of mages, but their deaths boldened the necromancer and now he slithered, the fangs dripping venom on the houses of Fedosia. Eugene shuddered to think what would happen when the last of the Guards was no more, but in the end, *nothing* mattered but his boy.

"It's all right, boy," said Eugene. "I'll find another way. But if it comes down to it, you're more important, that's all. You'll have many more friends, many others who'd want to be your brother. You're a prince, my boy, and you'll be a tsar. Don't let Elfurian bastards tell you otherwise."

"It's good you believe that." Grigori rose, stretched, and petted Eugene's shoulder as he passed by him. "Now, be a good dog and go fetch me a Guard head."

※

A month after Eugene left the Chartorisky port, he arrived at Seniya with four hundred sentinels, all of the prince's remaining sentinels after two battles—defense of Raven and the assault on White Palace, both times with fucken Guards—and five thousand soldiers for good measure, and waited for the train from Bone Country.

He rigged the tracks with Wrath and the train engulfed in fire as it blew through the station and derailed, crashing with a great thundering noise, and setting aflame the timber yard and the granary near the station.

The train being a metal thing didn't burn too well. Eugene didn't concern himself with the fire he caused and waited for the druzhina to spill out to escape the thick black fumes towering to the grey sky, but nothing. Not a single soul exited. Then he had to wait for the fire to burn out, which took all night because setting Wrath near stocks of timber hadn't been the brightest of ideas.

Eugene waited in the yard as soldiers put out fire all throughout the city, sentinels too, because it was a Shield city that he just turned to cinder. All the snow melted, and soot covered men walked around shirtless it was so hot.

Then in the morning, instead of snow, ash fell. Forgoing all that, Eugene entered the smoking carcass of the train and found it empty, well mostly empty. Five souls had died. Their warped gear said they'd been Durnov puppeteers, operators of the train, and their severed heads said they'd been dead before the fire and the crash.

Eugene had brought Ignat because though the fucker was mouthy, he hated the Pulyazin and was an efficient killer, but it turned out to be another bad idea because now the boy wouldn't shut up. "Great plan, old fuck," Ignat said, his silver hair grey with soot and grime.

"Where are they, then?" The commander of the Shield legion frowned at Eugene while they stood in the ruins of what *was* once Seniya.

"Sipping tea in Ivory Fortress," said Ignat. "I *told* you Fedya Pulyazin doesn't travel west. He didn't even come to see his wife when she was first betrothed to him, second wife, I mean. Do you know why? Because the warmer the weather, the more expensive their alchemy, and he isn't wealthy, just smug. They're home, old man, laughing at you."

"Shut up," Eugene hissed. Grigori had been mistaken, he supposed, but how was he to get Lev now? Go to Bone Country? But that would have to wait till spring and now he had to explain the damage to Seniya to the ministers. Fuck.

"This makes no sense." Luka frowned. Aleksei let the sentinels chat like ladies having afternoon tea, and this was the result—everyone felt the need to chime in. "What are the Pulyazin going to eat this winter now? The prince had been sending them grain and they intentionally destroyed the train. With the puppeteers dead, it wasn't going to stop even if we hadn't set it aflame."

"How did it come all the way here, then?" another chatty one asked. "If the puppeteers had been dead since Bone Country how did the train journey across the tsardom on its own?"

"How fast do trains go?"

"Twice the speed of a galloping steed, I think."

Eugene turned out the voices because his head hurt. He hadn't smoked since yesterday and his body ached. He searched his belt pouch for his pipe and had been loading it when Ignat grabbed his vambrace, and Eugene sneered, lifting his gaze from his pipe because the boy had purposefully approached from his blind side—the courtesy of the Chartorisky who'd tortured him.

"Hey, old fuck, we're going to ride along the rail and look for tracks, all right? Don't burn anything else down while we're gone."

"Who said you could leave?" Eugene barked, then bit his pipe while he lit it.

"Captain," said a younger one. "We're going to look for horse tracks along the rail before it snows." He pointed at the sky. "It's possible they were on the train and just got off before Seniya. We're sure Lord Lev can figure out how to stop a train and rig it to keep going after the puppeteers were killed. I have seen the lord make a *lash* on a dare. It's all just alchemy. Guards are different that way. They *speak* alchemy."

"And where would a few hundred druzhina hide in the west?" asked the commander, finding it unlikely. "This is Shield territory, and now they have no way of going home." He gestured at the train.

"They weren't coming to hide in the first place," said Ruslan. "They were coming to assassinate the prince, and if they just got off twenty, thirty miles before Seniya, now they are a full day ahead of us toward Krakova."

"Not us, just *us*," said Ignat. "The legion is walking, yeah?" He tapped his thigh. "And if they're mounted, which I'm betting my nut sack they are. We're the cavalry, yeah?" He tapped himself. "Just four hundred of us. Even fight, I'd say, but what was it that we called city patrol back at Krakova?"

Guard Patrol, even Eugene knew that. They were bought and sold by the Guards, because the pay they received from the throne was minuscule compared to their earnings running errands for the archmage.

This was turning out to be a shit day and Eugene prayed to the dead saints, funny how that was, that the boys found no tracks along the rails, especially not hundreds of horse tracks riding toward Krakova.

"Get to it," Eugene snapped. They were wasting time holding their dicks and discussing possibilities.

"Suck my cock," said Ignat, and Eugene finally lost it and clocked the boy on his mouth. He spat blood at Eugene and laughed. "I'm coming for the other eye, old man."

"Drop dead." Not meaning to waste time grappling with a boy, Eugene backed off and calmed down.

"I'll *see* you in hell." Ignat walked away but continued to yell. "That's where cowards go, hell. You're a weasel who sold out your crew to save your skin. Then blamed the Chartorisky for your own belly turning yellow. In the end, where is your vengeance? You murdered an old man and Lady Zoya but where is Lord Daniil? He's sharpening his claws in Elfur, that's where. The real tragedy is when he returns and rips out the throat of a Shield, it's not going to be yours, but the prince's…"

The boy went on and on, his voice growing further but not silencing. Eugene exhaled, then lit his pipe. He was shaking so bad, he needed the relief. Anxiety tore him, and he tipped his face to the morning sky.

Please, don't let there be any tracks.

Twenty
Break You

Charger eyed Sofia suspiciously, pushing about the hay she put down for him. The ill tempered creature acted as though she would poison him, and she rolled her eyes at the black horse. Aleksei had obtained a few horses from the Chartorisky stables for the low, low price of free, and the stables at the Red Manor were half occupied. He had gotten mares and was looking for a suitable stallion. He'd also bought Sofia the gelding she liked. He was white and reminded her of Lev's Rhytsar, though Aleksei said they were nothing alike. She had named her horse Orchid. It didn't matter he wasn't fearsome. She wasn't going to war, not charging on a horse anyway.

After feeding and watering the horses, she closed the stalls and strolled down the long aisle carrying a bucket of bristles and singing. They meant to get a few dogs soon, but for the time being, she locked the doors. The trees sheltered wolves and the Red Manor was surrounded on three sides by silver birches, green in the summer, beautiful auburn in the fall, but quite naked like bony hands in the winter.

Aleksei's friend Countess Katya had invited them to a dinner party tomorrow, had sent an official invitation with Sofia's and Aleksei's name, and she meant to drag Aleksei to it. The countess was being kind initiating them back into high society because though Aleksei got invited to plenty of dinners, he couldn't go with Sofia on account of her being a murderer. Everyone knew she killed her husband and had taken a lover twelve years her junior, and at court, that was more scandalous than her being a Guard and living with a Shield.

They'd buried much of their silver in the forest like simple folks, but she kept a little jewelry boxful to pay out the wages of the servants she employed. She was the governess of the Red Manor now, except for the stables... Any groom she found, Aleksei didn't like, so she left that to him, and he was still yet to find stable hands. The trouble was Charger would either bite or kick the handlers and Aleksei wouldn't let them whip the horse.

The servants' quarters had quieted down for the night as Sofia left her snow boots by the door and wore slippers so as not to track mud through the beautifully polished wooden floor. The gold icons of the saints greeted her in the foyer. The sacred relics of her family, which she had to squabble with Luminary Matvey to obtain, watched over the manor, and she hadn't had trouble with the stranger since the craft town inn, nearly two months ago. The Church of All Saints in Krakova had more gold than plain surface but the old parson fought Sofia tooth and nail over the few things she'd wanted.

Perhaps Matvey meant well wanting to keep the relics in the church, she'd thought at first, but he turned out to be a deviant, a charlatan, because she'd heard from the courtiers he was selling the archmage's items in private auctions and demanded her uncle's things, but the luminary sent her forgeries.

The archmage's gold cuffs, rings, chains, everything, the old fraudster had switched out with worthless metal just turned yellow with potion, not even that good of a forgery. Sofia had only meant to keep them safe in a wooden trunk but as soon as she picked up the cuffs, she had a feeling they weren't gold. She asked Aleksei, and he couldn't tell, so he tried using it for alchemy—forgery. Old bastard! She confronted the luminary at service during Day Solis and made a scene on purpose and now he avoided her like the plague.

She fumed each time she passed by the trunk of junk in her foyer. She'd throw them out but was keeping them as evidence. Not that the archmage would have given her a single coin had he been alive, but these things should belong to Lev.

The relics were gold though. She had them tested by a jeweler because Aleksei wouldn't touch them, saying, *'I can't use the saints for alchemy! What if that angers them?'* And that was the reason the old bastard couldn't sell them off. No Fedosian would ever dare melt saint icons for alchemy gold.

Sofia strolled through her home, went to the bedchamber, and found Aleksei behind his writing table. He was so used to living in the bedchamber that he hardly used the rest of the manor. Sofia had asked him to translate the skin book to keep him occupied, and he was doing that, with numerous volumes of codices splayed out over his table and on the floor around him. She pecked him on the nape as she passed him.

"In our past lives, Charger and I used to be sworn enemies," she said, as she shed her wool cloak and equally heavy dress on the bedside chair. "I won, I suppose, because he was reborn a nasty horse, and I the companion of a count."

A month ago, Niko had come by with a pitiful face, knocking on the window and wanting to know if Aleksei still loved him.

'I wish you would have listened to me about the Chartorisky,' Aleksei had said. *'But you're still my brother, and I'll never not love you.'*

A prince, even the crown prince, couldn't grant the title of duke, because in Fedosia a duke would outrank a prince, but Niko would be ennobling Aleksei count during the winter solstice when he'd be granting lands and titles to a few commanders and nobles in his capacity as the heir apparent.

As soon as Eugene left, taking all the sentinels to Seniya to meet with Fedya Pulyazin, a liar as far as Sofia was concerned because he did *not* have Lev's head, Niko stopped being difficult and came around Aleksei again, acting like the child he was, and barraging his brother with silly questions.

'Do you love Sofia? What if she died? Will you find a different wife, then? What if she left you? Would you still love her? I was introduced to a Vietinghoff lady today. She was very beautiful. More beautiful than Sofia and younger. Do you want to meet her?'

A tang of jealousy over his brother's love, Sofia thought, but innocent otherwise.

Aleksei looked up from his writing and smiled, the stunning scarlets catching the candlelight. Then he turned sour and moaned, "How does anyone learn this shit? Light alchemy is ludicrously complex."

"Being a Guard helps, I suppose," she said. Lev had always claimed it was easy, and it was for *him*.

"Do you know what I was thinking?" Aleksei set the writing quill down. The logs crackled in the fireplace behind him, and in the bright orange hue he turned into a dark silhouette as he got up.

"You were thinking of selling Charger." She tried her luck.

He came over as she was by the bed, putting on her nightgown, and stood there looking at her for a moment before reaching out and combing her curly hair back. She'd taken the pins out and now the locks were free.

"I'll sell him if you want." His eyes wandered over her body as though she was a mare he was considering purchasing.

"It's a joke, Aleksei," she whispered. "What were you thinking?"

"That I love you," he said. "Also, when the cold months pass, we should go up to the Bone Country and meet Lev. I'll act as Niko's envoy, and you'll be there to protect me."

It was slipping his mind he killed Pyotr Guard. Sofia couldn't protect him, but she didn't mention it and kissed him instead. She had decided to go to Usolya in the spring but not with Aleksei. Ignat or Dominik, and some ministers and advisors who could speak on Niko's behalf but *not* Eugene. Hate was a strong word, but she didn't like him anymore.

Aleksei took a step forward, and she took one back, waltzing toward the large piece of furniture behind them draped in red velvet—the bed, her favorite thing about the room. The trees had been budding green when she first came as a visitor to the Red Manor after the Royal Ball. Soon, spring again, soon the prince would turn sixteen, and it would mark one year they'd loved each other.

"The saints must favor me for I am the most blessed." He kissed her and her world tipped. It would end up with him on top of her, and she ached for it, badly, desperately.

He didn't have scars to hide for she'd seen them all, and no longer a sentinel, he didn't have so many buckles, straps, and belts for carrying weapons. The drawstring cotton trousers went down easy enough.

Back and forth, back and forth, they breathed, as the flames in the fireplace licked slowly at the dry logs, the heat taking hold, then it grew, popping and crackling, becoming all consuming, before it simmered down to embers, giving heat without the brightness...

"What are you doing?" He laughed.

She'd been lying as if she'd died. "Debating whether I should get up and wash or sleep."

"Sleep." He pulled the blanket over them, then whispered in her ear, "I fucken love you. I'd die if you ever left me."

"Where would I go without you?" She took his arm and made a pillow of it. "Don't go doodling in the red medley. That is the only place I can't follow you."

"Mhm." He buried his face between her shoulder blades.

"Tomorrow we're going to Countess Katya's dinner, right?" she asked.

"If you insist." Sleepy, he dragged his words.

"I insist."

"Mhm."

Sofia resisted sleep so she could fall into it all at once, then she dreamed of Elfur again, and saw her father again. Fire, and he burned. She called his name, and her hand outstretched, she ran toward the pyre. The archmage caught her and dragged her away. She remembered the shadows were so dark that day.

"What are you doing?" Aleksei mumbled.

"What?" Sofia woke up.

"What?" he asked. He'd been asleep as well, and they'd woken each other.

"Nothing," she said. "What were you dreaming about?"

"Why?" he asked.

"You were talking in your sleep." She turned to face him and traced his collarbone with her finger.

"I thought you were at the writing table. I could hear the pages shuffling." He blinked, trying to wake up. "Never mind... What I've translated so far makes very little sense."

"What does it say so far?"

"The woman who wrote it, she carved it onto her own skin while she was losing her mind," he said. "She was playing with someone else's light, and three mages came and stole it from her…"

"Stole her magic?" She nuzzled her nose against his.

"I guess." He combed her hair with his hand. "It's your book. Anyway, she cast a dark spell upon the mages, and stole their alchemy."

"A lot of thieving going on," she said.

"Yeah, then she used the dark spell again because a merchant ripped her off, I think. She only used it twice, the second time, she began going mad, she thought she was being possessed, and the third time, he came and took her."

"Who's he?" she asked.

"The dark mage."

"What dark mage?" Sofia laughed.

"You know what, I have no idea. It's the symbol for a mage, I know that. Then that symbol for light inside dark. I can't find anything like it anywhere in the light codices and have been translating it as a dark spell."

"Makes sense." She hiked a leg over him, then climbed on top of him. "Are you tired?"

"Not anymore."

"How's this?" Sofia asked in the dressing room. Where there used to be a painting of Duke Burkhard with his hunting dogs above the mantle, Sofia had put up one of Saint Aleksander the Wise, staking her Guard flag in the Red Manor. Awfully proud of it she was too, for she didn't think there had been a painting of a Guard in a Shield estate in the last century.

"Like the spring flowers, my lady," her maid said. She was helping Sofia dress.

Sofia had tried the latest fashion of wearing a twirling wire under the skirt, but it made Aleksei harass her, lifting her skirt in the dining hall and trying to fit himself inside the wire while laughing hysterically. *'How do you sit? How do you use the privy? How are you going to fit inside the carriage? Is it supposed to wobble?'*

She gave up on it rather quickly and reverted to puffy underskirts keeping the shape of her dress. It was their first time attending a social event together, and she wanted him to behave. In the spring, they had been at several balls together while he was on duty and she was married, but tonight they would be arriving and leaving together. That made her happy.

Aleksei wore a currant red velveteen tailcoat with black leather trousers, making her nearly die when he came into the dressing room.

"Is that not cold?" she exclaimed about the trousers, secretly jealous at how good he looked. She'd been preparing for hours and not two drumbeats ago he'd been walking about in a dressing gown, and she had to yell for him to change thinking they were going to be late. It took him *no* effort to be stunning, and she frowned at the imagined number of younger women swooning over him. Not only he wasn't a sentinel anymore, he was to be a count. Her frown deepened.

"It's lined with wool," he said. "But I can change if you hate it that much. You look upset."

"Never you mind. We're going to be late... Do I look old?"

"I don't know what you mean," he said.

"Never you mind," Sofia grumbled. As she put on her gloves, in the corner of her eyes, she could *clearly* see the maid mouthing something to Aleksei.

"You look like spring flowers, my lady," Aleksei said.

"More like mature flowers at the end of summer before the petals shrivel and fall off the stem," Sofia said. "I'm wilting."

"What are you mumbling about?" He laughed. "Is it the trousers? You're still frowning at them, or me. I'll change."

"It's nothing. Let's leave."

"Are you going to be upset the entire time?" He held out his arm for her to take.

"I forbid you to be with anyone else!"

"Of course. What is with you?" He looked curious.

"Let's leave. We'll be late," she insisted, taking his arm.

"If we go by a tortoise?" he asked.

"Shut up." She shoved him out the door. They were going to their last social event. He was going to be stolen from her walking about in public like this. No dinners, gatherings, balls, teas, nothing! She was going to lock the doors to the manor after tonight.

She'd been speaking to herself which she hadn't realized, and he turned and shook her. "What are you murmuring about? How are you so adorable? I'm going to break you in half!"

Twenty-One
Hello, Soful

Countess Katya was Aleksei's friend who lied for Sofia the first time she'd spent the night at Red Manor. She expected the countess to be a pleasant host, and she'd been right, but her guests—uuf.

Sofia all of a sudden was the center of attention, being whisked away to this room and that, being introduced to more people than she could remember the names of, and was invited to more card games and afternoon teas than she could keep track of. The women pulled her tongue about the red den, about the prince, about Aleksei, Lev, the luminary... She was still a murderer and they'd never be her friends, but she was a sensation and courtiers loved those.

Eugene had taken most of the sentinels to Seniya and she hadn't seen Ignat since the Chartorisky port, but she ran into Dominik. They exchanged smiles, but he was in the middle of swindling a card game and stealing a baron's heart, so she didn't interfere.

Seeing Ania Illeivich, who was now married and was introduced as Ania Petrovna, was a dreadful moment, but the girl pretended not to know her. Later, in privacy, Ania approached Sofia and they had a civilized talk, where Ania confessed the Illeivich estate had been compensated by Papa to sweep the count's death under the golden rug. At the end of their conversation, Ania remarked, "I suppose you tolerated him for as long as you could."

They parted, wishing each other pleasantries, though they were insincere.

So passed the evening in a dizzying manner, not the greatest thing to happen, but it was Sofia's first step in fitting into the social life of Krakova, and seeing an Illeivich girl had been a freeing thing. She wouldn't say she worried for the girls daily, but it had been at the back of her mind.

She lost Aleksei and found him in the music room surrounded by two dozen women. "I want to go home." She frowned, and that was the end of their time at the countess's party.

During the ride home in the carriage, he said, "What happened? You're unhappy."

"How am I to compete with so many women?"

"For what?"

"You…" She sighed.

"I didn't realize I was a prize. Thank you, my lady." He smirked. Silent for a moment while Sofia brooded, then he asked, "Sofia, would you marry me?"

Sofia had been fanning herself with her glove and that slipped from her hand. "What?"

"I can't have children. But if that's all right, would you marry me?"

"Only if you don't keep other women."

"All right, I'll limit my infraction to Day Solis, solstice, my birthday, the prince's birthday, harvest festival, spring…" He couldn't go on and burst into laughter.

She slapped his knee. "I'm serious, Aleksei. I'm sorry but I'm—"

He flung from his seat and kissed her, then held her face. "Only you, all right? Only you for as for as long as I live. Only you till I die, then afterward I'll gaze up at your star and think only of you. I love you, and you only. My mind and heart don't split when it comes to you. They are wholly yours, my lady."

"Where have you gone that you're looking up at me rather than be beside me?"

"Hell," he said. "But that's all right because I had you."

"Well, then I have no interest in being a star. I'd rather be in hell."

"I'm sure that can be arranged." He kissed her. "Marry me, Sofia. Marry me. I love you."

"I think I shall," she said confidently.

※

The fire burned in the brass brazier, the patterned tiles of the bathroom flickering in the light. The long copper chains holding the crystal lamp to the star studded blue ceiling chimed, rubbing up against one another as it swayed. Aleksei kept tapping it with his *lash* extended into a quarterstaff.

The warm bathwater smelled of lavender, and fresh calendula Sofia obtained at an eye gouging price floated on the surface. She leaned back into Aleksei and put her foot up on the rim of the copper tub.

"Should you be getting your gear wet?" she asked.

"Probably not, but it sounds... I can see the reverberation." A tap and a chime followed. "This is fucked up," he whispered.

Sofia laughed. She'd been getting more creative with her potions. Had a talent for it, according to Baltar, and this one she called Divination.

'Are you sure? I'm already mad,' Aleksei had asked when she gave him the potion with a mild hallucinogen, but he trusted her with these

things. Divination was based on Euphoria which he knew and liked, and since his dismissal from the imperial sentinels she'd been brewing creative potions for them which had started therapeutic, but turned experimental.

Selling her talent to Baltar, who upsold the potions at dinner parties and afternoon teas, she made small fortunes which she saved, meaning to buy Aleksei a couple of purebred Fedosian shepherds for his birthday. The dogs were the size of small bears and were meant for killing wolves, so they could cost a bit.

"Do you want a miniature pony?" Sofia glided her hand along his thigh, then over his knee. He had a lot of scars, but she hadn't seen a fresh injury on him since Chartorisky Port, and that was good.

He laughed. "No, why?"

"Thought you wanted one."

"When I was like nine." He retracted the quarterstaff and let the darksteel drop. He stroked her hair, a better use of his hand. "They look like horses, but they are tiny. I find them endearing, but no, they're useless," he said.

"What do you mean they look like horses? They are horses."

"If you say so."

"I'm sure they say so too, Aleksei." Twisting back, she found a kiss. "You can see sounds, you say? Do you want me to play the piano for you?"

"Too loud," he whispered. "People are asleep."

"Do you mean the servants?" Sofia asked.

"They are people."

"Don't forget that when you're a count." She turned to face him, water sloshed out of the tub, and she ran her hand up the side of his face. He closed his eyes to her touch. "I have an idea." She leaned forward but withheld the kiss. "Say yes."

Scarlet eyes opened. "What is the idea?"

"Say yes," she said.

"I see. It's something I'm not going to like, is it?" he asked.

"Say yes."

"All right, I trust you."

The water had been growing cold, so they moved into the bedchamber, Sofia grabbing a vial as they passed by the apothecary. That room used to be empty but was now stuffed as though Pyotr Guard lived here. Little by little she was turning the manor more Guard, building herself and Aleksei a livable home. She'd started an indoor garden and soon she wouldn't be buying calendula or lavender.

Sofia sat down on the bed, dried her hair, and waited as Aleksei stoked the fire. Less than a hundred miles from the Zapadnoi Morye, Krakova winters were soft, and a single fireplace was enough to warm the grand bedchamber with a tall ceiling and large windows.

The curtains were still open from the day, and she considered getting up to close them, but the manor was isolated enough to not worry about strangers peeping in, so she let it be. They only had a short decorative fence, and the gate was left mostly open, but it was a Shield dwelling in Shield territory, and everyone knew a sentinel lived here.

"The canopy is moving." Aleksei sat down beside her. He was in the cotton trousers he slept in and didn't have a shirt on. "It's waving at me like a banner."

"Here, drink this." She handed him a vial of potion.

He looked at the pink liquid suspiciously. "Will this turn me into a frog?"

"No, that is reserved for princes."

"Not good enough to be a frog, you say?" He drank the potion and waited, and when nothing bad happened, he asked, "What is it?"

"A different type of divination. I haven't thought of a name yet."

"How much better will it be, would you say, than being a frog?"

"Worse, sad to say. You'll be eaten by a heron."

Aleksei shuddered. "They frighten me."

"The bird?"

"They're fucken huge, Sofia. Have you seen one? Especially when they fly, and they look like an evil old man draped in a cape."

She couldn't stop laughing. He was silly.

"Always so many at once, they stand around in flooded fields, looking like a herd of necromancers." Ranting about the evil herons, he got up, put his shirt on, then stood by the bed taking deep breaths. "Yeah, I feel that." His pupils were large, making his eyes darker. "Fuck, I feel that."

"Good, come here," Sofia whispered. She'd been thinking of naming this potion Pleasure, but that was too simple, wasn't it? Trance, perhaps?

When he returned to her, she ran her fingers through his locks. His eyes rolled up and he lay back on the bed, whispering a long, "Fuuuck."

She traced the angles of his face, the curves of his neck, and dragged her nails down his chest over the soft fabric of his shirt. Twirling her finger around the cotton lace of the drawstring, she undid the tie, then pushed down his trousers.

His inhales were deep and quickened as she got on him, but he caught her chin when she kissed down his navel. "Don't do that." He sat up.

"You already said yes."

"No."

"Why?" she asked.

"Why do I need a reason?"

"You don't," she said, though she knew the reason. He thought he was dirty, a thing he wouldn't let go, and didn't want to come in her mouth. He probably thought that was vulgar. He was wrong but she didn't want to argue about it. His deepest wounds weren't the scars on his body, but perhaps time would heal the unseen as well.

In the meanwhile, she straddled him.

His hands tightened around her hips, and he whispered, "You're my divination."

※

They'd fallen asleep with their limbs entangled. She hadn't felt the cold because Aleksei was a furnace, but seeing her breath steam in the pale morning light, she frowned, half asleep. Cold front, she supposed, and peeled off the blanket to get up and start the fire. The windows were completely frosted over, and it was freezing.

Someone would come in at dawn to tend to the fire because Sofia and Aleksei liked to sleep in, but they hadn't done so this morning and the fireplace was a sad, dark place of ashes and ruin. She grabbed her cloak, hopped over the icy floor, and bent by the fireplace to stack some kindling. It was ridiculous to be shivering indoors and she thought to have a stern talk with the steward about being diligent with the heating.

She got a little fire going, and as she sat at the table by the fireplace, waiting for the flames to take hold before adding wood, she saw the wine in the cup had frozen. She turned the cup over and a solid block of ice plopped out.

"Aleksei, go check on your horses. It's damn freezing."

"Yeah?"

"Go check on your horses," she said again.

"Yeah," he mumbled but continued to sleep.

Seeing as Sofia was up anyway, she thought to go tell a servant to heat the stables, but she'd add wood to the fire first, so the room would be warm when she returned to bed. She'd been sliding the frozen wine over the tabletop thinking of going skating when it sounded as though the window took a heaving breath and the fire went out. She lifted her gaze.

Silently, the frosted window shattered so finely it blew inward like a shovel full of snow someone had chucked, and it flurried white in the red bedchamber.

A man with a white cloak stepped through the window, his long hair also white when he removed the hood, and he held a spear made of ice. But for his dark eyes, he looked like a winter doll.

"Aleksei." Sofia backed away from the table as more men entered. They were dressed as sentinels, but their gear wasn't darksteel.

"Yeah." He sat up and rubbed his face, struggling to open his eyes. He reached for his trousers on the floor, then looked up, awake now, because there was a blade tip pressed against the hollow of his neck. Scarlet eyes swung, assessing the room.

"Get dressed, captain of the sentinels, I insist." The pale intruder sat down with an elbow on the table. "I'll wait."

Recovering from the strangeness, Sofia turned toward Aleksei but a steel to her throat stopped her from advancing.

"Don't do that," Aleksei hissed, getting dressed.

"Then don't make me," said the pale man.

"What do you want?" Aleksei scanned the room. He was looking for his exoskeleton, but the pale man had it.

"Do you know what happens to darksteel when it freezes?" he asked, then slammed the exoskeleton against the wooden table, breaking it like black glass. "Don't try me and I'll let your lady live. The opposite is also true, Captain."

"Fedya Pulyazin, I assume," said Aleksei. "What do you want?"

The gold on the Pulyazin lord wasn't visible, but Sofia assumed it was under his fur cuffed sleeves. She remained standing, not hysterical but afraid all the same. She wanted to ask the lord about the message he'd sent claiming her brother was dead, but this was hardly the time.

A man with short, earthy brown hair dressed as a sentinel but clearly not one, circled the maquette of castles Aleksei had along the wall. He tapped on Raven and the miniature castle frosted over. With a flick, the tiny walls of the little castle collapsed.

Noticing Sofia watching him, he bowed. "I'm Isidor, my lady. I'm captain of the druzhina, and I'll be keeping you company."

Sofia grimaced and looked away, returning her attention to the strange man with ice claws tapping the table as Aleksei put on his shirt and the felt slippers he wore around the manor. The room didn't grow any colder for having a broken window. It had already been freezing.

"Good," said the lord. "Now, fetch me the skeleton key to Raven and we'll be on our way."

"I don't have it," said Aleksei.

The lord clicked his tongue, twisting his neck to Sofia. He strummed the table. "Are you certain that's the answer you want to give me?"

"I don't have it," Aleksei said. "The captain of the sentinels has it, and that's no longer me."

"Here's my deal, Captain," said the lord. "Skeleton key for the lady. If it's true you don't have it, Isidor is in luck because he likes zapadnik women. Isn't that so, Isidor?"

"For a few nights, sure, my lord. Most of my men too."

"I will fucken kill you," Aleksei whispered, the narrowing red gaze stalking Isidor as he circled Sofia. There were half a dozen men between them, all armed.

"A grand threat for a boy holding up his trousers with his bare hands," said the lord. "I already have hundreds of men in your city disguised as civilians. Give it a little time and they'll grow to thousands. I may not have as many druzhina as the prince has sentinels, but they aren't there, are they, Captain?

"Whether you give me the key or not, Raven *will* fall. I'm trying to save lives, that's all. I'm not here to murder Fedosian royalty, but whether you believe me doesn't matter, so long as you believe I can kill you, then give your lady to my men to share.

"So, produce for me the skeleton key of Raven, Captain. I shall not ask again."

Aleksei clenched his fists, and his knuckles were white as he sneered. There were nearly twenty men in the room and probably more outside because they could hear voices. He was weighing his odds against so many alchemy users, a tall task even had he been armed, but he wasn't, and whispered, "It's inside my right vambrace."

His vambraces were stacked together on the mantle, and a druzhina fetched them for his lord.

"Inside?" Fedya asked, inspecting them.

"Inside."

He'd said right but Fedya held them together, and in his hands, the darksteel froze, groaned, and warped, the gold alchemy popping out and separating. He smashed them on the table, scattering them into frozen shards, and a cast iron key fell out intact.

Sofia remembered such a key. She'd held it when Eugene freely gave it to her. There was more than one, she assumed, and the prince must have the other. But how did they know Raven had such a weakness and that Aleksei would have a key to it? The Pulyazin didn't travel west. Without the train, which was fairly new, the journey from one end of Fedosia to the other would take six months.

"Thank you." Fedya took the key and tossed it to Isidor. "Now come with me." He exited through the window he broke.

Aleksei had to raise his hands, showing non-aggression, because they kept shoving him.

"If you would, my lady," said the druzhina who nudged Sofia from the back.

The Red Manor had two wells, an indoor one in the kitchen and an outdoor one behind the manor, by the servants' quarters. Treading snow in their slippers, they were being taken to the outdoor well. There were more druzhina there and they had the servants kneeling on the snow. At least they'd let them grab their cloaks and let the mothers comfort their little ones.

"Get on it." Fedya tapped the stone curb of the well.

"I gave you what you wanted. You said you'd leave." Aleksei turned.

"I said I won't harm the lady, and I won't. Now, step up."

Two large men picked up Aleksei by the arms and set him on the curb. He was *struggling* to restrain his temper, trying not to get himself killed, when they bound his hands at the front. His jugular pulsed as he scowled. His eyes glowed red for a beat but when he blinked, he'd regained control.

A man in a brown cloak came up from behind Aleksei, his hood pulled down. He walked around the well and came in front of Aleksei. "The only reason I don't kill you is my sister is still alive." Lev pushed Aleksei.

That well was fifty feet deep and Sofia screamed when Aleksei fell into it. The Pulyazin men slid the lid over it, the grey stone frosting, and turning completely white before a wall of ice formed around and over the lid, growing and growing into a mound.

Lev pulled his hood down and danced toward Sofia, his demeanor playful, but he looked more like the archmage than himself, and Sofia realized it was his eyes. They used to be the color of summer sky and now they had a gold tint, not quite yellow as Uncle's had been, but they were tainted by magic. The light in them had gone out and she was looking at a stranger.

"Hello, Soful." He held out his hand, and he was wearing gold enough to buy the Red Manor.

Twenty-Two

Ridiculous

The dining hall had two fireplaces, but both were black. Lev tossed a wooden chair into one then casually flicked Dragon's Breath. He walked through the hall, touching and inspecting the Guard relics Sofia had along the wall and above the mantles. He used to have a single gold bracelet for his alchemy, but now wore heavy cuffs on both arms, exactly as the archmage used to. The only difference was he wasn't wearing rings on his sword hand.

Sofia sat behind the table, following Lev with her eyes, and waiting for the tea a nervous servant was making.

"The water is boiling, my lady," she whispered, afraid of Lev.

Lord Fedya took his men and left to storm Raven, but Lev had enough city patrol at Red Manor to be his private army. They'd all gathered to see that Lev Guard had truly returned. But in the dining room, it was just Sofia, her brother, and an anxious young woman fumbling cups because Lev had looked at her.

"Aleksei must be freezing," Sofia said.

"Oh." Lev set down the icon of a saint on the mantle and turned to her. "I can have quicklime tossed down the well. That will heat things up, you think?"

"Please don't do that," she whispered.

"Then don't say his name again, mmm?"

Was she supposed to apologize? Be afraid of Lev? She didn't think so, but it was hard to interact with this person he had become.

"So, Soful, Songbird, how have you been?" He settled across the table from her as the steward came running with the wine Lev had asked for. Lev took the bottle and shooed the man who was rather glad to be dismissed.

Sofia did the same and let the servant leave and took over her tea. "Do you want tea, Lev?" Sofia poured hot water from the samovar into the cups and let the tea steep.

"I saw you had an indoor garden. It made me think of Father," he said, pouring wine into his cup. "Why do you have church stuff here?" He gestured at the saints.

For months, Sofia had been wanting to speak with him about the stranger but now that she was looking at him, it was hard to do because the conversation had to start with how she killed their uncle. This wasn't the best time, she decided.

"Luminary Matvey had been selling off church property, I heard, and wanted to save them," she said.

"Get the fuck out of here. Are you serious?" He called in the patrol and demanded they bring him Matvey, but mercifully, the old man had left for Murmia.

Lev saw blood just then, and Sofia realized she should be *very* careful speaking with him, lest she cause harm to others. He dismissed the captain of the patrol as he would a servant, but tossed a pouch of silver and the man caught it like a dog who fetched, with a grin, nonetheless.

"Anything else for you today, my lord?" the captain asked.

"Take the day off, Captain. Let me know when the sentinels return to the city, but don't worry, I don't expect your men to engage with them. I have druzhina for that. And tell your mother I said hello. I remember she didn't miss a Day Solis when Uncle was alive."

"Oh, she'd be so delighted to hear my lord remembers her. You've made her year, my lord." He left with a bow.

"Where's Semyon?" Sofia asked, stirring some sugar into her tea.

"With Zoya, I suppose." Lev flicked a silver coin on the table and watched it spin. It rattled.

"Zoya passed, Lev."

"I know," he said.

Then, she realized what he was saying. "Oh, I'm sorry." She reached across the table and touched his hand. He stopped fiddling with the coin, lifted his gaze at her, and was himself for a brief moment, but then it was gone.

"Have you seen Grigori around?" He pulled his hand from Sofia and she straightened in her seat, bringing the teacup to her lips.

"Not in Krakova. I heard he was at Chartorisky Port, but that was..." Sofia counted back the days. "More than two months ago."

"Mmm." He strummed the table. "Were you at the White Palace when my father died?"

"Yes."

"How did he do?"

"He drank with Clodt in the music room, laughed, and went to see Auntie in his armor and holding his sword," she said.

"Clodt," said Lev, staring out the windows as though the old captain of the knights was out there in the courtyard. "What did him in, finally?" He was asking who killed his father.

Sofia studied her teacup. "Watchmen."

"I see."

When she stole a look at him, Lev was in a reverie. Being back in Krakova must bring up memories. Unlike Sofia, he grew up here.

"Lev, I'm glad you're well. People kept telling me you've..." She exhaled and wiped a rogue tear making a path down her cheek. "I'm glad you're here." It was true, and she nodded, but she hadn't forgotten Aleksei. "So... What are you going to do?"

"I've come to meet my nephew." He swished wine, didn't like the taste from the grimace on his face but kept drinking it. "But first things first, I'm here for the necromancer."

"Necromancer?"

"Grigori is a necromancer. Elfurian, I think, but that may be an act. We'll see once we find him."

"What about the prince?" she asked.

"He's my nephew. He's family." He smirked.

"You want tsar regent," Sofia said.

"The birds in Krakova tell me Duke Rodion and his whole family suffered the Shield ailment of the head rolling off the shoulders, is that true?"

"It is."

"I suppose the old age and natural causes the queen died of was contagious and her watchmen suffered the same fate?"

"I heard," she said. "I don't know how that happened." They sat in silence, listening to the burning chair crackle and pop. "Lev," she begged. "It's freezing outside and Aleksei—"

"He's fine, Soful," he whispered. "If I see him, I'll kill him, and I'm trying not to do that, all right? A lot of people died because of that necromancer and I'm kind of... angry about it, all right?"

"He didn't know," Sofia insisted. "I believe you, but I don't think anyone knew."

"That may be. We'll see." He finished his wine and got up. "It was good to see you, Soful."

"Where are you going?" She got up with him.

"Raven. I just wanted to catch up with you and gather my calm." He smiled. "I'm better now. I *probably* won't kill their fucken prince on sight, *probably*. Enough Fedosians have died. I'd rather avoid more carnage." He was supposing Raven had already been taken by the Pulyazin.

"Lev, will you wait a moment while I change? I'll go with you."

"No, I'd rather you stayed out of the ugliness. I'll send for you once I've had the blood washed from the floors."

"Lev." Sofia climbed up on the table and slid across it, because it was too long to go around, and embraced Lev as tight as she could. "I missed you." When the hug ended, she ruffled his gold hair. "Let me just grab my cloak, it will only be a moment." Without waiting for an answer, she turned and ran.

There was a bigger problem than Lev realized. He was going to kill the prince and didn't know it yet. Then there would be a *bloodbath* in Krakova once the Shield forces arrived, and it would end with either Aleksei or Lev dead.

Sofia had seen Niko cut his finger on paper of all things, and the bleeding stopped normally. He wasn't afraid of getting injured, didn't restrict his physical activity, and the illness that prevented his blood from clotting only came up when people were asked to remove their jewelry and weapons, things with gold, around the prince. Niko wasn't ill, but he corrupted gold when it touched him. There was much yellow metal at Raven which appeared to be gold but couldn't be. Aleksei might or might not know, but Eugene must. The reason the queen allowed Eugene to live, Sofia thought, was that he forged them all, took the gilded and gold furnishing of Raven, and replaced them with fakes, and that was a grand endeavor.

Lev had a lot of gold on him which would turn black when he touched the prince. A bad thing to happen even if he hadn't been looking for a necromancer specifically. Whatever else Niko was, he was a Shield prince first, and Fedosia would bleed dry should Lev murder him.

Her mind in a frenzy of worry and imagined terrible possibilities, Sofia rushed past the foyer to get to the bedchamber in the other wing. She meant to put on a simple dress and grab her wool lined cloak, but the wooden truck the luminary sent her caught her eye and she had an idea.

"That was an incredibly long time for you to be still in your sleeping garment." Lev leaned against the doorframe.

Sofia had made an improvised potion stand in the far end of the music room, and stood behind the apothecary table, mixing her concoctions. "Come on in, Lev. It'll be only a few more moments."

He took in the powder blue walls, the gold and crystal chandelier, the white veils hanging from the tall windows, and the ceiling meant to look like cotton puffs of cloud, and smiled. He came in. He mindlessly ran his hand along the carved crest of a velvet chair as he slowly made his way toward Sofia.

The music room of the Red Manor had a lacquered white upright piano. Lev knocked on the fallboard, then he lifted it, took off his cloak, tossed it on a settee, and sat down on the piano stool.

"I remember this room." His fingers fluttered across the keyboard, teasing out a tune as light as a summer butterfly. "This needs to be tuned, Soful. Where's the tuning key?"

"I don't know. Yani tuned it last."

"Yani? I hope he didn't charge you. He owes me a lot of money." Lev played the song he wrote when he was eight years old. It was called Lavander Garden and it had been for his mother, Sofia remembered. "You know they tried emulating the White Palace with this room. A baroness had it decorated before for her birthday party so she could feel as though she was hosting it at the palace. The courtiers are sad people."

Yes, Sofia knew, which was why she was in here. They hadn't done a shabby job and the room felt like a piece of home.

"Do you know Baltar?" Sofia asked.

"I am from Krakova." Lev sighed as his hands dropped from the keyboard. "The tuning is bothering me. I'll have a word with Yani about ripping you off. He was lazy with it. This always happens when I'm not around. Just because Guards are thought wealthy, people assume they can swindle us. Happened to Mother a lot because she was kind, like you. It doesn't hurt to be an asshole once in a while, Soful, so these pompous fucks who call themselves the 'high society' take you seriously... About Baltar, he's equally likely to sell you snake oil than he is a miracle. It depends on whether he likes you."

"I'm learning elixirs and potions from him," said Sofia. "Look," she held up two vials, "one is Euphoria, the other is my own making. Which one would you like?"

"Are you peddling potions with Baltar?" Lev brightened and marched over to Sofia's little setup and prodded through her ingredients. "How are you doing it? I suck at this shit. Once I tried making a potion for a shindig I was hosting and nearly killed everyone."

"Well, I have to be good at *something*." Sofia handed him the lime blue potion which was Euphoria. He downed it and returned the empty glass. "You're good at a lot of things others aren't."

"Yeah, like what?" she asked.

"Being nice to people you don't like, for one. You also have the patience of a saint." He picked up another vial and sniffed it. "It smells like sugar. What is this?"

"Baltar calls it the Unicorn. We *may* have been selling it at gatherings."

"Get the fuck out of here." Lev drank it. "Tastes exactly as it smells. I can't believe you invented a new potion while I was away. How did you learn elixirs so fast? Uncle had acolytes for this shit. Perhaps not to make *this* kind of potions, but it is a study field on its own merit."

"Talent." Sofia smiled. "I am Guard."

"So you are." Lev spun, his movement flurried though the attire he'd been wearing was simple and for riding. "Woah, Soful, this is pretty good." He went back to the piano. "We should get going, though. I actually should have gone with them. The patrol said Grigori wasn't at Krakova, but who knows."

"How do you know he's a necromancer, Lev?"

"He turned the Menshikov into monsters and brought back Vasily and the Apraksin retainers as soulless, among other things."

"That's terrible. What happened at Usolya?"

"Later, Soful. Get dressed, let's go." He played a note and whispered, "I can *taste* that." He moved down the cord, sustaining the notes with the pedal. "This shit is wild."

"I'll go get dressed, then." Sofia cleaned up her potion stand, then pretended to find the wooden trunk she placed by the settee. "Oh, Lev, here." She dragged the trunk along the parquet boards, scratching her floor.

"What the fuck is that? Better be a handsome man in there. It's big enough."

"It's Uncle's things," Sofia murmured, now regretting having made a scene at the church about the gold being forged. But Lev hadn't had the time to gossip with courtiers, she hoped.

"Archmage?"

Lev came, and as they sat on the floor like children with a treasure trove, digging through the trunk, Sofia held her breath waiting for him to notice. Lev would know, surely. But he was high, too high. He tossed a ring across the room to hear the 'music' it played.

He put on the archmage's gold cuff and held a ball of light. The alchemy was working because he had real gold on the other arm, but soon he switched that out for the forgery as well. Then he slipped on ten gold rings and rubbed his hands together, laughing. "Do I look as ridiculous as he used to?"

"If Uncle was ridiculous, it wasn't the gold." She ruffled his soft blond locks as she got up. "I'll be right back, all right?"

"Yeah." Lev lay down on the floor and stared at the blue and white ceiling, reaching up as though trying to touch it. "Aren't we all ridiculous down here, Syoma?" he whispered.

Sofia left to get dressed, and on the way she checked to see what was happening with Aleksei. A few of the male servants were chipping at the ice with an axe but they were nowhere near reaching the lid. It would be a few hours at least.

Twenty-Three
Games We Play

Rodion's men hadn't wanted to die for the prince. Uncle used to say loyalty couldn't be bought with silver, an astonishing thing to admit for a Guard.

Soldiers of plain sword, the men who came from the den had laid down their steel and fled as soon as the castle was breached. Sofia didn't understand how Eugene missed the Pulyazin, but it had been the mercy of the saints because a fight between sentinels and druzhina would have been... brutal. This wasn't to say lives hadn't been lost, and Sofia bent down to close a young man's eyes in the throne room of Raven. Like the others around him, he'd died looking up at the ceiling of painted saints.

"Go to them now, they wait to honor your bravery." She fixed the hem of his red tunic, the mark of a Shield soldier, and wiped a strand of hair sticking to his young face with dark blood.

Lev walked down the long hall of white granite pillars, his boots leaving bloody prints, toward the throne of Fedosia. He pulled down the

Shield banner behind the dais, then tossed the hem of his cloak before sitting on the throne.

"The last Guard to sit here was Aleksander the Wise," he said, his voice echoing through the hall.

The room smelled of blood, and Sofia covered her nose with the sleeve of her dress, wondering if Aleksei was able to get out of the well by now. Freezing in the wet dark, imagining the worst possible things because of the threats the Pulyazin made, he must be going mad. She worried his fragile sanity might break.

Lord Fedya brought Lev the gold scepter of Fedosia and Lev twirled it like a baton. "Come here, Soful."

"It smells like blood." The pillars of the white hall were splattered with death.

"Open the fucken window then," said Lev. "Come here." It was good he was so high he wasn't noticing the forged gold all around him, but it wasn't so good he was a nasty drunk and he'd been drinking since they arrived at Raven an hour ago and was drinking still.

The druzhina were in the throne room as well, and not bothering to move the dead, they were stepping over them.

Isidor had apologized for his lewd words, but it was not accepted, and when he grabbed her elbow, Sofia hissed, "Don't touch me."

He let go and backed off, raising his hands.

"Saints watch, Lev. The Fedosian throne has never been usurped," said Sofia.

"And it never shall be," said Lev.

Sofia had been midway between the red dais and the entrance of the long hall when a druzhina announced, "Prince Nikolas, Your Grace." They addressed Lev as though he was the archmage.

Dressed in all black, Niko had blood on his face, but it was a spray and not a wound. He frowned at Sofia as he passed by her, his steps not making a single sound on the polished parquet floor. Fearful for the prince, because she didn't know if the scepter Lev had was real gold, Sofia held her breath.

"I want a physician for my sentinel," Niko said. "Where is Baltar?"

Lev pretended to search inside his cloak, then blew a raspberry.

"Who's hurt?" Sofia asked.

"Dominik." The prince's frown deepened. "Has he killed Baltar? Where is the old man?"

Sofia had seen Baltar alive and well, tending to the injured druzhina while fascinating himself with the Pulyazin alchemy, and said, "Lev, please send the physician. Dominik is my friend."

"Have a lot of sentinel friends, don't you, Soful?" He grimaced, but said, "Lord Fedya will see to it that he receives the care he needs." The Pulyazin lord bowed and relayed the order to his men. Lev continued, "Now that you're here, Prince, let's have a word, you and I." Playing with the scepter, Lev sat crooked on the throne, hitching a leg up on the gilded armrest. "Would you say it's true you were sired by the ghost of Saint Neva of Guard?"

Sofia looked at the prince and nervously chewed her lip. But Niko held his own, replying, "I wasn't there, but that was what the queen said."

"All right then, let's pretend as though your mother wasn't mad," said Lev. "That makes you a Guard, Nikolas. And I'm saddened to say, I'm what passes for an elder of our house these days. So, be good. Let's not shed any more blood. When your men arrive at the capital, you will tell them to stand down because you would have accepted my guardianship as your elder. You will assemble the *Boyar Duma*, missing the Chartorisky and the Menshikov, and give me tsar regent. You will also produce for me the necromancer known as Grigori. Do those three things and you may live. Miss any one thing, and Fedosia will have one less house. That, I promise."

"I don't know where Grigori is," said the prince, not denying he was a necromancer, and the expression the boy wore, he'd known it to be true. Many things went through Sofia's mind but now wasn't the time for doubt.

"That's unfortunate for you," said Lev. "You and your mother *knowingly* sheltered a necromancer, and because of that sin, Vasily Apraksin, Semyon Skuratov, Bogdan Menshikov, and countless other Fedosian lives were lost. Though I find your house responsible for their deaths, I'm being *immensely* merciful because you are a kid. I presume it wasn't your doing but the mad queen's. However, if you don't find me Grigori, it will not go well for you or your men.

"Today, I'll send the physician to your wounded. Today, I'll allow you to gather your thoughts. But if you know where Grigori is and don't tell me, I will hang everyone you know in the garden where you can see from your window. Are we clear, Nikolas?"

"He..." Niko winced as though it hurt, and his nose bled. With a gloved hand, he covered his mouth. "I don't know where he is."

"If you know where he is, tell him," Sofia chimed in because the look Lev had just then reminded her of the archmage. He'd gained cruelty, her brother, that he hadn't possessed before his journey eastward.

"I can't," the prince whispered, closing his scarlet eyes. He was about to break down, so Sofia went to him and took his hand. She didn't care about the etiquette, there was none left anyway.

"We'll find him, Lev."

"You speak a lot, Soful."

"Don't turn into Uncle. You're better than him," she said.

Blond brows furrowed, and the gold flaked eyes underneath regained something resembling awareness, but then Lev scowled it away. "Come here, nephew."

Niko stood frozen because only now it occurred to the child it may have been an unwise thing seeking Lev out. Sofia stole a look at the gold scepter on Lev's lap. Though she'd never seen Niko hold it, it could *not* be real, could it?

"The prince agrees, Lev. May I take him to his quarters? He's a child," she said.

"Come here, nephew," Lev repeated.

The room had fallen silent, and Fedya's dark eyes trained on the prince, his head crooked. "His Grace asks you to approach, Nikolas of Shield."

Sofia didn't know how Lev had obtained the devotion of the northern lord, whether it had been a miracle or a trick, but reverence it was, true and genuine. The company Lev kept wouldn't question him, ever, and that was how the archmage's delusions of grandeur began.

All eyes on them, Sofia nudged Niko forward. The prince was covered from neck to toe, and the boy knew, hopefully, not to touch Lev.

"Yes, Uncle." Niko stepped forward.

"Kneel for me, nephew."

Niko obeyed, taking a single knee in front of the throne. Lev straightened in his seat, and Sofia tensed when he reached with the gold scepter, but Lev touched Niko on the shoulder with it, resting the gold on the thick black cloak.

"Thank you, Prince." Lev rose and he touched Niko's crown as he walked by him—many rings, none gold.

Sofia exhaled, releasing the bottled anxiety. How did the prince live his whole life like this? She found pity for him. No wonder the queen locked him away. No wonder he could never be in the same place as the archmage. Uncle couldn't have worn more gold had he been made of it.

"Aleksei of Shield, Your Grace," a druzhina announced.

Niko got up and turned to the door. Sofia twirled and sprinted, blowing by Lev and flying into Aleksei's arms.

"You're all right," he whispered.

They were surrounded by those who increasingly felt like enemies, including Lev, so she quickly collected herself and gave Aleksei the space to look stern and composed.

"Prince," Aleksei called.

To Sofia's relief and Aleksei's as well, Niko responded with, "Cousin." He came to Aleksei and immediately crumpled, turning into a child holding back sobs.

"It's all right," Aleksei said. "It'll be all right." His scarlet gaze narrowed at Isidor who was speaking with his lord by the red dais.

"Good that you've joined us, Aleksei." Lev stepped to a song in his head and played with the gold scepter of Fedosia. "I will be tsar regent till the prince becomes of age. Assemble the *Boyar Duma*."

"Understood," Aleksei said. He had placed Niko behind himself.

"You're the elder of your house now, I suppose. Funny how that worked out," Lev said. "It's probably best the Shield forces remain at the border. If they leave the Narrow, Elfur will come pouring through it."

"Agreed," Aleksei said.

"When the sentinels and the red legion," Lev smirked, "return from Seniya, there will be no trouble. Lest they risk the prince's life needlessly." Lev stopped fidgeting and looked at Aleksei. "You will bring me Grigori, alive, and your prince will remain in the same condition."

"Give me time, I need my men," Aleksei said.

"Reasonable request. You have three days."

"Lev," Aleksei frowned, "Fedosia is enormous. I need more time."

"God created all that is, was, and shall ever be in seven days. The savior conquered hell in three. You have *three* days to produce Grigori. After that, your prince shall lose a limb for each day you're late." Lev pointed at Aleksei with the scepter. "Listen, simpleton, if you think you can buy time till the stragglers arrive from Seniya, you must think I'm as stupid as you. If the red legion crosses the Krakova bridge and you haven't delivered Grigori, the first thing I will do is cut off your cousin's head, with a dull saw so it hurts." Lev spun and sauntered back toward the throne. "Fuck you, and your house. Go fetch me the necromancer you fed, or I'll kick in your teeth, Aleksei, quite literally, so you'll be better at sucking cock."

"Oh, and by the way," he twirled, "I want Grigori alive, *alive,* ALIVE, do you hear? If I can't question him, there is no deal, so don't bring me some black bones or a face bashed in so badly it's unrecognizable. Grigori, alive, that's the deal. The next I see you, which will be within three days, you will have the necromancer for me, and until then, I'll hold onto your prince, and Soful will stay with me as well. Now, piss off, red dog."

"Three days," said Aleksei. "If he's in Krakova, I'll find him."

"Nope," said Lev. "I don't care if he's on the other side of Fedosia or the bottom of the Zapadnoi Morye. That's your problem, not mine. Three days, *wherever* he is."

"Lev, I want to speak with Aleksei," Sofia said.

"If that's how he wants to spend his time, what do I care? I've been itching to kill off the Shields anyway." He pitched the scepter at a marble pillar, making a boom as though a cannon had gone off, then plopped onto the throne, and yelled, "Wine!"

Sofia had never been to the prince's bedroom. His bed was narrow and against the wall, the size meant for a child, and above it was a collage of hundreds of saints pressed on silver leaflets. There was blood on the floor where Dominik had been lying, and Niko sat on a little stool praying to the wall of saints.

"Baltar says he will be all right," Sofia comforted the prince. She'd brought a bucket of water to clean the floor and got to it. Many of the servants had perished during the assault, Raven was still in disarray, and she didn't want to bother people over a thing she could do herself, but the smell of blood was potent enough to taste the copper.

She got up from the floor to open the window, realized Niko's windows didn't open, and cracked the door.

"Who will be all right?" Niko asked.

"Dominik," said Sofia, wringing a bloody rag into the bucket. "Isn't that who you're praying for?"

"No. Should I?" The prince frowned. "But they don't listen."

Night had claimed the city, but Aleksei hadn't returned. Sofia whispered, "Pray for your brother."

"Many of the soldiers didn't fight. They ran away rather, and I hear now they're looting my city."

"I don't claim to know what inspires loyalty, but I suspect it might be a thing that takes time," then she thought of the Pulyazin addressing Lev as His Grace, "or a miracle. Don't take the traitors to heart but many also died for you, Niko, and if they have living family, it's customary they are compensated."

Sofia peeked out the door and gave the dirty bucket to a druzhina posted there. Then she went to the washing table to clean her hands.

"Niko, do you want tea?" she asked.

"No, I want a soul." The boy cried, upset at his wall of saints.

"Hush!" Sofia rushed to close the door, then went to the prince and whispered, "Don't say such things with Lev around. He *will* kill you... is it true what he said about Grigori?"

"I can't talk about him." He shook his head.

"Why? Can he hear you?"

The boy punched his own head and startled Sofia. "Always here," he said. "Always here."

She looked into his eyes, and he didn't appear to be redlining. She didn't know if the... soulless redlined or even counted as a Shield, but those questions would have to wait till they weren't in earshot of druzhina.

"Have tea," she said, and got up to bring it.

The door opened and jolted them both. Sofia never thought the day would arrive she'd be afraid of Lev, but here it was. It wasn't Lev, though, but Aleksei returning.

She embraced him and felt better as though no trouble could exist in the world while she was in his arms.

"The sentinels arrived," Aleksei spoke with Niko while he held her. "Give me command, Niko."

"Eugene?" the prince asked.

"Yes. He's huffing and puffing trying to get into Raven. I need command, Niko. Eugene can't find Grigori. It's my city. Also, our situation is delicate, you realize. I can't have Eugene instigating a fight with the druzhina. They'll kill you the instant trouble starts."

"I'm jailed here?" Niko asked.

"Niko." Aleksei let go of Sofia and approached his brother, taking a knee before the prince. "Trust me to handle this and give me command."

"I can't." The prince's voice had grown so quiet it was hard to hear a foot away. "I'm sorry."

"What's the matter, Niko?" Aleksei held his face. "Tell me."

He shook his head, crying. "I want to see Eugene. Please send him to me."

"I can't." Aleksei rose. "It's not my castle at the moment."

"If I send him a letter, will you take it to him and not read it?" Niko asked.

"Yes."

"Promise?"

"I promise." Aleksei cupped his brother's neck. "Don't cry, brother, it'll be all right. That, I also promise. Lev knows we will *eviscerate* him if he harms you. Fedya can't help. This isn't his home. Now it's just a matter of who gets what piece of land, which title, not who dies, all right?"

"I love you as a brother."

"What do you mean as a brother? I am your brother. Now, write the damned letter. I need to have a word with Sofia."

They stepped out into the corridor where it was dim and smelled of blood. Druzhina were down the hallway because this was a dead end, but not right outside the door. He pushed her against the wall and kissed her.

"Are you all right?" he whispered.

"Yes. How are you to—"

Their mouths met again, exchanging familiar greetings and sharing the same air. He wore his sentinel gear, and the exoskeleton tugged a few strands of Sofia's hair as they got tangled in the metal, but she didn't mind it, and pulled him closer and tighter, squeezing him with all her might.

He held her nape and whispered into her ear, so soft even the shadows wouldn't hear. "I'll be taking Niko and leaving Krakova tomorrow night. Will you come with me?"

"What?" Sofia breathed. "What happened to..."

"They are listening." His eyes flicked to the druzhina at the end of the corridor. "I love you," he said much louder, kissing her, and pressing against her. "Please tell me yes."

"What happened to finding Grigori?" she mouthed. It occurred to her the Shields had surrendered Raven too easily, but she'd hoped for... peace, nonetheless. Three days was an unreasonable demand in the vastness of Fedosia. Perhaps Aleksei would have considered had Lev been more sensible with his ask.

"How the fuck do I know where he is?" he asked.

Yeah, he wasn't wrong. Sofia nodded. "I'd follow you anywhere."

"I'll see you tomorrow. Stay with Niko and make sure he's in his room tomorrow at midnight, but don't tell him anything till you have to, yeah? He talks way too much."

They stood in the dark hallway, their foreheads touching, and Aleksei caressed her cheek. The moment passed, and he took a step back. "Niko, letter?" he hollered.

The prince peeked out of the room with an envelope in his hand. "You promised," he said.

"I did." He took the envelope and tucked it under the new vambrace he had. The alchemy on it was the same as any other sentinel, missing the Durnov symbols.

"Be careful," Sofia said.

"Of course, my lady."

Sofia nodded, and together with Niko, she watched as Aleksei's long strides carried him away. "All right, then." She patted Niko's shoulder. "Now let's have tea."

Twenty-Four

Father

Eugene realized they lost the city as soon as the patrolmen in their plain armor had the gall to detain Imperial Sentinels on the Krakova bridge. They'd been running around too freely after the queen's demise, extorting coins from the nobles and merchants for 'protection' while they allowed mayhem, caused them in some instances, and the fat captain had begun to believe he had an army for hire—and someone had hired him. The Guard coin pouch ran deep, and now the prince was a hostage in his capital, or so he thought, because he hadn't believed Raven would fall so quickly. But it had. Someone had let them in, more traitors. People didn't fear the prince was the trouble. Commoners heard hangings and lashes but not sweet words and that included the captain of the patrols.

So, Eugene's evening began as shit, progressively grew worse with every street he rode through as commoners flung rocks and garbage at the sentinels, then took a complete dive into the bottomless pit when he was accosted by Pulyazin druzhina at the gates of Raven. He had to stand down because otherwise, they would have killed his prince.

As night fell, it grew too cold to sleep by the riverbank and Eugene stuffed his men into a common inn in the poor district, a warehouse full of drunks they had to kick out. It had straw on the floor for sleeping and a single stove doubling as a fireplace. No one had eaten or slept in days and tempers ran high. The red legion was some five days behind them, and Eugene's options were extremely limited till they arrived.

He sat on the barrel and was trying to eat some porridge when Ignat kicked straw in his eye. "Hey, blind fuck, there's lice here."

That was the end of his patience. Eugene punched the insubordinate brat, they rolled around on the straw drunks had spat on, pissed on too probably, and Eugene had mounted Ignat, raining down his fists, when he was picked up like a child and thrown against the table, which he tripped on, and went toppling his legs above his head.

Aleksei stood over him and hissed, "Get your shit together." The boy was in his sentinel uniform.

"The prince?" Eugene got up and dusted himself off.

"Where's Grigori?" Aleksei asked.

"Fuck if I know," Eugene grumbled.

"Fuck if you know anything," Ignat yelled.

"Enough," Aleksei snapped. "You realize patrol is stealing your fucken horses?"

A dozen sentinels dashed out the door, but the remaining eyes blinked at Eugene and Aleksei from dim corners.

"It reeks like a pigsty in here." Aleksei sneered, then spoke in a clear, loud voice. "Can everyone hear me?"

Sentinels called out from the far corners to confirm they could hear.

"The prince has restored my command, so I'm your captain now," said Aleksei.

"Thank the saints for that," Ignat muttered.

"Just your word?" Eugene asked. "I'll be seeing that order now." He looked at Aleksei's empty hands, but the boy ignored him.

"If I don't call your name you take the night off, go stay with a patron or a friend, or do whatever you wish so as long as it doesn't involve antagonizing the Pulyazin or the city patrol. Find plain clothes to wear. Tomorrow, gather at rendezvous seven to receive further orders.

"If I call your name, I'll see you at Red Manor."

Aleksei proceeded to call a dozen names which didn't include Eugene's, and sentinels filed out of the inn. Feet shuffled on the bare floor as hushed voices discussed plans for the night amongst themselves.

"What are you doing, boy?" Eugene asked.

"Cleaning up after your fucken mess," Aleksei barked.

"Whatever you're doing, you *will* include me." Eugene grabbed Aleksei's cloak when the boy began walking away from him.

"I can't have you if you won't hear me," Aleksei said, the cold red gaze flicking down to Eugene's grip, warning him.

"All right, all right." Eugene raised his hands because he did fuck up. "What are we doing? Seeing as how I'm tagging along whether I'm invited or not, it'll be better just to brief me."

"You *will* follow orders," Aleksei said. "If you can't, I *will* put a steel through you. I don't have time for your bullshit. Come to Red Manor only if you understand that. Otherwise, you're better off going to see your lady friend. I promise you that, Eugene."

Eugene sighed and contemplated his life because he took Aleksei at his word. It had been a while since he saw the baroness and thought he owed her a visit. He'd been wondering what to do when Aleksei turned at the door and produced a sealed envelope from his cloak.

"Almost forgot." He held out the envelope to Eugene. "From Niko."

Daylight grew shorter. Eugene thought the sun had only risen, he'd blinked, and it was setting again. He sat on a gold settee in the music room of the Red Manor, where the prince had danced with Sofia what seemed like a lifetime ago, and thumbed over the four words his boy had written.

Kill Lev Guard, Father.

When Eugene was a boy, he'd taught himself a little alchemy and used it to get by. He'd started thieving, then robbing, had his share of nights in dungeons and public lashings, but real trouble found him when he began forging silver coins with alchemy... The Chartorisky retainers came for him. The rest, everyone knew. He lost his eye and his honor, as little of it as he had, to the Chartorisky. Ignat wasn't wrong that he sold out his crew. There was only so much pain a man could endure before he found his breaking point. Everyone had one, no matter how brave they thought themselves.

Because of his talent in alchemy, he was given a choice between turning sentinel and being flayed. He chose to keep his skin. Eugene was good at looking out for Eugene. He'd been twenty-five at the time, too old to start meaningful training by any measure, but failure hadn't been an option, not if he valued his life. He hadn't minded when they took his ability to sire children, he thought he'd never want them anyway, more mouths to feed. Funny how time and a boy who called him Father could change a man's priorities.

He'd known something was wrong with the boy long before he put Burkhard through the wall. He could move physical objects with shadows, which Eugene had thought was dark art, and had many talks with the prince about not using it. The church burned you for that, prince and peasant alike. It was only later he learned, from Grigori nonetheless, the art was reserved for a powerful soulless only. The magic wasn't alchemy and he'd never seen it before because those possessing light, or so called the living, couldn't perform the feat. That didn't make him love the boy less, only worry for him more.

The House of White Guard was on its last leg, and he had no qualm kicking it out, but whether he was able to was the trouble. When he tried to discuss his plan to assassinate Lev and reclaim Raven, Aleksei's answer was, *'No, you will follow my orders.'*

Eugene folded the letter and tucked it under his leather armor when Aleksei came in. He'd somehow destroyed his custom gear, had been wearing a standard one yesterday, but the smith appeared to have come through, replacing his custom vambraces with the added Durnov symbols, and Aleksei sat down across from him, adjusting the alchemy and synchronizing it to his *lash*. The alchemy of movement needed a lot of tinkering and tweaking.

"You didn't want to eat or get shuteye in a warm bed, Eugene?" he asked, looking down. "We're going to be on the road for a while. I need your skeleton key, by the way."

The plan was to steal the prince, hightail it out of Krakova, and let the red legion purge Pulyazin out of the city. Except for the dozen riding with the prince, Aleksei was leaving the sentinels behind to support the legion so the commander didn't suffer extraordinary casualties against the druzhina. A reasonable plan but…

"We should do away with the Guard boy while we have the chance," Eugene said. Elbows propped on his knees, he rubbed his neck.

"We won't have peace if we do that," said Aleksei.

What peace? The boy assaulted Raven, twice now. The real reason Aleksei wouldn't touch Lev was he didn't want to upset Sofia, and Eugene didn't see it changing for the foreseeable future. He could tell him about the prince's precarious position being hostage to a necromancer, but he'd also have to tell him he was neither the prince nor his brother. Then there was the matter of Grigori wanting Sofia and that would never fly with the kid. So, Eugene was on his own.

"What happened to your gear and your key?" Eugene asked. There were three keys: the queen, the captain, and the prince. The prince had given Eugene the queen's key rather than ask Aleksei for it when he dismissed him as captain.

"Lost it," was his answer, and Eugene didn't find it satisfactory.

"You gave it to Lev," said Eugene, and Aleksei's red eyes flicked up, displeased.

"Key, Eugene."

"Say pretty please."

"Now."

"That works." Eugene mustered a smile and reached into his armor.

Every door in Raven yielded to a single key, and so did the three-inch thick, four thousand pound steel gates separating the sections of the tunnels webbing underneath the castle and veining out through the city. It wasn't a flaw. By design, the hundreds of doors opened with the same key, done so they remained functional without having to carry around a wheelbarrow full of keys. Could they be bypassed by alchemy? With enough gold, everything was possible, but it would be a painstakingly slow and one hell of an expensive journey through the dark. You could easily get lost, wander for days, and die without seeing sunlight. It was vast, was the point, and the easterners hadn't scratched the surface of it, but to be the captain of the sentinels, you had to have mapped it in your mind. Eugene didn't, but Aleksei did, and four hundred sentinels could have easily marched back into Raven, yet the captain chose to run.

'*Shut up and follow orders,*' Aleksei would bark at Eugene whenever he voiced his concern. The kid had changed. Sofia Guard had him under her thumb. So much so that Aleksei gave his skeleton key to Lev. But that was neither here nor there because they'd arrived directly under Raven.

Aleksei said something, but Eugene didn't hear him. Instead, he thought of his boy as he tapped his face armor, and the plate came down. The alchemy on his vambraces glowed, and Eugene pulled down the iron ladder, ready to climb to his last fight.

Kill Lev Guard, Father.

Twenty-Five
Define Gone

THE LIBRARIES OF ALL houses were mostly collections of the various volumes of light codices. It was almost as though their simple alchemy could be summarized in a single book, but they wanted to appear well read. Literature existed. Lev liked poetry, but every library he'd been to had the same old codices the church produced, and the library at Raven was no different. But for the section on herbology and elixir which he might look at later, the two floors of shelves were stacked with the same books Lev had seen at the White Palace. He'd brought his own reading though, and had simply sought a quieter place to sit alone, away from the druzhina bombarding him with questions he didn't have the answers to.

They wanted to see the miracle again, but Lev only ever had one true lover, and his heart was spent. Necromancy was a tempting thing when you missed those who had departed, but it was his good fortune he'd seen what the dark art had done to Vasily. It hadn't been Vasily, but something strewn together from his corpse. He'd died a lord and returned a serf, and that was offensive.

Not wanting to sit in darkness, Lev lit all the candelabras, placed his bottle of wine on the reading table, moved aside the bust that had been there, which showed how little the Shields used their library, and settled behind it with the fascinating thing he'd found—the human skin book.

Aleksei of all people had it and he'd tried translating from the language of spells. Lev had gone through his notes, and he hadn't even been close. The very first line was 'To conjure a darkling,' and he'd translated it as, 'To cast a dark spell.'

It was his lack of understanding of basic alchemy. There was no 'dark' spell as all spells were cast with light. There was 'dark' alchemy, which was probably his confusion, but dark in that case simply meant forbidden, not implying void of light. *All* known alchemy used light, even the so called 'dark' alchemy, and the shadow magic the serf Vasily played with wasn't of this world. It came from the other side of the *dver*.

Also, the symbol for 'light' could mean soul, life, energy, sunlight, purity, even gold in some instances, and Aleksei had jumbled them all. The mages would write things like 'a woman of light' when they just meant a virgin.

The book began with her confessing her light (heart) to someone only referred to as 'he'. She gifted her light (chastity), received his light (devotion), conceived light (love, not pregnancy) something, something happened, illegible because the skin had warped and chewed the ink, lost her light (she died), he gifted her life (without the soul, because necromancy), the church found out and robbed him of his light (killed him). In all these instances, Aleksei had interpreted 'light' simply as 'magic', and that had been as far as he got. Also, he'd confused faith the person (mage), faith the establishment (church), and faith plural (synod), funny how none of those was the congregation.

The trinity or three faith symbols stacked meant archmage, not many mages, and Lev smiled because Semyon had made the same mistake when they were children and had asked how one person could be many mages. The blond bear had tried learning the spell language to impress Lev, but sadly, that was not how that worked. You had to be a Guard to understand this shit and that was the point. The whole thing was one long inside joke, a nod to the Guard mindset, not a way to communicate. So, not really a language.

The book had pages and pages of torture the 'he' suffered, and the extent of the viciousness made Lev think he had been a mage. It was incredibly easy to slip from light to dark as they were the two faces of the same coin, and if necromancy in general was deemed the cardinal sin, a mage turning dark was the absolute sin for which he must suffer hell to atone.

Not understanding what this had to do with conjuring a darkling, Lev had been subjugating himself to the story of a man whose testicles were torn off, and grimacing, when Isidor found him. He closed the book with a groan not knowing which was worse, enduring the druzhina or reading about torture.

"May I trouble you for a moment, Your Grace?" he asked, pulling a chair to sit down and troubling him already.

"Only if it's important." Lev took a long drink from his wine cup. It was good to be back in Krakova. If nothing else, the wine was better.

"I hope you don't think it too forward, but I find Lady Sofia exquisite." The captain's breath was warm and sour. He'd eaten or drunk something that didn't agree with his gut. None of the Pulyazin men had been to the capital and they were being overwhelmed by the 'luxuries' of life.

"Keep in mind she's my sister." Lev frowned, finding the company, the smell, and the conversation distasteful.

"I know, Your Grace. That's why I'm asking for your permission to have her."

Lev's right eye twitched. "She's not a horse. I can't *give* her to you."

"But she is a woman."

"Really?" asked Lev, and heard the sarcasm whistle as it flew over the dirty brown crown of the druzhina. "The way it works here," he tapped the table, "is that you can ask for my permission to court her but whether she accepts, that's up to her." He hadn't been thrilled when Uncle married her off to some old bastard and didn't mean to do it again.

"Court..." Isidor twisted his neck side to side, releasing the cricks, then cracked his knuckles. "In Bone Country, we just marry."

"You want to marry Sofia?" Lev didn't know why he was still entertaining this conversation other than that he was trapped. "Let it be known she murdered her last husband."

"I can handle her." He grinned.

That was it. Lev closed the book, gathered Aleksei's notes, and got up from the table. It had proved too much to hope Isidor would know his place and leave. He wished Konstantin was here to put the fucken druzhina in his place so Lev didn't have to be rude himself. He *was* rude but didn't want to appear it.

"So, may I court her?" Isidor rose as well.

"By court, if you mean ram her, absolutely fucken not. I'll feed your pecker to the dogs while it's still attached to you."

Things like this made him feel unsafe, demanding a spectacle as though he was an exotic animal from the Paradise Islands, and threatening his sister. This was why the archmage used to perform light shows, to fool buffoons like him, but Lev didn't have the patience for the horseshit.

Grumbling to himself because Semyon wasn't here to listen to him whine, he meandered through the dim corridors holding a single lantern and the cursed book till he realized he was lost. He'd ended up on the Shield side of Raven, dark as doom and black as hell.

He wandered through a hallway with an entire watchman stuck inside a wall. They'd left him there, Lev guessed, because they couldn't pry apart the armor to scrape out the corpse. Blackened and dried, it'd been months since he died. What did this? The walls glittered as the darksteel caught the passing light of the lamp.

He'd been complaining in his head to the ghost of his lover about the awful extensions the Shields had attached to what once was a Guard palace when he heard the distinctive click of a sentinel crossbow, threw the lamp, and ducked as the bolt whispered by and punched into the wall at the end of the hallway. He curled behind a thick stone candlestand as a plume flew into his face from another bolt, took cover behind a pillar, retreating still, more bolts each with a click that announced it. He couldn't see the bastard but could fry the whole corridor, and tossed...

No fire, nothing came out, but he'd opened himself by peeking out and flicking his wrist like a fool, and was rewarded by a bolt to the shoulder, the darksteel missing his heart by inches and tearing through the front and back as it passed clear through him.

Lev rolled and dashed into the only open door, a bedchamber without any windows, and cornered himself. The gold he had on wasn't gold, he *just* noticed—the perils of being a drunk asshole. Soful probably didn't know, but now he had a vendetta against the swindler luminary.

Lev drew his blade, held his single-handed weapon in guard, and pressed his back against the wall. Ideally, the free hand would produce magic but not only he didn't have the gold to pay for it, he couldn't even lift his left arm, and blood soaked through his sleeve and trickled down his fingers.

He thought it may be Aleksei and had been worried because there wasn't a way to counteract the *lash* without any alchemy or a long range weapon. But it wasn't him, and the sentinel blocked Lev's strike with his vambrace, and there was a penalty for that. The Apraksin saber slashed through the gold on the vambrace. Get enough strikes and it would damage the symbols and disturb the alchemy.

Lev didn't know if the sentinel was alone, didn't wish to find out in a room without a way out, attacked, flurried, and escaped.

Without a lamp or a single window, the corridor was as dark as an asshole, he was knocking unknown shit over, making loud clangs while dodging whizzing bolts, and ran to where he saw a sliver of light. Another fucken dead end, the throne room of the mad queen, and there was a tall window behind the darksteel throne, the moonlight spilling through it. Thank the saints the skies had been clear, and Lev could see semblances of shapes.

He hid behind a pillar and held his breath, waiting for his sight to adjust to the dimness. Lev heard the sentinel looking around for him, someone with an uneven gait, an old injury perhaps, and there was a penalty for that. Lev blitzed him, they crossed steel, and back and forth they danced.

Darksteel's superiority was in its adaptability to Shield alchemy, not durability or strength, and though Lev wasn't a hard hitter like Semyon, the sentinel couldn't block without damaging his weapon.

"You started too old." Lev slashed across his thigh and kicked him in the throat when he took a knee. "And you're blind in the left eye."

Getting up, the sentinel blocked with his vambrace—penalty.

"And you're too cocky." Hoarse as though he smoked all day, the voice wasn't anyone Lev recognized.

Sidestepping a spear thrust—another thing he kept doing, needlessly alternating between weapons, and it meant he couldn't figure Lev out—Lev caught the sentinel's hand with a strike, gushing red. Contact with the vambrace, another penalty, and now that one was useless.

"So what? I'm Lev of White Guard." He flurried. He liked doing it, and Semyon would call him a show-off. "It's not conceit when I'm better than you."

Lev circled left, to the sentinel's blind side, and swept his legs, his blade clanging against the face plate as he *just* missed his neck. The sentinel rolled away, crawling into the dark, and Lev pursued him, but he stepped on something that gave way under his feet. There was a fucken hole in the ground. He caught himself with his sword and scampered to climb out as flames chased him up. Fire licked at his boot heels as Lev pulled himself up, his sword gone, tumbling down the hell hole.

"Too cocky, kid. Told you so."

Knee to the face and star exploded. Half dazed, Lev kicked to get away. Another thing opened under his hand, nearly plunging him face first into another hole, and flames shot out and singed his lashes and hair.

"What the fuck is this place?" Columns of fire erupted, and the sudden bright flashes meant now he couldn't see shit.

"Red queen's throne room. She used to execute people here. Put them in the incinerator," the hoarse voice said.

The exoskeleton connected with his jaw, and Lev bit his tongue and tasted blood. Light danced in his vision, the remnant of glaring fire an inch from his face, and he couldn't see the way out or the sentinel.

By instinct alone, he caught the darksteel blade with a naked hand, and it sliced through his palm as he slapped the blade away from his heart and it pierced into his shoulder. To not let him slice through his entire torso, Lev pushed into the blade and grabbed it with both hands. Now he moved with the sentinel, finding himself at the end of a shit stick.

The sentinel kicked him back to free his sword, and the steel made a sucking noise as it exited his flesh. Lev twisted to miss a strike, the blade passing by close enough to hear the hiss but caught a wicked knee to the ribs, knocking his breath out completely.

Lev scooted till his back was against the wall and sat there grimacing with blood mist in his exhales.

"Go see your family, kid."

No alchemy, no weapon, the darksteel caught the silver moonlight as it swooped down like a diving goshawk, magnificent creatures. In his mind, the sun got in his eyes, spilling gold through the branches overhead. Semyon was on top of him. *Do you remember that, Syoma?*

The grating of a sword striking a shield jolted Lev out of the daze.

"What the fuck are you doing?" A bark, and the sentinel tumbled.

"Move out of the way, kid." He was getting up, and Lev frowned, trying to focus his eyes. Why were they so bad, suddenly? Did he get hit in the face? He wiped his eyes and saw blood. He had a cut on the forehead, that was all.

"Not a kid. I'm your fucken captain and you had orders, Eugene." Aleksei shoved his sentinel back.

Trying to get his bearings, Lev leaned against the wall and pushed himself up. The sentinel lunged at Aleksei and discovered the reason why Lev didn't like fighting Aleksei, that fucken *lash*. It was damn long, had no predictable geometry of motion, and had nasty teeth when it got you—he remembered the steeplechase.

Lev spat blood while the sentinel got schooled by his captain. He'd been shot, his left shoulder was chewed, and his palms pulsed hot from catching a blade with his bare hands—he'd had better days.

He'd been looking down when his breath steamed. It hadn't been *that* cold. He looked up and a spray of ice got in his eyes. More fighting, the Pulyazin arrived. Thanks for nothing, that took far too long considering they had Raven 'under control'.

Worse than nothing, all they did was occupy Aleksei, and now the lunatic sentinel came at him again. He'd lost his face plate, and Lev saw he had a scar along the left side of his face.

What was his problem, Lev would ask, had he been not too busy dodging swings, wide and slow now because the old man was tired. Out of form, blind, and didn't obey orders, what kind of sentinel was this?

Lev ran around the room, because he couldn't see the exit in the dark, while being chased by the one-eyed sentinel. Then there was light, bright and red, as flames erupted from the hell holes the room was rigged with, and Lev turned to see Aleksei kick a druzhina into the fire. Then the *lash* hissed by Lev's face and took a bite out of the wall between him and the lunatic.

"Stand down, Eugene! What the fuck!" Aleksei grabbed his sentinel while Lev fled, or tried to... Did this room not have a door? Then how did he get in?

"I knew you'd do this," said the sentinel, on his ass and on the floor when Lev looked over his shoulder. "You're not thinking with your thinking organ, kid." That got him a boot heel to the face.

Carefully, Lev peeked down the hole the druzhina had fallen into. It was too dark for a beat, then he saw charred black bones at the bottom of the glowing pit and jumped back as the flames erupted again.

Druzhina limbs were sprawled on the floor, and Lev stepped on something he assumed was a gut by the squelch it made. He spotted the door, finally, but now there were more sentinels in his face. Finding his throat at the tip of a darksteel blade, he raised his hands which were still bleeding. In the back, Aleksei and the lunatic fought—with words.

"Hello, Ruslan," Lev said. He knew a couple of the sentinels who'd joined the shitty party.

"Good evening, Lord Lev."

"Captain," one called, stepping over the dead druzhina.

"What are you doing here?" Aleksei cleaned and sheathed his sword.

"The prince and Lady Sofia are gone."

"Define gone," Aleksei turned, frowning.

"Not in Raven, Captain."

Aleksei looked at Lev for answers. Lev shrugged with his good shoulder. "Fuck if I know."

"Where is Fedya?" Aleksei came over, and now the gathering had turned into a shitty dinner party with men standing around and holding their dicks—well, that actually sounded like a good party—while Lev was losing blood and about to swoon.

"You probably shouldn't seek him out, Aleksei," Lev said. "You just killed his druzhina. Fedya likes men."

"I don't care what Fedya likes. Where's Sofia?"

Where *was* Sofia? Lev thought he was saying something, but no, he passed out. Hit his head on the floor and everything.

I was outclassed by a blind old man, Syoma. Without you, I'm shit like this.

Twenty-Six
I Told You So

The soldiers' quarters were a pitiful place with bare stone walls and rows of narrow wooden beds, flimsy like folding chairs. The sentinels had made it home, however, hanging keepsakes from the wall along with their gear. There had been only five sentinels at Raven during the Pulyazin assault, three were injured including Dominik, and two had sadly been killed. One of the dead had a silver locket hanging from the head of the vacant bed, a gift from a lady, no doubt. War was a harrowing thing, collecting lives unlived and leaving only stories to be told.

The quarters were tidy, everything folded and stacked, the floor swept, and it smelled of dry rosemary and lavender. Sofia wanted to check on the wounded and brought food. She'd asked Niko to dismiss them, explaining three sentinels wouldn't make a difference should the castle full of Pulyazin turn hostile and that they should go home to get better care. Dominik for one was from Krakova, but her true reason was she knew Aleksei would come tonight and didn't want the wounded to get left behind to be tortured for amusement once their prince fled.

Dominik had been lying with his cloak pulled over his head and got up when Sofia came in. He helped her carry the tray of food. They had a little kitchen area with a wooden table and a long bench where Sofia set the meals down. The corner was by the fireplace and warm.

"Thank you for your concern, my lady." He sat down to eat but the other two remained asleep. Perhaps they were sedated.

It was just some broth and bread, but it was warm, and she'd quarreled with the Pulyazin cook to get the small portions. The Raven had a multitude of cooks, of course, but Lord Fedya was paranoid about being poisoned and had barred anyone who hadn't come with him from the kitchen and storage areas.

Sofia added wood to the fire, turned the logs, then sat down with Dominik. "How are you feeling?"

"Not too well, my lady." He smiled though his face was ashen from the blood loss. "How is the prince?"

"He's fine. Also, he says you should go home." Sofia flicked her gaze to the sleeping sentinels. "Are they able to walk?"

"Yes." He studied her while he chewed bread. Keen, this one. "Did the captain say something?"

"He says to get out of here before tonight," she muttered, blowing on a spoonful of soup. "I'll speak with Lev in a moment and get permission. I'm on my way to him. Gather your things, yeah?"

He nodded. "Do you know what happened to Lord Semyon?"

"He died at Usolya, I heard," Sofia said.

"That's too bad."

"Yeah." Sofia let it sink in. "All of you are friends, aren't you? Lev, Daniil, Semyon..."

"We know each other," was his answer. "Eugene arrived, I heard."

"Same," said Sofia. She hadn't seen him.

"He's not fit for command. He can barely read. It was a mistake taking the sentinels to Seniya. We already have a garrison there. It's our city."

"You're a highborn, right?" Sofia remarked.

"My father was a baron here in Krakova."

"What happened to him?" she asked.

"Died in a duel over a card game. My mother remarried, chose some merchant who had money. Silver over title is the saying, I believe. He kicked me out and I had nowhere to go, so," he shrugged, "I came to Raven."

"Oh, so you *don't* have a home here," said Sofia. "Do you have someplace you can stay?"

He made a smug face—he had plenty of places to go to. And when Sofia asked if the other two had friends in the city, his answer was, "We're Imperial Sentinels."

After Sofia finished with Dominik, she went to find Lev, meaning to tell him to let the sentinels leave. She didn't expect a problem, but who knew?

Lev was in the domed room where Niko used to hold his assembly with the old serious men, the ministers of every conceivable thing. What they discussed, Sofia didn't know because she wasn't a minister, but Lev was splayed out on the wool carpet with a peacock, a bottle of wine by his side.

"It's odd." He sat up. "I thought this was Raven, but I find myself surrounded by our shit. Look, that's the bust of Uncle Pasha." He pointed and Sofia laughed. Niko had mistaken him for a saint perhaps. "And this carpet," he tapped his heel, "my mother had it made for the archmage. And that mirror is from the servants' quarters. The frame is yellow paint, but I suppose the dimwit child thinks it's gilded."

That, Sofia assumed Niko had done purposefully. The prince knew very well what was gold and what was shiny yellow paint and surrounded himself with the latter. Lev on the other hand still had the forged gold on. At this point, she was only waiting for him to figure it out and planned to blame the luminary. She'd had the entire conversation in her head.

"Did you know I pissed in that vase?"

"Why?" Sofia sat down on the carpet with him. She smelled dust and it certainly hadn't come from the White Palace this way. "Get up, Lev, the floor is dirty."

"It was Mother's favorite vase, and I was angry with her."

"So this was a long time ago and now just now? That's good." She got up and pulled him up. "What happened to your knights, by the way?"

"Freezing their balls in the nowhere country, supposedly rallying people for my cause. Without church couriers, it's impossible to know what's going on. They probably don't know I'm here."

Compared to yesterday, he was much more himself, and Sofia hugged him, patting his back as though he was still a child. The moment passed, then she asked, "There are three injured sentinels at Raven. They're doing nothing. Is it all right if they leave? One is Dominik, I think you know him."

"Yeah, yeah, sure. What do I care?"

"Can you tell the druzhina?"

"Sure."

Lev told a random Pulyazin soldier in the corridor and a breath later Isidor appeared demanding to know why as though it had been a serious infraction. Sofia didn't like him. He gawked at her and kept touching her.

"Do you know they make us big out in Bone Country?" Isidor asked.

"You're not that tall," Sofia said.

He flicked down to his privates and Sofia burned. She wasn't accustomed to men speaking to her in such a way. They also made them crude out in Bone Country.

"Is this how you talk to a lady?" Sofia asked.

"Pulyazin women, of course not, but you're a zapadnik."

That just meant from the west, but she assumed he meant it as a slur. Lev was speaking with another druzhina and didn't hear him, which was probably good.

Sofia had been walking away, when she heard, "I can kill the Shield boy if you're worried about him."

She turned and sized him up. Isidor was larger than Aleksei but not significantly. Either way, she didn't want trouble and smiled at him.

"You are so fine," Isidor said.

Lev caught that. "Fuck off, Isidor."

After they left, Sofia whispered, "Perhaps don't be rude. There are *so* many of them."

"So what? Who cares?" He should, was her point. But he missed it, and said, "If you fancy him, go at it."

"Lev!"

"I don't know." He threw up his arms. "It's not like you have good judgment in that regard."

"Never you mind... Aleksei asked for my hand, and I accepted."

"Nope." He took his wine and fled.

"What does that mean?" Sofia called after him.

"It means no, Soful. No, no, no, no, no..." The no trailed down the corridor and faded with his footsteps. But she could still hear it in her head, no, no, no...

Then she realized she didn't get to speak to him about Grigori or ask him to be more reasonable with his deadline and ran after him. She also hadn't talked to him about the stranger but that would be a *long* conversation, perhaps for another time.

"Lev!"

Niko had packed a leather valise and stuffed it under his bed with his cloak folded on top. Aleksei had spoken with him about leaving tonight, assumed Sofia, and pulled down the bed skirt to hide the bags when Isidor announced himself outside the prince's door.

Niko was curled up on the bed, the scarlet eyes staring blankly. A sad child these days, he often cried himself to sleep, and Sofia couldn't help remembering how much better he'd been doing when the queen was alive. Though she still didn't understand how, Niko did kill his mother to save Aleksei, which she was infinitely grateful for. She didn't want to disturb the prince and stepped out to see what Isidor wanted.

She closed the door gently behind her and stood in the corridor, clutching her hands in front of her. Servants lit the candles as the light grew scarce, and Sofia sat down on the red brocade settee along the wall when Isidor asked her to. The prince liked saints so much it was almost believable his father would be a Guard. An oil painting depicting the creation mythology hung on the opposite wall, God holding a wisp of light, the first ever soul.

Being polite, Sofia waited for Isidor to speak his mind as he was the one who'd approached.

"After Grigori is killed, my lord will be returning home, but he will be leaving men to tend to His Grace, and I volunteered."

"Oh."

"It was denied."

"Oh."

"So, I hope you like Bone Country because I'll be taking you with me," he said.

"Oh…" Sofia tried to think of a polite way of going about it. "I'm unavailable, I'm afraid."

"You're neither young nor virtuous, Lady Guard. I'd hoped you'd be gracious as I've given you a proper offer."

"I am." She blinked, trying to escape the most uncomfortable conversation she'd ever had with a stranger. "But you must ask Lev. He's the head of the family now. My father is deceased."

"That's reasonable." He rose. "Where is His Grace?"

"What? Now?" Sofia didn't have a fan so she flapped her hand instead. "Of course, now. I mean to have you tonight."

Thank the saints she wouldn't be here then. "I believe he was looking for the library. There are two at Raven and I don't know which…"

He got up and marched away, but not before turning with a grin. "I'll be back."

She took that as a threat. Suddenly it didn't feel like such a bright idea to have sent the three sentinels home. Now she had no one. She spoke with Lev about giving Aleksei more time to find Grigori because she hoped the situation could be resolved with fewer losses of lives. Lev being tsar regent wasn't the worst of ideas because Niko was… Well, he corrupted gold. But that conversation soured quickly. Lev's mood swung wildly and turned on a silver coin at the mention of the supposed necromancer. So many unbelievable things were happening at once—the stranger, Niko's trouble with gold, tales of necromancy, Lev claiming tsar, Pulyazin invading Raven—at times it felt like a very long, tiring hallucination.

Not that it mattered but she didn't believe Isidor's affection was legitimate. The captain of the druzhina fancied he was having some type of rivalry with the captain of the sentinels and Sofia was a part of it. Aleksei didn't care about Isidor and wouldn't have known his name had he not threatened Sofia at the Red Manor, so the competition was in the druzhina's head, but perhaps that was the most dangerous place for it to be.

Sofia returned to the prince's room and lit the candles.

"You shouldn't do that," he whispered.

Sofia thought he was speaking in his sleep and turned, but he was staring at the dark corner of his room.

"Brighter lights make darker shadows, did you know?"

"It'll be all right, Niko. Don't worry so much." Sofia smiled. "Do you want me to make you a tonic while we wait for Aleksei?"

"Lev is difficult to kill because he doesn't cast a shadow, but you're not like him. You're not a Guard."

"I look like my mother. She had dark curls." Sofia sat down on the prince's bed and ruffled his hair. "Lev is not a monster. He's a human man who has a shadow. Even the archmage had a shadow."

"No, different shadow." Niko frowned. "I mean shadow art can't touch a true Guard. But I can do this," he said, and Sofia's hand moved up against her will, and in the shadow cast on the wall, someone stood there holding her hand. She froze and couldn't get up or run. Her scream was stifled by an unseen hand. "So you're not a Guard." The scarlet eyes flicked to her, appearing nearly black in the lack of light. "That's too bad." He sat up. "You keep asking, so I'll tell you. This is how I killed the queen." He pointed at the shadow. "When I tear that apart. You come apart. It doesn't matter if you're a watchman or a bull, your shadow weighs nothing."

He got up and pulled out his bag and cloak from under the bed. "We have to go because Grigori told me to bring you. He's under Raven. He's been there the entire time. It's too bad Lev didn't look there. Monsters do hide in the dark."

He put on his cloak, shouldered his leather bag, lit a lantern, and carried it, saying, "I can see in the dark, but I need the light for the shadow."

Sofia said nothing. She was stunned. Her mind couldn't comprehend the horror as she felt like a stranger in her own body, a flea in a horse's mane taking a ride as she followed Niko behind a paper screen, the wall opening as the prince pressed on it.

"I didn't put that there. It was just the way Raven was built, where some rooms have a secret passageway. The room looks small because of this." He took her into the space between the walls and closed the door behind them. "I picked this room for this reason. Five other rooms in Raven do the same. The queen's bedchamber is one. I would sometimes go there when the queen had Aleksei, to see if he was all right because it wasn't the first time she hurt him."

They walked through the dark, tight space, then descended a wooden ladder, winding and suffocating, till a sudden surge of cold air greeted them. They were under the castle.

Through a maze of corridors, Sofia mindlessly followed the prince, a hostage in her body as he took her through iron doors, each opening with the skeleton key the prince had.

"I killed Burkhard because he tried to take Eugene away. I should have let him leave, then he wouldn't have died tonight. Grigori made me throw his life away. Eugene can't kill Lev. Your brother is superior in every way. He'll die trying, though, and that is what Grigori wants, for me to have no one.

"With this, I've betrayed Aleksei, though I love him so much. This is why the soulless are dangerous. We don't have a will of our own, not when it conflicts with our maker's. I've asked and asked the saints for light, so I didn't have to do this. But they don't listen. I've told you so."

Through the twisting corridors, Sofia followed the prince. She fainted, came to, and found herself walking still. There was no escape. Even if she died, her heart burst from the terror, she'd continue ambling after the prince.

They climbed, ascended finally, and the door above them was already open. The cold air smelled of tobacco smoke and the stars twinkled in the clear sky.

Niko closed the hatch and locked it after they came out. A black coach drawn with six horses waited, and a tall man in a hooded cloak smoked pipe outside it. She recognized the driver as Vasily Apraksin, though he didn't look too well with half his face terribly scarred from a burn.

"Oh, dear girl, you must be cold. Where are your manners, Niko?" The tall man had a calm, friendly voice, but as he removed his cloak and draped it over Sofia, she saw it was Grigori. Shamelessly, he still wore the white robe of a mage under it.

They climbed into the large coach. The shutters were closed, and Niko hung the lantern from a hook, the light rocking gently as the carriage moved to the knocking rhythm of the six horses at a canter.

"Grigori, I'm tired," said Niko.

"Chain her then." The smile never left Grigori. His pale blue eyes were large and haunting, jarring against his long dark hair and thick beard, but the smile made him warm, as though he was someone kind.

Niko put a collar around Sofia's neck, the chain on it bolted to the floor. "Please don't make him hurt you. I can't help you."

Sofia gasped as though emerging from the water and taking her first breath after drowning. She heaved and panted, reaching for the door.

"Please don't do that," Niko begged.

The door didn't open but Sofia screamed and screamed, and after her voice cracked and throat turned sore, Grigori said, "Good, now you've gotten that out of you. But do that again and I'll crush your voice box with the pommel of this sword."

Sofia wheezed, fanning herself with both hands. Talking about necromancy, reading about dark alchemy, and looking at a necromancer and a soulless sitting across from her inside the coach she was chained to weren't the same. The difference between this and Murmia was the incident at the church had been so unreal there was a chance it had been a dream, but this, she knew she was being kidnapped by a necromancer.

Where was the stranger when she needed him? Sofia manically pulled the door, rattling the handle and the latch but it didn't open. It must be locked from the outside. But just as she thought of him, Sofia heard the stranger. *"Give us a name."*

"Grigori."

"Give us a name."

"Grigori! Grigori!"

That wasn't his name was the reason the stranger didn't accept. Grigori didn't hear the whispers and thought Sofia called him, and looked at her, his patience thinning at her antics, but Niko's scarlet eyes had ballooned. His gaze swung between Sofia and Grigori.

"What is that?" he whispered, too soft for Grigori to have heard over the knocking of the hooves, the jingle of the tack, the slight squeaking of the wheels, and the groaning of the wooden boards, but Sofia had been looking straight at the prince and saw he'd heard the stranger. So it wasn't only in her head. Of course not, she'd known that, but she had a way of denying things till they kidnapped her in the middle of the night.

"Grigori," tested Sofia but the stranger was gone. The fear remained on Niko's face, though. "What do you want with me?" she asked the necromancer.

As an answer, he smiled, then placed the bite of his wooden pipe into his mouth.

Twenty-Seven

The Plan

Lev sat on the floor of the ballroom at Raven and whispered with Fedya while a string quartet played in the corner. The musicians were far enough they couldn't eavesdrop over their instruments, and there was no one else in the ballroom. They thought Lev was eccentric so this wasn't strange, but the conversation couldn't be overheard in a city where silver bought information. Lady Guard was missing, and they were searching for her. That was all. It could *not* be known they'd lost the crown prince. Otherwise, there would be war. Not the game of houses they'd been playing so far, but all out war for the throne.

Word was sent to a Shield commander called Volg to come keep order in Krakova, pretend as though it was affairs as usual. Lev didn't like his literal name was *wolf*, but Aleksei trusted him and that would have to do. Pulyazin couldn't keep the capital, not without holding the prince hostage, and Lev had no misgivings about that. Shield was a house of war with numerous garrisons in the west, and they'd swallowed the Chartorisky in a handful of days.

He'd pressed the prince's seal directing effort for the rebuilding of Seniya, the train station, giving orders for the Durnov to fix or rebuild their transportation machine, and for Fedya to take with him grain enough to survive the winter. He'd gone through the grain reserves, and they were woefully short. Everything had to move, including the grain trade with Elfur as though Nikolas was at Raven still.

"Yes, Your Grace," Fedya said to Lev's request to transfer Raven over *peacefully* when Volg arrived, and to brief him on the specifics which couldn't be written down or sent with a messenger.

At the end of an hour long conversation, the lord rose with Lev and bowed. "May the saints watch over you, Your Grace."

"May the saints watch over us all," answered Lev and headed for the door.

He was getting the hang of Raven now but would occasionally take a wrong turn and find himself at a dead end. The castle was built by a madman.

Only Dominik was in the soldiers' quarters, everyone else out searching for Soful though they'd known she wasn't in the city two days ago. The sentinel sat on a long bench by the fireplace, writing on a dark wooden table.

"Lord Lev," he said.

Semyon had been right that Dominik was pretty. He looked like a statue from every angle and even the curls of his brown locks fell over his face perfectly, so he could comb them back gracefully as he looked up.

Lev sat down at the table and poured himself wine from the clay pitcher. "Anything?" he asked.

"Vasily Apraksin was seen driving a black coach over the Krakova bridge. Multiple patrolmen saw him but assumed it must be someone else because the lord himself had been driving. They are useless like that, but we haven't been able to reorganize them since the queen's passing because of, you know, the war with you. We just don't have the resources."

"The bridge?" Lev asked, hopeful that there had been a carriage. Because then, maybe Sofia was still alive. He was afraid the necromancer kidnapped the prince but killed his sister and threw her in the sewer canal. That was still a possibility, but the news of the carriage was better than hearing three male riders left.

"Or it may be a decoy. We don't know," said Dominik. "If the church could help spread the word to towns close by it would be helpful."

"I tried. But the aviary is in disarray," Lev said. "Apparently, they can't wipe their ass without my uncle. What are we doing? Where's Aleksei?"

"Throne room," he said, then clarified, "Not yours, ours."

"We have yours and ours?"

"Her Majesty's throne room. That's one with fire pits in the floor. I heard you had some trouble there." He smirked.

Lev imagined Aleksei sitting about on the throne and frowned, and as he got up to go find Aleksei, Dominik asked, "Are you able to find your way, Lord Lev?"

He wanted to say yes but didn't want to waste time being lost, so he said, "Would you show me?"

"Of course, my lord." Dominik set the quill aside and rose. Then as they walked through the dim corridors of the Shield side of Raven, he said, "I heard Lord Semyon passed. My condolences. He was a friend."

"I bet he was," Lev said.

"Not like that, Lev." Dominik looked over his shoulder. "Skuratov loved you."

"You're very direct," said Lev.

"Sorry."

"No, that's all right."

One eternity later—Lev would have definitely gotten lost on his own—they reached the black throne room.

Aleksei sat at the foot of the dais, the throne behind him, red, black, and empty. All his alchemy alight, and his eyes burning like coal, Lev found Aleksei menacing but didn't show it and marched toward him. The half blind sentinel who nearly killed Lev was chained to an iron grate and didn't look to be doing too well, bleeding all over the place.

The darksteel dagger in Aleksei's hand moved on its own like a small creature wrapping around his wrist, around and around. Red eyes flicked to Lev, stalking him as he crossed the hall. He had no idea how Soful found him attractive. The fucker was temperamental, swung from insane to asshole, brooding always as though he was about to cry or kill, and sounded in pain even when he was just having tea in the sun. Women were strange.

"You need me," groaned the half blind sentinel.

"I disagree," Aleksei said.

The chain yanked the sentinel to his feet, many fine hooks burrowed into his skin. He moaned, then breathed blood. As Lev got closer, he realized darksteel snakes slithered everywhere, on the floor and wrapping around the pillars, as though the room was alive. Aleksei's *lash* had multiplied.

Lev questioned whether he should be approaching the bastard at all, but did anyway.

"What?" Aleksei asked.

"Although it may be more smoke without the fire, I think Grigori is Elfurian." Lev got right to it. "I think he's taking the prince and going home. He's insane enough to want war, and taking Nikolas to Elfur would certainly start one. Murmia is the closest port. I'm leaving, but I'd like you to give me sentinels." The port was warm, Pulyazin alchemy would be weak, this wasn't their neck of the woods, and leaving the city,

Lev would run into Shield forces. He didn't have time for the trouble and it was easier to travel with sentinels.

"Vasily Apraksin was seen crossing the Krakova bridge, driving a black coach, Captain," said Dominik.

"When?" Aleksei asked.

"We *just* found out, Captain. But three nights ago, according to the patrol. I'm still verifying..." Seeing Aleksei's reaction, Dominik wisely took a step back. Lev thought Dominik had been stalling in the soldiers' quarters, afraid to break the news to his captain. "They don't report to us, Captain," he explained.

"It's a coach, Aleksei," said Lev. "They have to stay on the road. I can ride them down, but I want men and horses." Three days was a great lead, but it was doable in Lev's mind.

"Apraksin is a soulless now, you say." Aleksei considered the claim. "What happened to your knights, Lev? Light users would be nice. We have no protocol on dealing with dark arts."

"Jerking off in the east," said Lev. "Not going to lie, communication has become a major problem since Uncle's death. I don't see how because he didn't use to hand feed the pigeons, and it occurs to me this luminary fucker is doing it purposefully to hinder me." He grimaced, remembering the fucker gave Sofia forged gold.

"Take me," breathed the tortured sentinel.

"You don't obey orders," said Aleksei. "Niko *was* at Raven when we arrived. They slipped out during your bullshit. Should the prince perish, it's your fault. Sit here and revel in that while you rot alive, Eugene." Aleksei rose. "We leave with a dozen. Make the preparations, Doma."

"Yes, Captain." Dominik bolted.

"You should probably stay." Aleksei gathered his scattered gear from the dais. "So Fedya doesn't get any ideas about sitting on the throne. It'll turn to shit if Volg arrives and Fedya doesn't surrender Raven.

"I trust him," Lev said.

"Famous last words," Aleksei said.

"What happens when the prince returns and this Volg doesn't surrender the power?" Lev challenged.

"I don't actually care," was Aleksei's answer, and they had been walking out together when the chained sentinel called from behind.

"Take me, Aleksei! Take me with you."

"What do I need old lying dogs for?" Aleksei snapped.

"I know his true name. I know Grigori's Elfurian name," yelled the sentinel. "If you can't catch up to them, you have no way of finding him without me. Take me, Aleksei."

Aleksei stopped, and Lev turned, unimpressed. "Is it Federik or Sebastian?" Lev asked. "The whole of Elfurian male populace is named so." He pulled Aleksei's elbow, then wiped his hand on his cloak when he realized he'd touched him. "You can't find a man by his name alone, Aleksei. Elfur isn't a town. It's an empire. Our time is better spent riding down Vasily rather than watching our backs with him behind us."

"He won't betray Niko," Aleksei said, hesitating and wasting time.

"Then give me his name, Eugene."

"Take me, Aleksei. You will need me," the sentinel said.

"Let's go, Aleksei. It won't matter," said Lev.

But he didn't listen. Aleksei turned and marched toward the sentinel. He grabbed him by the chains, tearing at the skin, and said, "Did you think Burkhard was cruel, Eugene? He wasn't. Should you lose me Sofia, I'll show you cruelty."

"No doubt." The sentinel wheezed. "Now free me, boy. We're wasting daylight."

To the half blind sentinel's credit, he was as tough as Skuratov iron and was mounted already, his pack horse saddled and beside him, when Lev stepped out onto the carriageway. No carriages, though, no time to stop, everyone would be riding with a spare horse. He checked his tack, stepped on his stirrup, and swung a leg over his tall white horse.

Aleksei's nasty black gelding side eyed Lev's mount. He recalled the steed from when the queen attacked White Palace.

"He kicks. Also bites," Dominik warned, gesturing at Aleksei's horse.

"I'm not surprised," Lev said. Everyone mounted, dressed in plain so they didn't immediately announce their arrival in Murmia. They were in front of Raven waiting on Aleksei, and when the captain burst out through the door carrying a saddlebag which he packed on the largest horse, Lev sneered. "Taking a last moment shit, Aleksei?"

"I'm bringing gold for your whiny ass," Aleksei said, yanking the harness to check the saddlebag. "I thought your alchemy was expensive."

It was. Lev packed boots, cloaks, change of attires, wine, opium, the skin book, and had also found room for gold cuffs.

"Brought a map of Elfur just in case." Aleksei jumped on his horse. "You don't have one, I suppose."

Lev had never even seen one. His whole plan was to catch Vasily on Fedosian soil, and if they couldn't... He didn't know.

"Let's go. Try not to cheat this time." Aleksei kicked his mount and the thing bolted.

Lev caught up. They'd trot as much as possible but galloping in this weather, unless they had the carriage in sight, would waste the horses. "You burned down my home, my father is dead, and you want to bring up the fucken steeplechase?"

"I'm sorry about Lord Pyotr," Aleksei said.

"Don't flatter yourself. Pyotr Guard killed himself."

"If you say so." Aleksei pulled up ahead.

They *weren't* trotting was Lev's guess. All right, he'd play. *Let's race to Murmia, then.*

Twenty-Eight
Slowly, Terribly, Poorly

SOFIA REALIZED THE HORSES weren't typical when they didn't eat, drink, or rest for two days. They could see at night, weren't squeamish about the wolves howling in the woods, and the only time the carriage stopped was so one of the occupants could piss. She once tried her luck fleeing into the woods, was captured immediately, and brought back kicking and screaming by Grigori himself.

He beat Niko with a riding crop for losing her, discouraging her from trying it again, but she did hiss, "His brother is going to kill you."

"A soulless has no brothers. He only has death and his maker." Grigori slammed the door and banged on the cabin roof. The calmness was skin deep, a falsity like the archmage's kindness, and he was a volatile and violent person.

If she ran, Sofia realized, this evil man was going to kill Niko. Whatever else Niko was, he was the prince of Fedosia, Aleksei's brother, and most of all, a scared boy.

Then her mind churned, trying to conjure up a way of killing Grigori. When she got mad enough to wish death upon someone, the stranger would creep in the shadows.

"Give us a name."

Niko squeezed her hand and flicked his gaze to the front where the driver's seat was. If Niko could hear the stranger, so could Vasily. She had no idea what was happening but thought only of where Grigori might be taking them and what he might do once he got there.

The Church of Murmia. Sofia shivered with the terrible memories. Beyond the red carpeted narthex she stood in was the nave where the archmage and his synod died. She lifted her gaze at the grand crystal chandelier that had come crashing down the cursed day. It had been repaired and hoisted up since. Right here, on this gold embroidered carpet was where Viktor Guard tore Aleksei away from her and shoved him out the door, and below her feet was the undercroft where he imprisoned Aleksei in the dark and tortured him.

Shadows flickered, making it appear as though the painted faces of the saints were following the nameless stranger, the dark cloaked man stalking their halls. Just as the archmage didn't see him, neither did Grigori in his mage's white robe and sash around the waist, picking up relics and icons of the saints, appraising their worth, then setting them down with a heaving sigh of annoyance. They were waiting for Luminary Matvey, and he was late.

Grigori had sent Vasily on an errand. Niko had accompanied them but stayed outside the door.

It had been a while so Sofia went to check on the prince and found him curiously peering in but keeping a distance as one would from an exotic but dangerous creature.

"It's going to look strange that you're outside when Matvey arrives, Niko," said Sofia.

"Should I pull my hood up?" he asked.

"He'll recognize you," said Sofia. "You didn't want to come in?"

"I don't think I can." Curiosity was getting the best of him though he clearly didn't like the church.

"See if you can invite him in, Sofia." Somehow that sounded like a test and Grigori turned, watching, waiting with his hands clasped behind the back. He'd left his sword on the rack by the door because it wasn't proper to be armed in the church.

"Come on in, Niko," Sofia gestured.

The prince tried stepping in, careful, then winced and ran out. "It hurts. I can't."

An awful smile split Grigori's face but he didn't share what that was about.

Matvey rushed out of the nave and gestured with an open hand. "Your Highness," he gasped. "They didn't tell me you were here. Thousand apologies, please come on in. Come, come." He ushered the prince in and that seemed to work as Niko relaxed when whatever he thought might happen didn't.

"Mage Grigori. Lady Guard," Matvey greeted.

Grigori was the queen's mage and it made perfect sense he'd be with the prince, but because he presumed Sofia was here about the gold dispute, he appeared disheartened now the quarrel involved a mage and the heir of Fedosia. The luminary smiled at his death as he followed Grigori out to the cloister where he was stabbed to death among the rose bushes asleep for the winter. Then his body was folded and stuffed into a wooden trunk and stowed under the seat of a black coach driven by a soulless.

After nightfall, Grigori took Vasily and the coach and left Niko and Sofia at an inn. They sat on a small stool by the fire as all the tables were taken by drunk sailors singing or brawling. No one approached Sofia as Grigori had tipped the largest man in the hall a silver coin to 'protect the lady'.

The pitiful boy holding a tankard of ale with both hands and staring into the flames said, "I can't let you go, I'm sorry. It's not even that I'm afraid he'll kill me if I do, but I'm just unable to disobey him. You wouldn't understand because people always have a choice, but I'm not a person. That's all."

"It's all right, Niko," said Sofia. She'd already decided she wouldn't leave him. If by grand fortune and the saints' blessings, she could trick Niko into releasing her, like asking to go to the privy, and successfully escaped, the necromancer would kill the boy. She had to find a way to kill Grigori and free them all, including Vasily. An opportunity would arise, sooner or later. She just had to be sure not to waste it.

Merry laughter of the men and ladies of the night who kept them company quieted as a sailor with a voice like a silver bell sang a prayer for the souls claimed by the sea. It was then followed by an exultation to the saints believed to watch over Fedosian waters, asking for mercy for those departing in the morning.

"I came to be as a child," Niko said, the flames caught in his scarlet eyes dark with sadness. "Suddenly there was light, and this world was beautiful. Grigori was the first person I saw. He told me I was a prince and that I was lost, and he'd take me home. There was so much to learn because I didn't remember anything. They told me it must be because I nearly drowned and that I would be better soon. I never got better. I was sick a lot and I wasn't allowed to go outside or play with other children.

Later, I learned Grigori was making me sick to keep me alone, so people didn't notice I was different. He also lied and said I have a blood illness so people wouldn't touch me with jewelry." He shook his head. "Aleksei would come, bring me things, teach me things, play with me, and keep me company when I was bedridden with fever.

"He made me feel not alone, and when I found out he was my brother, not cousin, I was happy. We played with shadows, not like I do now, but as children did with cutouts of things. Sometimes he would make a horse with his hand and make it gallop. One time we were shadow dueling with paper swords. He'd made a dragon with his darksteel because he was a sentinel then. I was supposed to rescue the princess... My shadow grabbed him and dragged him across the room.

"It scared him, and I knew I shouldn't have done that. Eugene had been telling me not to do that. He was always my protector, but because he also nagged, I hadn't taken him too seriously.

"Aleksei didn't speak to me for a while after that. I would sit by the window and see him in the courtyard with other sentinels, but he wouldn't come over, and when I called him, he'd pretend he didn't see me.

"Then one day he just returned, brought me a horse, he said, and wanted to teach me to ride. He never mentioned the shadow again, and I wondered if he'd dismissed it as a dream. He has waking dreams, you know, where he speaks and walks around but he isn't awake. That's his mind crossing into the red haze.

"I killed Burkhard, and he pretends not to know that. The night I killed my mother, he was awake when I came into the queen's bedchamber. He'd been crying for a while and I went to beg her to stop, but it was one of her mad days and she wouldn't. She was hurting him but that wasn't why he redlined. It was me.

"I tore her as I would a paper cutout dragon, and her watchmen too. It makes no difference how big or small you are. After they were in pieces, I tried to help him and that was when he redlined. He was afraid of me.

"He pretends that didn't happen. He's very good at that, putting things away and not seeing them again. That's how he deals with hurt. But his mind is so cluttered with the things he doesn't see, once in a while he trips on a thing, because they are still there, and becomes sad or angry.

"Because you make him so happy, I hoped one day you could help him clear out the mess... But life is more sad than happy, isn't it? Yet I still want to live because the other is just nothing. I have no soul to go to the stars and I've been here only a little while.

"It hurts I've taken you from Aleksei. It hurts I lied to Eugene. I will never be free of the maker, but I watched as Grigori promised a false thing to Eugene to use him. Unlike Aleksei, Eugene doesn't pretend. With his one eye, he sees more than anyone else with two. He's probably dead now because he walks too close to the truth.

"Grigori made me believe I was Nikolas so others would too, but when I was ten, he gave me revelation and I saw what I was..." He trailed off and fell silent as the singing of the sailors continued, drunker and louder than it was before.

Sofia would reach over and take his hand, but he wouldn't let her move. "Niko," she called, and he turned to her, blinking as though he was just seeing her. "It will be all right," she said.

"No, it won't. Sometimes living gets so sad I wonder if it's better to return to the dark. I'm sorry for all the trouble. It certainly wasn't my intention to hurt people when I came into this beautiful world full of things I wish I could do." Then the prince was quiet and listened to the sailors for a while.

"Do you know where it has lice in Raven?" Sofia smiled. They were in an inn, and it wasn't as awful as Aleksei had claimed the last time she'd been in Murmia.

She didn't expect the prince to know and had only meant to pull him out of the melancholy mood, but he said, "Dungeon. When Burkhard was alive, he used to imprison and kill people in the Raven dungeon. Why? It's no longer there."

"Oh, just the sentinels talk about lice more than expected," said Sofia. "I wondered why. That's all."

Niko thought for a while, frowning, and her plan worked till the prince said, "Not many. Just Aleksei, and it's because Burkhard used to lock him in the dungeon a lot. He got fleas and lice, got bitten by a bunch of things, and had to shave off all his hair. That was long ago, though."

Every story Niko told was more miserable than the last. "Do you want to get married?" she asked.

"No, but I want dogs to like me."

"Have you tried feeding them?" she asked.

"They don't like the soulless, Sofia." He pursed his lips. "Where is Grigori?" Calling the necromancer by his name, rather than addressing him as Maker like Vasily did, was his way of retaliating, Sofia thought.

"What happens to you when he dies?" she asked.

"I don't know, and don't tell me anything you don't want him to know."

She nodded. "Can you release me for a moment? I just want a drink. I won't run away."

He did, and she ordered a beer, but before she did that, she leaned forward and squeezed the prince's gloved hand. "It's all right. It's not your fault because it's not your doing."

"It doesn't make it any better, but thank you for trying."

Sofia's beer came, and Niko had been holding a full tankard the entire time. "To better days," she toasted. "Try it. It's quite good."

Niko sniffed it first, took a little sip, frowned, tried again, considered, then took a gulp and approved.

But for the fire crackling and some snoring of men who'd fallen asleep in their chairs, the hall had grown quiet at dawn when Grigori returned. He looked older than he had been yesterday, but life returned to his pale face and bony frame as he ate and drank and warmed by the fire. Then as they were leaving, he stabbed a drunk pissing in the alley, and the alchemy under the long sleeves of his robe glowed as the necromancer drained the life out of the unfortunate sailor, the man's hair greying, and his body shriveling and aging till it turned into an old corpse.

The vigor returned to Grigori. He had a spring in his steps, and hummed as he strode with his long legs along the wet, sandy earth, the horizon brightening over grey frothing ocean. Sofia, Niko, and Vasily followed him, all carrying his luggage.

The dawn was chilly, and the air tasted of the faint salt of the ocean and carried the pungent odor of Grigori's pipe which he smoked as he walked. Sofia didn't know if he realized the light was too weak to cast a meaningful shadow and Niko's hold on her was non-existent. But she didn't run. She'd see it through and try to free Niko and Vasily. All she needed was the necromancer's name.

When Grigori stopped and turned, Sofia panicked thinking he'd somehow heard her thoughts, but he took his leather bag from Vasily, and said, "You've outgrown your use to me. Go into the water."

"I can't swim, Maker," Vasily said.

"Walk then, go on, boy."

"Yes, Maker." He turned and walked toward the waves, whispering as they lapped on the cold beach.

Vasily reached the edge of the water and looked back at Grigori who said, "Go on, then. Go on."

He marched toward the blue horizon, trudging, then struggling onward as the waves became larger. A wave pushed him back and he fell but got up and fought on.

"What are you doing?" Sofia asked. "He can't swim, he told you."

Grigori didn't answer and just watched as he smoked his pipe. Vasily was going to drown, Sofia realized, and broke from Niko, tossed Grigori's luggage, and ran after him. Deceitfully calm the water looked but the waves were an immense force as they shoved Sofia back.

She didn't swim well and flailed in the freezing water, dragging her drenched cloak, as she yelled after the young Apraksin lord. "Vasily! Go back!"

He kept going forward, deeper, beyond Sofia's reach.

"I want to live! I want to live!" she heard him yell over the waves, and watched as he disappeared under them.

She floated there for a while, being pushed and pulled by the waves, nothing but the ocean and her.

Then she realized she was drifting out and turned back. She shivered as she walked out onto the beach where Grigori was stomping on Niko.

"There's no shadow, Grigori!" the prince was yelling.

"You have hands, boy. If you don't need them, I can cut them off!"

"No, please!"

Sofia wiped her face and got salt in her eyes. "You're a cruel bastard," she said as she passed Grigori. "There had been no need for that."

"The irony of *you* calling me cruel." He had Niko by the throat but dropped the boy, and his eyes shone with hatred when he turned to Sofia.

She took a step back.

"Moriz was my brother," Grigori said, retrieving his ruined leather haversack from the wet sand. "Now, let's go home."

"Home?" she asked.

He gestured at the port where sailing ships awaited. "Alten."

Elfur? Sofia balled her fists. Though the allure of her long lost home called her name, a faint voice in the breaking waves, the words of another were louder because he was closer, a shadow cast by nothing standing on the water. *"Give us a name."*

"Lothar of Dohnan," Sofia whispered.

"We do not accept. Give us another name."

"I've given you a name. Lothar of Dohnan." Sofia's wet dress was cold as it furled around her in a sudden gale.

"We do not accept the name of Dohnan."

"Why? Tell me why!"

The stranger left without answering.

Because she had said his name, the necromancer turned. "I'm pleased you know me, but now let's go. We have a boat to catch." Then he said to Niko, "Unless you want to go searching for Vasily, I suggest you gather Lady Sofia and follow me. If we miss our ship, I will kill you both. Slowly, terribly, and very poorly as far as deaths go. Now, get to it."

Twenty-Nine

Good, Bad, Terrible

Five dead horses with muscles and tendons ripped from overuse, and the sixth one walking around with flesh falling off and frightening the good people of Murmia... Lev burned them all. They found the carriage and there was a trunk under the seat with dried blood and stains but no body. Who did he kill? Was it Soful? The prince was too valuable of a hostage to stuff into a wooden box. Had his sister been turned soulless? And if she had, would he be able to do what was necessary?

Lev's concern with Aleksei was no longer that he didn't care for Soful because he *clearly* did, but that he was mad. They needed to have a talk and Lev pulled Aleksei aside after he beat a port patrol with the man's helmet for being mouthy and unhelpful. The man narrowly escaped with his life.

"Aleksei." Lev pulled him aside under a cotton tree naked for the winter. A rowboat carrying passengers glided by them in the canal. The city stunk and was sinking into the ocean while drowning in the sewage it reeked of. They were flushing the latrines into the water was Lev's guess.

"What?" the captain of the sentinels snapped.

Murmia wasn't a small city, and the sentinels had spread out each with their own task, and it was Lev's good fortune he was stuck with Aleksei.

"Did anyone ever tell you your temper isn't helpful?" Lev asked.

"Yes."

"So rein it back a bit, yeah?"

"Yeah." Aleksei exhaled. "What am I going to do if they already left?" Despite having brought a map of Elfur, his plan too had been to ride down the carriage. Five days into the pursuit, Lev couldn't understand how they weren't catching up to the necromancer till he saw the horses an hour earlier. Their mounts had the disadvantage of being living things with limits. Had there been any doubt among the sentinels Grigori was a necromancer, the sight of the horses extinguished it.

"I don't know," Lev said. "But let's first find out *where* they are. This whole thing may be a ruse from Grigori to get us to sail to Elfur like assholes while he circles back and takes over the throne, yeah?"

"Yeah."

"I really need that name from your sentinel. If I knew who he was, it'd help me understand what he's doing," said Lev.

"Yeah," Aleksei said.

A good thing about sentinels was they were used to taking orders and having knowledge of dark alchemy was giving Lev authority.

"This is a Guard city. The church would be the beating heart of it." Lev pointed a chin at the Church of Murmia, the grandest building in the city visible over all the rooftops. Uncle died there. The sight of it gave him chills, but it had to be done. "Let's go meet Matvey. He'll be able to help. If not, let's kill him."

"Yeah." Aleksei didn't like the building either and frowned at it. "What killed the archmage?" he asked while they walked toward the church.

"I... actually don't know. It may have been a thing he was working on. Sometimes alchemy bites back. Or it may be Grigori. What killed your queen?"

"Age," said Aleksei. "She passed in her sleep."

"Right, and I have a ten-inch cock."

"Right, and I've never seen you stumble around Raven in the nude, blasted out of your mind."

"Have I?" Lev pondered.

"More than once."

"Good times," Lev reminisced.

"For you, perhaps." Aleksei strode ahead and Lev picked up the pace.

"Did you ask Soful to marry you?"

"Yes."

"The answer is no, by the way."

"I could just kill you and throw you in the swamp."

"I wonder if this fucker even exists," Lev complained when Matvey wasn't at the church.

"I've seen him around," Aleksei said, taking him seriously.

They were in the nave and Lev tipped his face at the domed ceiling of the saints where the archmage had been... lodged. They'd repaired it since, but the paint didn't match and was more vibrant at the center than the faded saints further away.

"How may I help you?" A parson came out from the back and addressed Aleksei. Although an old man, he was new at the church. Lev hadn't seen him before, and he didn't recognize Lev either.

"We're looking for Matvey, Parson," said Aleksei.

"The luminary isn't here, I'm afraid. He's caught the fever. Is there anything I can help you with?"

"Where does he live?" Aleksei asked.

"Actually, let's not go there if he's sick," Lev interjected. "We're looking for someone and need help getting the word out to the innkeepers and sailors. Who is in charge here?"

"Well, the luminary," answered the parson. "But who might you be looking for? I can ask around."

"Sofia Guard." Lev dropped the family name to be taken more seriously, and as he understood it, Matvey and Soful knew each other. "She may have been traveling with—"

"Lord Vasily Apraksin and Mage Grigori," said the parson. "Lady Guard was here yesterday. She sought a meeting with the luminary." The parson looked proud. "I was here myself and it was wonderful to have met a living Guard."

Yesterday, that was good news and Lev felt the bright lights of hope shine down upon him.

"Where are they now?" Aleksei asked.

"I'm not sure, actually. Perhaps you can ask the luminary."

"The archmage lived in the church, no?" Aleksei asked, suspiciously eyeing the two-story inn conjoined at the sides with taller buildings like a child in between his parents. One was a brothel, clearly, and the other was some type of textile mill, rolls of fabric being carried in and out.

"Well, the parson said Matvey didn't want to get the chapter sick with his fever..."

"Church of Murmia has towers, Lev, rooms people never use," said Aleksei. "He could have locked himself in one if he was concerned. He'll get more people sick at an inn. I don't like that he lied."

"Maybe he just likes whores." Lev gestured at the brothel. One of the women loitering outside the door and fanning herself while soliciting the men walking by turned and sneered at him. "Not you, darling. You're lovely," Lev said.

Aleksei stood there scanning the rooftops and the buildings across the street. A carriage passed by, splashing slush on Lev's boots.

"Come on." Lev pulled Aleksei. "One way to find out."

"Don't eat, drink, or smoke anything he offers," Aleksei said as they stepped through the door.

"What am I? A dog?" Lev threw up his arms when Aleksei yanked him back and went ahead of him.

"If he offers you wine, you'll drink it. So, don't."

Well, he had a point.

Except for the candles lit enough to set the wooden inn on fire, the luminary's room wasn't half bad. Lev could see fucking a whore in it. Matvey was in a plain cloak and held a handkerchief over his mouth as he coughed.

Not wanting to get sick, Lev tried to open the window, but the shutters were stuck closed. Hence the candles, he supposed.

Aleksei remained by the door, scanning the room as though Grigori might jump out, and Lev introduced himself to the luminary who was a humble looking man who smiled and bowed a lot—swindlers rarely looked like swindlers. He'd have a word with the old bastard about forging the archmage's gold, but perhaps now wasn't the time. He sat down at the table and the luminary poured wine for him.

By habit, Lev reached for the cup and Aleksei snatched it from the table and set it on a stand.

"Breathe, Syoma." Slip of the tongue because Lev wasn't used to being in Aleksei's company and it was something Semyon would have done. Toward the end at Usolya, Semyon had been taking away Lev's wine, kind of a lot.

"Get to it, Lev," hissed Aleksei. He'd been anxious since he heard the parson say Sofia's name. Lev was too, but wine was how he dealt with nerves.

"You met with my sister yesterday, Luminary?" Lev leaned back into his chair and looked down at his lap, loading his opium pipe.

"Lady Sofia, yes. She was in the company of His Highness and Mage Grigori," said Matvey. Lev didn't have to be looking at him to know Aleksei was making him uneasy, pacing around the room and looking behind furniture, and under the bed.

"Where are they?" Aleksei was behind Matvey, and the luminary looked over his shoulder.

Lev gestured for the luminary to answer as he blew out thin white smoke, the scent a sweet release as death might be to a suffering man.

"The lady didn't share where they were staying but I heard the mage say they were leaving tomorrow. A packet ship for Elfur, I believe."

"Tomorrow from now or did he say tomorrow yesterday?" Aleksei asked. It was a reasonable question, but the luminary looked confused.

"I am to meet the prince later on today," said Matvey. "Why don't you sit down, Semyon? And we'll wait for them together."

Aleksei was in civilian attire with a plain brown cloak draped over him, and Lev had just called him Syoma, a common endearment for Semyon. So the luminary made an honest mistake mixing up the names, Lev would have thought, but here was the trouble…

Aleksei slammed Matvey's head onto the table, and the tip of a dark-steel blade pressed against the luminary's nape. "We've met many times, Matvey. You've been to my home. What is wrong with you?"

On the train to Krakova, Lev had gone over his interactions with the soulless, over and over, thinking how he could have done things differently. In hindsight, there had been so many signs as loud as the tolling of a church bell. For instance, Vasily wouldn't address anyone by name unless someone else called them first. The soulless didn't carry memories of who they were pretending to be, confirming nothing of the deceased remained except for their appearance. They came with language, not sure about literacy, and knew generalities of the world such as this was a table and Lev was a Guard, but any specific knowledge, such as what darksteel exoskeleton looked like compared to Skuratov iron, they had to learn for themselves. Where the boundary was and how that worked, Lev didn't know. He wasn't a necromancer, but Matvey was a soulless, sure and true.

"Hands, hands, Aleksei! Watch his hands!" Lev sprung up from his seat. "They carry poison, be careful!" He ran over the table and some chairs because he'd suddenly forgotten he had a blade.

Shadows moved across the wall, yanking Aleksei back, and Lev reacted by... burning the place down.

"We could have questioned him," Aleksei said, while they watched people toss water into the fire, trying to keep it from spreading into the brothel next door. Folks at the fabric mill were trying their best to save the rolls they had.

"He was going to kill you. It doesn't take much. I saw Vasily slaughter four druzhina in a beat. *Druzhina*, Aleksei, and Vasily was a scrawny bastard."

Aleksei frowned, his face dark against the orange of the blazing inferno. "What was that? The shadow... alchemy?"

"Wouldn't call it alchemy. There is no gold or trade. It's something *some* soulless do."

"Doesn't have to be a soulless, though, right?" Aleksei turned to him.

"Have you seen that *anywhere* else?" Lev asked.

He shrugged.

"That's what I thought. No one else does that. Shadow alchemy is *always* in reference to a powerful soulless, and by 'powerful' I meant they speak and at least pretend to be human. I've seen others who were just walking corpses. The Apraksin retainers, the last I saw them, had been reduced to simple grunts, and they used to be rowdy bastards." Lev tapped Aleksei's shoulder. "Come on. Let's go find out what packet ship is leaving tomorrow, *without* tipping the fucker off. All right?"

"Yeah." He'd grown uncertain. Something was on his mind, but what did Lev care?

The ocean was a void at night, pitch black and endless. Lev didn't want to be surprised by another soulless and ceased his inquiries at the dock after dark and headed to the church. He gave his family name and warned the parsons Grigori was a necromancer. They didn't know what to do with such a wild claim, but they let Lev shelter on the hallowed ground.

Restless, he paced in the nave in the deep of the night. Hearing the heavy wooden door slam with a thud, he waited, drawing his saber in the house of the saints. It was Dominik, he'd come in without needing permission, and the gold on his vambrace was bright and shiny still. Lev sheathed his sword.

He sat down on the gilded steps to the gold wall of the saints, where he left his wine, and stretched out his legs.

Dominik walked the length of the aisle. Taking in the sight, he whistled. "Guards sure are wealthy."

"There's a cup over there." Lev pointed.

"That's for sacred water. It's probably blasphemy." He sat down next to Lev, knocking on the gilded steps. "A Shield sitting on the altar. This is also probably blasphemy."

"Probably." Lev took a drink. "Where's Aleksei?"

"Trying not to lose his mind. Captain walks very close to the redline. It's better to give him breathing space when he gets agitated."

"What happened at the Red Den?" Lev asked.

"What happened at Usolya?" he asked.

"Vasily Apraksin turned into a soulless and killed Semyon Skuratov."

"We're walking through living lore." Dominik gazed up at the saints. "We found Vasily at the dead house. He'd drowned and washed up ashore. Except for some burn scars, he looked like himself. It's strange. You'd think monsters would look different."

"What do monsters look like?" Lev asked.

"Like us, apparently." Dominik shrugged with a single shoulder.

"I take that back, actually." Lev took a drink. "The last I saw Bogdan had two heads. It *wasn't* an attempt at creating a soulless. The dark alchemy was botched purposefully. Just jumbled parts except they'd animated because of the presence of the *dver*."

"Like an incomplete alchemy?"

"Yes, exactly that," said Lev.

Aleksei and his dozen sentinels entered and strode down the aisle. He was starting to feel like an ally because Lev felt better seeing him. The same couldn't be said for the scarred sentinel, though. Lev didn't appreciate how the old man had come after him as though they had a personal vendetta. And how did he know Grigori's name when no one else did?

"We searched every anchored ship. No one has seen Sofia or the prince," Aleksei said. "And there is no packet ship leaving tomorrow...

Fuck." He sat down on a carved wooden chair by the collection plate on a stand and grimaced as he rubbed his knee.

Lev had his own injuries too, but drinking helped, opium helped more.

"Port patrol will assist us in combing the city at first light, Captain," Ruslan said.

"Captain, I spoke with a stevedore who'd seen the prince," Dominik said, rubbing his hands and looking at the calluses on his palm.

"And?" Aleksei asked.

"Should you go into the red, no one here can pull you out," said Dominik, warily. But he had a way of speaking the truth, Lev was learning. "It will be a deleterious way of dealing with the crisis, Captain."

"I know that," Aleksei said. He appeared calm but Lev saw the sentinels back away from their captain, not drawing attention to their movements and floating away quietly.

"The stevedore remembers a boy with red eyes," said Dominik. "Remembers him because of the unusual eyes, and it drew his attention because a 'tall bastard' with a longsword was beating him. He remembers Lady Sofia because she was the most beautiful woman he'd seen all his life, and because she tipped him ten silver coins when he carried her luggage to her cabin. He'd never had such wealth.

"She was traveling with the tall bastard and the boy with peculiar eyes. They boarded a packet ship headed to Elfur, he doesn't know which port, and left this morning. The beautiful lady had said she was traveling with her uncle.

"I paid him four coppers to take a truth potion and retell the story. It did not change."

As Lev watched, Aleksei's eyes turned bright red. He closed them, and sat quietly, shifting the cross of his legs but nothing more.

Lev frowned at the scarred bastard. He looked gutted but that could be an act. Lev knew nothing of him. "I'll have that name now, Eugene," Lev said.

"You may have it in Elfur," he said. "There must be a ship leaving soon. We're going to get the prince back."

"Dog," said Lev. "My sister tipped the stevedore so he would remember her. When she says Uncle, she doesn't mean the archmage or my father. I already have a name, but I'd like to hear you say it. That is, if you know it at all."

"Who the fuck do you—"

"Name, Eugene," Aleksei whispered, barely audible but he was heard. His eyes still shut, he rubbed his temple.

Eugene fidgeted, his hands and eyelid twitching, then he sat down on the red wool carpet, took out an opium pipe with shaking hands, and lit it. He exhaled slowly, then said, "Fuck if I know."

Aleksei opened his eyes, and they were normal. Still looked like old blood but typical for a Shield. Lev frowned at himself for having gawked at him for so long. He cleared his head with a shake.

"Who speaks Elfurian?" Lev asked. Dominik raised his hand and that was it. "Aleksei?"

He shook his head.

"And here I thought you were a highborn," said Lev, then realized this wasn't the time. "All right. We're going to go get my sister and your prince. If you don't speak Elfurian, I don't need you, unless your name is Aleksei. The larger our number, the more attention we will draw. So, Aleksei, pick one more sentinel. Not him." Lev pointed at Eugene. "Let's get our shit in order, and we leave on the next ship. If you have any questions, shut up, because I don't give a fuck."

"Ignat, Dominik, stay," said Aleksei. "Everyone else, return to Raven. Esenov is now acting captain. Dismissed."

The sentinels obeyed their captain except for Eugene who remained seated. "Aleksei, take me. I will be useful."

"You're dismissed for good, Eugene," Aleksei said. "I'm letting you retire rather than ask for your life because when Niko returns, he'll be upset should he find you dead."

"My life has no meaning without that boy," said Eugene.

"That's what makes you dangerous, Eugene," Aleksei said. "Because Niko loves you, I'm being a friend right now. But that will change if you test me. Tonight is not the time."

Eugene sat there smoking, taking his time, but with a heavy sigh, he finally got up, grabbed his gear, and headed toward the exit after the sentinels. Then turned on his heels, having decided on something, returned, bent by Aleksei, and whispered in his ear.

"I understand," said Aleksei.

Eugene straightened, nodded, and headed for the door. He looked back once more, narrowed his one good eye at Lev, then stepped out and closed the door behind him. He'd been the last to leave, and only Lev, Dominik, Aleksei, and Ignat remained in the nave.

"Lothar of Dohnan, that's the name I got," said Lev.

"Like Fredrik of Dohnan, the Elfurian King?" asked Dominik.

"House of Dohnan is a large clan with dozens of nobles, mostly minor, but a few are very powerful, like King Fredrik," said Lev. "The trouble with Lothar is *supposedly* he was executed by Fredrik himself four decades ago, and why would I know such a fact about an Elfurian noble, you say?" Lev tapped his pipe on the gilded dais. "Because Lothar of Dohnan is the last known High Priest of *Vrata Nochi* before the church of necromancy was disbanded and its priests executed. Where dark alchemy is concerned, he is an equivalent to what my uncle was, an archmage.

"His brother Moriz stole my aunt Yelizaveta and took her to Elfur. If you ask Soful, she'll say her father loved her mother, and if you had asked anyone else in my family, they would have said he took her forcefully. I don't know.

"Now, there's good news, bad news, and terrible news. The good is he's Soful's uncle. He's *probably* not doing vile things to her. We all thought it, and now I've said it. The bad news is we're dealing with a high priest, and all you got is me. The terrible is I can't think of any other reason for a Dohnan to abduct a Fedosian prince than as a declaration of war.

"So, before hundreds of thousands of people die and both countries turn to cinder, let us four assholes try and stop it. We'll most definitely fail. Write your mothers a letter, I'd say, but you are sentinels, you have no families." He blew a raspberry. "Any questions?" There weren't, they just stared at him. "So, why you, Ignat?" he asked. He wasn't familiar with the sentinel.

"I'm handsome, dauntless, and I never lie." He winked. He was not handsome. That was a lie. He was so blond his lashes were white. He looked like Fedya had the man been two decades younger.

"Aleksei?" Lev asked.

"Going to need a moment, Lev." Aleksei got up and headed for the door.

"Is you being temperamental going to be a continuing theme?" Lev asked.

"No." And out the door, he went.

Great. Lev emptied his cup.

"Is you being drunk going to be a continuing theme?" asked Dominik.

"Yes," Lev said, and poured wine. "And don't forget high."

The voyage to Hohendahl, the largest civilian port of Elfur, was fourteen days in good weather, and Lev's shoulders sagged at how tiny the cabin was. More cramped than a coach, the bed secured to the bulkhead was narrow like a wooden coffin.

He clunked his bags on the top bed and whispered to Dominik who was settling into the bottom one, "Watch my shit, yeah? There's a lot of fucken gold."

"Sure."

Lev headed out, passed merchants with obnoxious perfume in the tight passageway, the wife of one smiling at him, and went up the ladder to the deck. He'd never been on the water and the constant yawing was making him feel drunk though he wasn't, and he wanted to barf.

While he was retching over the railing on the sunny wooden deck of the passenger ship, someone handed him a handkerchief. It was Aleksei. Lev took it. "Thank you."

"Can you swim?" Aleksei asked.

Growing suspicious he might throw him overboard, Lev backed away from the railing and bumped into another perfumed woman. The odor assaulted his nose.

"Why?" Lev wiped his mouth.

"I've never been at sea," Aleksei said. "In case this thing sinks, I need to know who can swim and who can't."

"I swim," Lev said. He could swim in the lake and was hoping it was the same, or at least close enough. "Can you?"

"Yeah," said Aleksei. "So everyone swims. That's good at least."

"Soful doesn't," Lev remarked. "Not very well, I mean. I tried to teach her but she just splashes and goes nowhere."

"My brother can't swim." Aleksei put his hands on the railing and squinted at the port city. "We'll see, I suppose."

"You keep saying brother, do you mean cousin, Aleksei?"

"Sure."

"He's Burkhard's kid, isn't he?" Lev stood with his back against the railing, trying to get comfortable and conquer his unease with this floating coffin.

"I never said that."

"Right." Lev puffed his cheeks. "Sure as hell he isn't Saint Neva's child. Nikolas looks like you, and you look like Burkhard."

"Fucken hate him," Aleksei said.

"Burkhard?"

"Lev." Aleksei turned to face him. "I'm not educated. I don't know shit about Elfur and the same goes for dark alchemy. I'm wholly depending on you, and I'll protect you with my life. It's your call where we go from here and what we do, but don't stab me in the fucken back, all right? We can do that once we're back in Fedosia."

"*If* we get back." Lev sneered.

"Don't do that."

"Just so you know, I'm full of bad calls," Lev said.

"Don't do that, either," Aleksei said.

The bell rang, the gangway retracted, and the mooring lines were cast off. Sudden fear threatened to overwhelm Lev and he battled the urge to jump over the railing and swim back as the ship began moving and the passengers hooted and clapped.

What the hell was he doing going after a high priest? He was in over his head and grossly inadequate. He wished he hadn't known who Lothar Dohnan was. Sometimes ignorance was bliss.

"Just so you know, during my last encounter with Lothar, I lost and got Syoma killed. I don't know how to kill a high priest. Soulless, sure, but not a high priest."

"The same as you kill any other man, living or not," Aleksei said. "You're not alone. Just get us close enough."

"Right." Lev exhaled. "I'm going to be sick, a lot."

"That's fine."

Lev leaned over the railing and looked at the frothing water, hissing as the ship sliced through it.

I'm going to Elfur, Syoma. Lev squinted up at the sun and found a smile. *I hope you're watching. I hope you're impressed. I may come see you sooner than I thought, so, save me a seat next to you, yeah?*

So, this was courage, being scared shitless. Lev laughed. A thing was often defined by its opposite, wasn't it? Courage by fear. Light by darkness...

Hold on to your feathered hat, Lothar of Dohnan, because Lev of White Guard is coming to define you.

Tsar and the Throne

Coming next...

Far from home, trust is frail and betrayal is lethal.

Lev arrives in Elfur with the sentinels, including Aleksei, whom he despises. Elfur is vast, and navigating it will be an art form in itself. As leads dry up and Lev makes questionable decisions, tempers flare and the old rivalry between him and Aleksei threatens to shatter their fragile alliance.

Sofia and Niko are held hostage in a foreign land. Sofia schemes to escape, but she can't leave Niko behind. The fates are cruel so far away from the saints and she finds herself at the mercy of an Elfurian prince.

The inevitable approaches: the ancient feud between Fedosia and Elfur must be settled in blood—but whose blood, only the saints know.

Author Newsletter

Thank you for reading and taking this journey with me. If you enjoyed the story of Sofia and her Aleksei, I invite you to join my newsletter. Sign up to be the first to know about upcoming releases, special offers, and to read ARCs before the books are published.

https://brienfeathers.com/feathers-monthly/

Also by Brien Feathers

IF YOU ENJOYED THE Fedosian Wars, I recommend checking out both my Sun War Trilogy and the Fallen Duology, as they are all inspired by the same setting—Russia—just at different points in time. The Fedosian Wars draws inspiration from the Tsardom era, with the story set around the mid-1800s.

In the Sun War Trilogy, we're right after the Bolshevik Revolution in the early 1900s. The tsar in that story is a warlock, and his court clashes with the militant People's Party—mundane bloods, or folks without magic.

The Fallen Duology moves to the WWII era, where a war with dragons has devastated the Soviet like country of Rosya.

All three series are dark fantasy (that's my jam) with romance, and I hope you enjoy them.

If you wanted a straight romantic fantasy without the grit and the grime, check out my Royal Diviner Trilogy. That one draws inspiration from feudal Japan. In it, the goddess of storm banished from the Immortal Court to the human realm falls for a vicious warlord. It still has sex and war, but the world isn't as dark as the other two.

You can find more about my books here:
https://brienfeathers.com/books/

Milton Keynes UK
Ingram Content Group UK Ltd.
UKHW041817151124
451262UK00005B/637